# LOOSE LIPS

# LOOSE LIPS

Fanfiction Parodies of Great (*and Terrible*)
Literature from the Smutty Stage of Shipwreck

Compiled by
## Casey A. Childers & Amy Stephenson

**GRAND CENTRAL**
PUBLISHING

NEW YORK    BOSTON

Grand Central Publishing
Hachette Book Group
1290 Avenue of the Americas
New York, NY 10104
grandcentralpublishing.com
twitter.com/grandcentralpub

First edition: September 2016

Grand Central Publishing is a division of Hachette Book Group, Inc.
The Grand Central Publishing name and logo is a trademark of Hachette Book Group, Inc.

The publisher is not responsible for websites (or their content) that are not owned by the publisher.

Library of Congress Cataloging-in-Publication Data has been applied for.

ISBNs: 978-1-4555-6642-6 (trade paperback), 978-1-4555-6643-3 (ebook)

Printed in the United States of America

RRD-C

10 9 8 7 6 5 4 3 2 1

# Contents

# Contents

# Foreword

## *AU, M/M, F/F, Fluff, Angst, Feels:*
## *The Secret Language of Fanfic*

## by Seanan McGuire

Hello. My name is Seanan McGuire. I am an award-winning *New York Times* best-selling author. I have more than twenty traditionally published books available all over the world. I am so prolific that I had to create a semi-secret second identity, the mysterious Mira Grant, in order to keep up with myself.

And I love fanfic.

I love the predictability of it, the author who you know writes only to make sure that Harry Potter and Hermione Granger will get the happy ending they feel J. K. Rowling denied them, telling the same story over and over again, each time in slightly different clothes (or without them).

I love the elegant, incredible ingenuity of it, the authors who unpack text and subtext and take stories off in directions the original creators would never have dreamed of and might never have been allowed to go. Modern storytelling is studded with "roommates" and "gal pals" who were never allowed—due to morality clauses or corporate demands—to be the romantic leads that they were destined to be. But in the hands of the fanfic author, Kitty Pryde and Illyana Rasputin can finally live happily ever after; Angel and Spike can finally talk about their pre-Buffy relationship without veiling it in subtext. The game changes.

I love the raw possibility of it all, the self-inserts and the original characters and the visions and revisions and the chaos and the *beauty*.

Fanfic is a community effort, the people who love a thing seizing it and saying, "I love this so much that I want to rip it apart and see how it works from the inside out." It's the biology class of literature, and we are all kids with scalpels, and we are all frogs, and it is all glorious.

Like all good communities, fanfic has its own lingo, which is constantly evolving in both frequency and usage, so I think we need to define a few things. After that, we'll talk vocabulary. And after that?

We'll get to the smut.

### Question #1: What is fanfic?

At its absolute simplest, fanfic is fiction about characters you do not own and did not create. I am aware that by this definition, most of the Disney canon is fanfic. So is most of Shakespeare, *The Iliad*, big chunks of Arthurian mythology, and pretty much any comic being written by someone other than the original creator. Some people are comfortable with this definition. Others feel that it's too broad and want some legal framework.

Their definition is generally "fanfic is fiction about characters you do not have official permission from the intellectual property holder to use." So the new X-Men comic from Marvel is not fanfic, because the IP holder (Marvel Comics) has licensed their characters to both writer and artist. Meanwhile, *Wicked* is not fanfic because *The Wonderful Wizard of Oz* is in the public domain, meaning no one owns those characters, meaning no one can have a license, meaning anything you write can be published.

Confused yet? Yeah, so are most of us.

### Question #2: So, like, how is this legal?

Parody and fair use and no one really knows, so we all spend a lot of time shrugging and looking faintly baffled before moving on to the never-ending porn buffet.

## Question #3: Why waste your time playing with someone else's characters?

If you're someone who wants to be a professional writer one day, fanfic is a great way to learn a lot about the craft of writing. I learned so much from my time as a fanfic writer. I learned about writing dialogue, writing description, and, yes, world building, because while the first stage of fanfic may be like "in *My Little Pony* she's a girl like Megan, only it was Wind Whistler, not Firefly, who flew over the rainbow to bring her back to Ponyland, and she has adventures just like the ones they have on the show," the second stage of fanfic is "what if Veronica Mars and Lilly Kane were huge fans of Josie and the Pussycats?"

The third stage is "what if the crew of *Serenity* were high school students putting on a production of *Oklahoma?*" We get a little weird from there. And all these things, every one of them, will teach you how to write.

If you're not someone who wants to be a professional writer one day, fanfic is a way to write and share your stories and be part of a community and remember that literature is for everybody. Stories are for everybody. If you want to do nothing more than share your vision of Emma Swan and Captain Hook's great romance with people outside your head, you can do that.

Fanfic is magic.

Now let's talk about that lingo I mentioned before.

When you're writing new stories about familiar characters, you sometimes need new ways to describe what's going to happen. For example, the infamous *slash*. Originally devised by fans of Captain James T. Kirk getting it on with Mr. Spock, *slash* stands for a romantic pairing between same-sex characters. (Usually. Some people use *slash* to stand for any romantic pairing, because we're *rebels* in the fanfic world, and no one actually gets to police how words are used.) *Femslash* is a slash pairing with women. Most romantic or smutty fanfic will have their pairings listed at the front, like "Hamilton/Laurens" or "Veronica/Lilly."

*OTP* means "one true pairing," or the pair of characters the author believes are truly meant to be together. It's possible to have multiple OTPs, one in each fandom the author works in. *OT3* means "one true three," or the threesome the author believes is truly meant to be together.

*Fluff* means nothing really terrible will happen; *angst* or *darkfic* means the opposite. Ratings—PG, R, NC-17, NSFW—mean just what they would mean for any other piece of media.

Confused yet? Well, there won't be a test after this book, but if you come away burning to dive deeper into the wonderful world of fanfic, you'll encounter all these terms and so many more during your journey through our archives. It's a great big fannish world out there, and you're more than welcome to join us. We have booze. We have cookies.

We have a remarkable number of ways to say *penis*.

**Excuse me, I am a fainting flower and don't like that kind of language.**

If this is the case, you have picked up the wrong book, and I strongly recommend putting it down and walking away. (Author's note: I'm pretty sure you're not supposed to tell people to read something else in the introduction to a fancy new book of fanfic and porn, but one of the best things about fanfic is that we do not believe in vague disclaimers. We like to put it all out there, so that you can tailor your reading experience to your own deepest, weirdest, most non-canonical desires. That leads to a better fanfic community for everyone. You enjoy what you read more and writers get more positive reviews, which encourages them to keep writing—everybody wins!)

Porn has a long and storied history in fanfic, going back to the night so many centuries ago when an older sibling, tired of listening to the same fairy tales over and over again, decided to make up their *own* fairy tale, one where it was a glass butt plug instead of a glass slipper, or where Rapunzel really enjoyed using her hair for bondage. The beat went on. The beat always, always goes on.

If you can name two characters, the odds are good that porn has been written about them. Fanfic is like a bespoke bakery of porn. You want your jelly roll with chocolate cake, buttercream icing, and a raspberry drizzle? We can do that. You want your threesome with light bondage, fisting, and a few literary allusions? We can do that too. We are porn connoisseurs living in a golden age of access and easy sharing, and we're going to do it. We're going to write about the butts.

What you are now holding in your hands is the equivalent of a *Chopped* cookbook, only with a lot more dicks. So many dicks. A heaping smorgasbord of dicks. Also butts, vaginas, boobs, scrotums, fingers, tongues, and basically any other tool you could want to use in our porn kitchen. And that metaphor got away from me somewhere in the middle of that sentence, but that, too, is the nature of fanfic: because we're doing whatever the fuck we want, sometimes things can get a little wild.

(See? I said *fuck*. Now that's the sort of literary freedom that you can't get in every introduction.)

When Amy contacted me, a known fanfic enthusiast, to participate in the first *Shipwreck*, I admit, I was a little hesitant. A lot of people don't "get" fanfic. They either think it's silly and frivolous—which it can be—or that fanfic authors aren't real writers—which is bullshit—or that it's all nerds giggling and blushing while writing "he had a penis it was amazing he let his best friend touch it OMG."

(And if you wrote that line in your first ever fanfic, more power to you. It took me years to admit that the people whose sex lives I wrote about were probably having sex with actual body parts and not with psychic powers. Except when I was writing about telepaths and didn't have to worry about all that messy biology. We all start somewhere.)

So, yeah, I was worried.

I didn't need to be.

*Shipwreck* is a celebration of story. It's an acknowledgment of the fact that, yes, we are all grown-ups with dirty, dirty minds, and sometimes we like to hear stories about the characters we already know doing filthy, filthy things with each other. It's a party that happens over and over again, and I dare anyone who isn't sure about fanfic to remain unsure after they spend an evening in a room full of consenting adults howling with delight over the many, many euphemisms for masturbation that *Shipwreck*'s many devious minds can come up with.

Like any good fanfic adventure, *Shipwreck* wears its disclaimers—or "tags," in the fanfic parlance—on its sleeve. No non-con, or non-consensual sexual activities; no underage characters (which led to a frantic e-mail during the second round of *Pride and Prejudice*, where I asked Amy, "Wait, Lydia was underage in the novel. Do I have to avoid Wickham fucking her?"); no intentionally harmful humor. All pieces are read and reviewed for content before the event. When you come to *Shipwreck*, you are entering a profane, foul-mouthed, absolutely safe space. You can relax into the pornography.

And oh, the pornography! The book you hold in your hands right now is full—absolutely full—of beloved characters doing terrible things to one another. Some of them (most of them) are funny. Some of them are poignant and sweet. Absolutely all of them are filthy as hell, because this is an *erotic* fanfic competition, thank you very much, and what's the point of being told that you can be as dirty as you want to be if you're going to keep things clean?

Beyond this point are words that can never be unread, images that can never be unseen, and stories that have never really gone untold, even though it often seemed like they did. We've always been here, telling them to ourselves, over and over again, while people tried to pretend that fanfic was just a phase.

Now we're ready to tell our stories to you.

Strap in. It's going to be a bumpy ride.

# Introduction

*Closes book*

Why, hello. Welcome to our library. We were just admiring our vast collection of leather-bound books. Leafing through them. Sharing our thoughts.

*Sees you eyeing the door*

But I've forgotten my manners. I'm Amy. Make yourself at home in the Georgian wing chair there while Casey tends the fire.

*Motions to Casey, who's struggling with the old-timey chimney flue*

But now, as to the reason you've joined us this evening, let me set the stage. The year was 2013. Daft Punk's "Get Lucky" was topping the charts, and San Francisco was falling in love with erotic literary fanfiction thanks to me and Casey. Our little show called *Shipwreck* washed up on the first Thursday of every month at an independent bookstore, the Booksmith, in the Haight-Ashbury in San Francisco (there goes the neighborhood).

Fanfiction...is complicated. Some authors love it; some hate it. We, and this might be obvious, love it. Fanfiction is when fans of a work—in this case, a book—write their own stories based on the characters or the world they love. It's the cat's meow of the Information Superhighway, and like so many huge phenomena on that crazy web, it's also widely ridiculed. But it seems safe to say we've all at least thought about writing fanfic when the story ends before the characters you were super into got to bone. If you were REALLY upset that they didn't bone, you might write a story that takes place six months after the story ends or ten years before it starts. Or maybe you hated the love story, so you picked up the main character and dropped her into another universe entirely to have new adventures without the jerk she wound up with in the real story.

Or maybe you read *The Maltese Falcon* and you couldn't stop picturing Effie Perine quitting her thankless job and starting up her own detective agency with Lisa Simpson and Hermione Granger and calling it Girl Friday Private Eye. If you wrote that story, it would be fanfiction, and we would love to read it (please write that story and send it to us).

You get the point.

So why the name *Shipwreck*? The first half, the *Ship* part, is from shipping culture. *Ship* is short for "relationships" in the fanfic community (e.g., "I ship Dagny Taggart with an aging Holden Caulfield"). The *wreck* half is giving you fair warning that you're in for the literary equivalent of a complete trainwreck. A friend suggested the name—a friend who's got a story in this collection. It felt perfect. It stuck.

*Pours a finger of single malt scotch and raises a toast*

Anonymous friend, whomever you may be, we are forever in your debt.

The concept of *Shipwreck* is simple. We pick a book from our splendid library for each show and invite six writers we love to help us completely wreck it with erotic pastiche (and, like, plumb the depths of their imagination for dick euphemisms—as in *Appendicks*). Each writer is assigned a character and given time to write ahead of the show. Then comes the big night. The stories are read aloud by our thespian-in-residence to preserve author anonymity and to foster grandeur—always grandeur. The audience votes for their top three favorites. The winning writer comes back the following month to defend their title.

*Crash offscreen as Casey wrestles with a television cart*

AMY: We had a video prepared.

CASEY: The VCR ate it, I think.

*Casey pulls an arm's length of ribbon from a videocassette as evidence*

AMY: Awww. Don't worry, champ. We can use words.

Our Thespian-in-Residence is Baruch Porras-Hernandez. He always starts the show by taking the mic and asking a simple question in his booming, seductive baritone: "Is everybody ready for some PORN?"

The answer—always—is a screaming, deliriously ebullient, YES. He sips his whiskey while the screaming subsides and then settles into an oversized armchair to deliver dubious erotica for about an hour.

Think Masterpiece Theatre, with glitter canon orgasms.

*Casey interrupts*

Oh, hello. I was just lighting the fire in our resplendent library. Here, have a pull on this fine Turkish shag in my pipe while I transport you to the heady year of 2013. Lorde's "Royals" was choking the airwaves and—

AMY: What are you doing?

CASEY: Setting the stage for—

AMY: I already did that.

CASEY: Oh...How far did you—

*Shipwreck* began as a three-event series to round out the sleepy summer months when nobody is on book tour and Booksmith's events programming lags. The first show had fifty people. The second had more. The third: even more. We kept it going. Within six months we had to start moving every shelf out of the back of the bookstore to accommodate all the regulars and the first dates and the would-be contributors and the stunned tourists who wandered in and stayed with their hands over their kids' ears. Shows started to sell out weeks early. People on social media started saying things like, "This is the most despicable literary event possible (@nathanielwagg)," and "It used to be we had to sit in dark, sticky booths to get these kinds of sleazy thrills (@courteousflush)."

Local rags started writing think pieces about us. One (and this is true) was titled "Why We Can't Have Nice Things: Erotic Literature Contest at Booksmith." We'd announce a book for an upcoming show and the store would immediately sell all their copies. We took the show on the road—all the way to New York City! Our faces were even on MTV.com, which, if you were a '90s kid, is a big fucking massive mind-blowing deal.

To quote the profile about the show on KALW and sum up the evening's ambiance quite succinctly: "this is the largest group of people I've ever seen in a bookstore, enjoying themselves raucously."

*Produces book of clippings to ease your skepticism*

And it *is* raucous. People cosplay, they bring props, they make signs. During *Little Women*, someone brought a bag of limes and quietly rolled one up the aisle every time a lime was mentioned. People wore shark costumes to *Jaws*. A writer brought two Dorothy costumes during *The Wizard of Oz* and changed midshow. Another writer brought about eighty succulents to *Great Expectations* to give it an authentic Miss Havisham vibe. We even embraced our inner neighborhood haunted house with strategically placed dry ice for *Frankenstein*. We went from a literary event at a prestigious bookstore that looked completely dignified to an outsider to what was essentially a mini-con: it's fanfiction come to life.

That's Who, What, and How. What remains is Why? Our favorite part. The Why is that fanfic creates a back door into a one-sided conversation through which anyone can enter. It takes the vast collection of leather-bound volumes down off the shelf and reveals it for what it is: books of words, written by people, that make us feel a lot of things but also leave a lot of people behind or out completely. We fanfic because it's fun to join the conversation about books we genuinely love. We erotica because it's essential that we take neither ourselves nor the canon too seriously to appreciate what lies beneath—the lovely and often problematic personalities, times, and observations of the Great Books by which we measure our world. *Shipwreck* lives in that space in between the sharp intake of breath at the beauty of the thing and a sarcastic exhale, a *pfft*, at its presumptions.

We talk back, basically. Something fans have been doing long before we got here (long before the internet, even) but seldom so—

CASEY: Out loud in a room full of embarrassed spectators?
AMY: Right!

Along the ride, we've poked some gentle fun at fanfiction, but the truth is, we love fanfiction. We've always had it out for Holden Caulfield, not E. L. James—fanfic was just the vehicle we used to get there. We're taking books apart by putting figgy pudding in places that figgy pudding was never supposed to go (apologies to Mrs. Cratchit).
*Crosses room to bask thoughtfully in the warm light of the hearth*
And here's the thing we're maybe most proud of: The show did all of this without being mean to people who didn't deserve it. We're not perfect, but we've worked our asses off at keeping this adventure safe—always consent, always inclusion, at all costs. Our tagline is "We're not dicks; we just like dick jokes." We do our best to stand by it.
So that's *Shipwreck*.
Now here it is in book form, and we couldn't be happier. All that remains is a simple question.
*Clears throat*
Are you ready for some PORN?

# Classics

$\mathcal{W}$elcome to the Classics section, in which, inevitably, *The Great Gatsby* comes first. When we launched *Shipwreck* in 2013, the Baz Luhrmann movie was making the rounds, and it only made sense to lead with that foot. A year later when we took the show to New York, we couldn't resist taking Gatsby's yellow car out of the garage for another spin. Why?

We learn this book as teenagers, when we're tiny doe-eyed babes who think this is what grown-ups are like. Gatsby's preoccupation with and unrelenting pursuit of Daisy maybe makes sense when you're in high school. To a person with an incomplete frontal lobe, Jay Gatsby's obsession comes off as romantic, and generally indicative of what True Love™ looks like in the sophisticated world of jazz parties and Rolls-Royces (Rollses-Royce?).

But then you read the book again as a grown-up with fresh eyes, eyes that have devoured countless think pieces and formed Serious Opinions on the white cis male hegemony we're all trapped in, and a few things jump out at you. As a grown-up, and even more so if you're a female grown-up, you probably want to fire Jay Gatsby out of a cannon into the sun, because oh my God, dude, seriously. Get a hobby, join a bowling league, do SOMETHING besides pine for a married woman with an alcohol problem and an extremely neglected kid.

The undeniable fact is, no matter how your life differs from the denizens of the western Long Island in the 1920s, this goddamn book resonates with people. Amy can tell you that in ten years of bookselling, she's never gotten through a shift at the register without ringing up at least one copy of *Gatsby*. T-shirts, matchboxes, pencil cases—if a piece of merch bears that signature image of the sad flapper with the naked girls in her eyes, it immediately becomes a bestseller. People. Love. This. Story.

So, there's your context. In this chapter, we learn how to care for Gatsby's car, we hear what Myrtle Wilson's remaining tit thought in its last moments of existence as a plot device at a gas station in Queens, and we down endless, endless champagne.

This is maybe a good time to clear up any potential confusion as to why certain authors in this book seem obsessed with ludicrous minutia and inanimate objects: We assigned them ludicrous minutia and inanimate objects. For *Gatsby* it was a certain billboard advertiser; for *Gone with the Wind* it was those fancy velvet drapes. Maybe we're jerks for this sort of thing, but our defense is twofold. First, even the most well known of books have only a handful of memorable characters. Second, nothing highlights the sexual imagination of a great writer like being stuck with a metaphor for a dance partner.

From *Gatsby* we move to *Great Expectations*, or #DeepDickens, as we now call our December shows. Not to put too fine a point on it, but the parallels between Pip's dogged pursuit of Estella through changing fortune bears more than a passing resemblance to *Gatsby*. Literature loves its creepers after all. Oh! Also, Miss Havisham makes an appearance via our first ever choose-your-own-pornventure submission (spoiler alert: All roads lead to Miss H getting her groove back).

From there, we drive our phaeton to *Pride and Prejudice*, with apologies to Darcy's horse, where we live out our vicarious and all-too-modern need to see these staid Regency types muddy up their skirts and set aside decorum. Pair with pearls to maximize clutching opportunities.

Then we mount the decks of *Moby Dick* to call Ishmael a fuckboy to his weather-beaten face. Like the source material, these pieces explore the deeds, loves, and faith of hardened seamen. Unlike the source material, there are a couple of women in the pages.

From Nantucket we turn our attention southward—after a brief layover in the passive-aggresivity of *Little Women*—to Tara in *Gone with the*

*Wind*. We chose this book for our one-year anniversary show, with all past winners competing. We really did assign the velvet drapes to one of our writers (see "Maybe we're jerks" above). In addition, a dashing, if short-limbed, predatory lizard leaves his calling card, and we catch a glimpse behind the doors of an Antebellum-themed orgy for maximum ick factor.

*Animal Farm* is next, and it is so gross you'll probably never again read the words *farm to table* with the rustic appeal intended by marketing copywriters. You will, however, come away with a healthy respect for the tenacity of farmhouse cats.

Next is *The Picture of Dorian Gray,* and we like to think of Oscar Wilde up in heaven, lounging in a trunk full of cash a la Rihanna in "Bitch Better Have My Money," jeering, "What was that about gross indecency?" Come for the dandies hurling themselves at fainting couches. Stay for a lesson in the loveways of anthropomorphized art.

And finally, back to #DeepDickens for a Christmas massacre that ensured nothing but coal in our stockings (or, in this case, up Bob Cratchit's ass [yes]).

Let that serve as your bar napkin roadmap as we turn our sights back to the glittering shores of the Long Island Sound, where if you listen closely you can just make out the dripping of tiny male tears beating back the wants and needs of any other characters on or around West Egg.

# THE GREAT GATSBY

## "Gatsby" by Seanan McGuire

In the end, Gatsby's problem was a simple one—perhaps too simple. Simple things are often harder to see when set against a backdrop of the spectacular, like trying to find a single spider in a garden filled with roses. But it is the spiders that will hurt you, in the end. Gatsby's was a garden filled with spiders, and all because of that one simple thing: No matter how many high-class whores and wild-eyed youngest daughters he brought into his bedroom—or into his hotel suites, rather, for the bedroom was reserved, ever reserved, for the gloriously golden fantasy who had long since claimed her marital privileges, if only in his dreams—Jay Gatsby never learned to fuck like old money.

Old money could afford to purchase pussy like it was nothing. Great teeming seas of heaving breasts and open legs, each with their own mysteries to suck and sample. Old money could try every perversion and permutation of the sexual world before most men could dream of more than a trip to a carnival coochie show, where a woman whose best days were further behind her than an old farm horse might pull her sequined skirt a little too high, granting them a glimpse of the mysteries that lay tucked and dreaming twixt her thighs. Old money could buy the carnival, buy the coochie show, buy the broken-down

7

old dancing girls, if it saw the need. Old money had no need for mystery, for poetry, for anything but prizing wide the legs of the world and ramming itself balls-deep into the dark and hidden places. Old money was carnal, cruel, jaded, capable of almost anything while genuinely concerned with almost nothing.

Gatsby learned this the first time he traded one of those top-flight call girls for a doe-eyed dame with legs like a road to heaven and a cunt like the Promised Land. He'd expected their bodies to come together in erotic verse, his hands and lips and cock writing the depth of his love for Daisy on the body of a nameless stand-in whose pleasure he would pursue almost as apology, for what was fucking without love?

Instead, he had been ridden as hard as a jalopy, pressed broken and sweating into the sheets while the force of nature he had invited into his bed worked through her anger at her father, at society, at the world. She'd kissed his cheek before she left him, told him that he was "sweet," and slipped, still nameless, out of the room while his prick lay quivering against his thigh, coated in the smell of her.

The fucking of old money, he had quickly decided, would take more effort to master.

So it was more expensive whores. So it was more dissatisfied daughters (and the occasional dissatisfied wife, a rarer, more dangerous beast to bridle, what with the risk of husbands coming home, but most of them had gone so long without a proper fucking that they welcomed him in with open arms). So it was more cheap, impersonal trysts in closets and in cloakrooms and once, when the champagne had flowed particularly easy and the night had grown spectacularly late, in the backseat of a stranger's car. Lacy undergarments, rumpled curls, and a dozen, two dozen, a hundred beautiful cunts all blurred together into the faint taste of salt and the bruises on his hips. And still—still, for all of that—he came to their beds eager and alert, watching their moods, desperate to please them and to be pleasured in return. If Jay Gatsby had been a soldier before he found his fortune, his cock was a soldier still, surmounting beachhead after beachhead, maidenhead after maidenhead, in search of that perfect degree of jaded detachment.

New money fucked like sex was still something precious and rare and difficult to come by. The tendency of Jay Gatsby to put the pleasure of his partners before his own was whispered through certain secret channels, until he found himself surrounded by flocks of hopefully smiling girls in fringe and sequins, their jaded eyes bright with the thought of tasting—and being tasted by—something new. He was kind to them all, because kindness was a part of the persona he had so carefully constructed, and he thought he kept them at a pleasant distance even when they had their legs wrapped around his waist and their fingers buried in his hair. He was detached. Cool. Untouchable. He told himself that, and he kept telling himself that, and no one believed him, least of all the girls who left him bruised and aching on the floor.

Gatsby cared too much to ever understand the world that he had chosen, that had never chosen him.

When Daisy finally came to him, pale and perfect and trembling, he thought the world was finally setting itself right: that at long last, the story he had been composing for years was beginning to be told. He fell upon her with all the lessons he had learned from his nameless girls—but, ah, this was no hired harlot; this was no bored and bloodless heiress. This was Daisy, his Daisy, and when she spread her legs for him, his heart stopped, just like it had on that long-gone North Dakota day when the lady at the carnival coochie tent had taken his quarter and shown him her secret, hidden labyrinth of pleasures. How could he be detached? She was everything that he had ever wanted and more, and she wanted him, and all he cared about was pleasing her as a woman should be pleased. His tongue was Theseus in search of the Minotaur, and when he found the hard knot of its lair at the top of her cunt, he bore down until she moaned like Ariadne in the dark. When she left him come morning, her dress clutched around her and her knees still weak, he knew that she had been most thoroughly and sincerely fucked. And that, in the end, was his undoing, for there is no hiding such sincerity in a world of pasteboard and façade.

A man may change many things: his name, his standing, the cut and fabric of his shirt. But he cannot change the nature of his prick or the memory of a carnival dame with her skirt hiked and her eyes shadowed by the ghosts of the sweet young girl she once had been. Jay Gatsby fucked with sincerity. He fucked like new money, like every lay was precious and not his due. Perhaps if he had learned to do differently, he would have fucked for longer. But not, perhaps, with half so much brilliance.

# "Caring for and Using Your New Car" by Jeffrey Cranor

So you just bought a brand-new automobile. Congratulations, car-buyer. Auto-haver. Drive-taker. Stick-shift fiddler. Road-rubber. Asphalt dry-humper.

You have joined the prestigious club of horseless carriage own-ers, but what next, rich guy? You certainly know how to spend your money...how to release the burning leather throb in your pants pocket. But how do you take care of the darn thing?

Well, relax, muffler-lover. Just follow these three simple guidelines for upkeep of your new car:

## PART ONE: Engine maintenance

Check your oil every three to four weeks. To do this you'll need to open the hood. Just reach your hand down below your seat. Between your legs you'll find a thin, hard wire. Tug on your wire until you hear a mechanical thump.

Now step to the front of your vehicle and place your fingers under the open edge of the hood. Raise the car's top slowly, because what is underneath is extremely hot. Slowly. Yes. Slowly lift its top.

Now bend forward. Lean forward, deep into the purring hollow. Find the dipstick. It's a small firm knob. It's very difficult to find. Move your face around the engine until you locate it. You will know when you do.

Don't move so quickly. Slow down or you'll miss it. Go up a bit. No, up. Up. There. There. That's it. You've…Nope. That's not it. To the left some. Maybe move your hands about a bit. It's a small iron loop, okay? Maybe if you put your fingers in there to feel about. Yes.

Yes! That is it!

Now pull that dipstick and check the oil level. That's it. That was pretty good for your first time.

But look at you. Covered in oil and holding your dipstick. You're a sticky mess.

Do you have a towel? You probably should have brought a towel. Definitely wipe that thing off before you put it back in.

## PART TWO: Proper body care

Care for your paint job like you would care for your own skin. You wouldn't NOT take a shower, would you? You wouldn't forget to put on lotions and powders, would you? You would never leave the house without a quick spritz of pleasing aromas—or as they sell in France: Axe body spray.

So why would you not also give the body of your car a similar caring touch? A car is an extension of your own self. Like you, your car is elegant, sleek, hard, pricy, loud, not as valuable as when it was new, covered in bird shit sometimes, an indifferent capitalist monolith, and supremely beautiful.

Wash your car with warm water and soap once a week. Use a terry cloth to rub out the dirt buildup. Get on your knees and put your hands along the long chrome bumper and stroke it clean. Stroke it till it squeaks. Wear old clothes so you can get a little dirty. You don't have to worry if you splash a little warm soapy water down the front of your too-tight white shirt.

But be careful! You accidentally spilled a whole bucket on your shirt, and trying to rub it dry with the already soapy sponge is not helping.

In fact, it looks like you tore the top of the shirt a little, and now it's splitting down the middle, your hard chest pressing out, shiny and smooth with sudsy foam. Maybe you should just rub your soft, wet pecs up and down the warm shaft, just so you don't waste any soap. Yes. That's it. That's a very good rhythm. Just lay your slick skin against the hard metal tube and glide back and forth in smooth, even motions.

That's the art of cleaning the chrome. Next, let's shine that paint job. So you got a yellow car? Well, how fashionable. Nothing says "disposable wealth" like a yellow car. Nothing says "I don't give two flapper fucks; look at my yellow fucking car, you proletariat dogs" quite like getting a yellow car. Plus, dirt doesn't show up on yellow quite like it does on darker colors. But blood does. Sometimes the American Dream just wanders into the middle of the road and you simply don't have the time—or the empathy—to hit the brakes before *splat!* American fucking Dream symbolically streaking across the symbolic yellow fenders of your symbolic automobile...parentheses hubris.

But as long as you wax regularly, you oligarchic titan you, you should have no problems keeping your outer appearance clean.


## PART THREE: Proper operation of an automobile


We've talked about maintaining the engine. We've talked about keeping the car's good looks, but now the most important part: How do you even use a car?

This is an important question on the minds of many first-time 1920s car buyers. You must be asking yourself the obvious question: How do I fuck this car? I'd like to rev my odometer needle into the red. How do I go about fucking this vehicle?

First off, never fuck a car. Very few cars are ergonomically designed with fucking in mind. Also, while they are not sentient, and are thus unaware of being fucked, no car has ever agreed to a fucking. Third, even if it could agree to being fucked, I repeat, it is not sentient and thus could not enjoy nor reciprocate the enjoyment of fucking, which is a necessary part of fucking. Finally, it's likely you are saying, "But what about the exhaust pipe?" And that's a terrible point, as no human can fill an exhaust pipe with their member. Your flesh shaft would just lie there, pitifully small in the much larger metal shaft; imagine a breadstick getting an MRI.

But while car fucking is out of the question, fucking in cars is completely acceptable. In fact, 75 percent of car owners never actually drive their cars; they just fuck in them.

Fucking in a car is fun and easy. First, ask someone if they would be down for some mutual backseat cum sessions. Second, that's vulgar and probably didn't work. Try asking them more subtly, like, "Hey, I like you. We've been dating awhile and I think we've reached a point in our relationship where it is time to sit in a backseat and touch each other until we explode liquids across our bare skin, surprised faces, and plush leather fold-away seats, heaving and breathing and feeling the lights of the city far below our sweat-dipped bodies." Third, okay, that approach didn't work either, so look, just pull into this rest stop and jerk off. Hurry up. Okay, you can clean yourself with those Carl's Jr. napkins that have been in the cup holders for...God, you can't even remember the last time you had Carl's Jr.

Well, anyway, congratulations, you've just fucked in your new car.

And that's it. You are now ready for the thrill of car ownership. You can put on your racing goggles, open those windows, and ease down your trousers. It's time to hit the road.

## "Eyes of the Beholder" by Mara Wilson

Clara couldn't see a thing.

"You broke them again?" her mother scolded. "No man will ever marry such a clumsy girl!" But it hadn't been entirely Clara's fault this time. She could never tell her mother what had truly happened.

Fred—poor Fred, the skinniest boy on the wrestling team—had taken her out driving, just the two of them and a flask. In the midst of their petting, Fred, flush with hooch, had asked her if she wanted to try that thing he'd heard Flora did to Skip. Clara had enjoyed it more than she had expected—yes, it ruined her perfect Louise Brooks lipstick job, but there was a look in Fred's eyes she had never seen before. He was enraptured, and for once, he didn't look as though he, too, was wishing for a superior specimen. But it had all fallen apart when, in the height of ecstasy, he had knocked off Clara's glasses and stepped on them. Fred had driven her home in a panic, too embarrassed to look at her. Or maybe he had; it was hard to tell without her glasses.

Poor old Dr. Goldfarb didn't work on Saturdays, so Clara's sight was entrusted to a perfect stranger. Now, all alone in a small, dark, and unfamiliar room, she knew her mother was right. Clara buried her face in her hands. She had tried so hard! She had bobbed her hair, but her finger curls never stayed. She had tried to smoke but had only given herself an attack of the vapors. She would never marry an Ivy League man, never even leave Queens, never go driving with any boys ever again. With her long, thin, ivory fingers over her eyes, Clara began to sob.

"Sit up, please." The voice was warm, deep, authoritative and seemed to come from everywhere. Clara looked up, but the room was dim, and there were only blurs.

"Doctor?" she said. "I . . . I'm sorry . . . I just . . ."

"Went and got your glasses broken," said the voice. "But it wasn't your fault, was it?"

"How did you know?" she said before she could stop herself.

"I see a lot of patients," said the voice. "Now pick up the paddle to your left and look straight ahead."

Clara blushed. The paddle looked like a smaller version of the paddle Sister Hyacinth had used to spank her at St. Mary's School for Girls. How humiliating it had been, her skirt pulled up, the paddle coming down again and again, feeling all the other girls' eyes on her... She could feel them still.

"Is something the matter?"

"No," she said. "I was just thinking of... What should I do?"

"Hold it over your right eye and read the chart."

"Um, E? R? B?"

A blur moved in front of her eyes, adjusting the chart.

"Do that again."

"B... D... S..." The letters were much bigger and much easier to read this time.

"It's better when it's bigger, isn't it?" said the voice.

"I'm sorry?" blurted Clara.

"You're very nearsighted."

"Oh. Yes," she said, feeling embarrassed. What on earth could she have been thinking he meant? She covered her other eye and tried to focus on reading the chart. The room felt warmer, and there was a scent in the air, something decidedly masculine.

"Move forward and put your chin on the chinrest." She moved her chair, reaching vainly in front of herself.

"Here." And then his hands were on her, guiding her. His touch was warm, even through his gloves. His hands were large and strong, the first grown man's hands ever to touch her.

"Yes. Right there," said the voice, and Clara felt one of his hands slip down her neck. Was it her imagination or was he letting his hand linger where Fred had left a mark? She shivered.

A chair moved. She could feel his knees on the outside of her own.

"Try it now."

The scent was stronger now, bringing to mind all the same improper visions that played in her head when she was alone in bed at night or when necking became tiresome. Her nipples grew harder, pressing up against her chemise, and she pressed her legs together, trying to quiet the aching need growing deep between them.

"Is that better?"

"Yes," she whispered. Something other than the chart appeared on the other side of the lenses, and for the first time, Clara saw the owner of the voice. This wasn't a perfect stranger. She knew those eyes. The color was somewhere between ice and steel. Younger than she had expected, yet somehow ageless. They had peered down on her from billboards in Queens, and once—her heart quickened at the memory—while she was out with Fred. That had been the night they'd first...

Clara gasped. Without even thinking, with her face still immobilized by the machine, she had begun to rock herself against the chair, feeling the hard, smooth, polished wood against her most intimate areas. Pleasure flooded her body as new lenses clicked into place and the eyes on the other side became clearer.

"Do that again," he said.

"Do...do what?" Her heart did the Charleston in her chest.

"You know what," he said, and his voice was as icy and powerful as his eyes.

Tentatively, she rocked herself forward again, her bare knees kissing his clothed ones.

"Yes...," he said, his voice all around her. A jolt went through Clara's body, and she reached out for him, gripping his knees. He took hold of her hands and gently led them down to her own sex.

"Please," she moaned. "Please..."

"Do it," he said, pushing his chair just out of her reach. "I want to see you."

As quickly as she could, with trembling fingers, Clara shimmied out of her knickers. Her knees were still touching as she slipped her hand down onto her sex, already wet with her desire. She traced along her folds, gently at first, then with more pressure, stroking herself until there was nothing but that electric ecstasy enveloping her. Her legs parted, as of their own accord, and even with her eyes closed, she could still feel his eyes on her. He watched her as he had always watched her.

"Yes, that's right," he said, his voice husky with desire as she slipped a finger into herself. "Right there..."

Clara moved faster, harder, pulsing, luxuriating in her own slick

softness as she heard his breath quicken. His enrapture only strength-
ened her own, and she moaned as she had never done with a man
before. There was only her and him, his scent and his voice and his
eyes...his eyes...She threw back her head as a final, penetrating wave
of bliss washed over her.

Clara opened her eyes. Still shaking, she pulled up her knickers. His
hands were on hers, holding a small piece of paper.

"Take this to the front shop," he said. "Get a rimless pair—you'll
look marvelous."

"Thank you," she said, taking it. "Thank you for everything."

He crossed behind her, out through the door and into the daylight.

"I'll be seeing you."

## "Daisy in Profile" by Joseph Fink

So to start off with, my name is Daisy Fay. I'm five foot something or
other, and I'm always surrounded by flowing white cloth. It's kind of
my thing. My measurements are enough, yes, more than enough, and
none of your business.

What does one usually say in these things? Favorite food? Happiest
memories?

There was this one time when I was absolutely paralyzed with happiness. Or, not happiness. What's that word for when someone has a
tongue on your clit and a slowly increasing number of fingers inside
of you, and it's been that way for twenty minutes or so, building and
building? It's like happiness, but it's...Oh that's right. G-spot orgasm.
I was paralyzed with a G-spot orgasm. Then I was flailing around and
kicking with a G-spot orgasm.

By way of thank you, I ejaculated all over the young officer's face,
which I was just then making use of, and he responded, "Glad to oblige,
old sport," or rather, since I shoved his tiresome mouth right back into

my East Egg, "Grrgh to obbgge, olff sprtt." He had this vibrator on me, a big, fast yellow one, and as I came, I thought, *Well, this could about kill a woman.*

And, yes, I am very open to experimenting with my West Egg as well.

My favorite kind of food is anything with gold leaf on it. Have you ever seen someone come on gold leaf that is itself on food? It is truly one of the most decadent things. I once had a husband with whom that was a nightly ritual.

Actually, he had a hard time coming on anything that wasn't gold. He'd gotten so caught up with the idea of wealth that he wanted to actually fuck capitalism itself. I had to paint myself to look like an Academy Award and shove a diamond in my twat just to get him to fuck me.

Oh, speaking of which, I have a daughter. I'm very much a proud mother. Her name is Pimmy or Puny or Pussy. I'm not sure. Honestly I forget her sometimes. I find that most people do.

"I don't even remember Daisy having a child," they'll say.

"I have the same problem," I say. Then I sit on the person's face and neither of us has any problems at all. Until little whatshername starts crying or wants food or something annoying like that. Ugh. Kids, right?

What else should I say? More favorites?

My favorite city is Chicago. So many skyscrapers but without all the emotional men who seem to hang around New York. One time I was in a skyscraper and I had the most fascinating conversation with the man who worked the elevator.

"Keep your hands off the lever," he snapped.

"What, this?" I asked as I jerked off the lever with both hands.

"Yeah, what are you even doing?" he said.

"Nothing at all," I said, adding a twist to my two-handed elevator lever jerk technique and licking at its wooden tip. "I certainly could not imagine what you are talking about."

"That's gross," he said. "I have to touch that thing every day."

But that did not stop him from changing out of his elevator outfit into an outfit issued to him by God herself. He had a brute of a cock. A great, big, hulking physical specimen of a cock.

I told him to get back to work at once and he did. And while he was working on one end, the elevator lever worked the other. As big and stiff as the elevator man was, he had nothing on his elevator's lever. Unfortunately, the movements we were engaged in caused the lever to move up and down, and thus the elevator itself to career wildly between floors, occasionally opening the doors to display to an entire gape-mouthed office the sight of me bent over, naked, and burning the candle at both ends, as it were.

What was I talking about? Right. I like Chicago. What else?

Do you always watch for the longest cock of the year and then miss it? I always watch for the longest cock of the year and then miss it.

Let's see, what more about me? Maybe talk about my friends?

I had one friend once, won't say who she was but she was a famous athlete if you call golf a sport, and let's just say that I let her take a few swings at me.

Or I won't just say that. Do I seem like the type of person to deflect with a sports pun when I could tell you about the time she had me upside down on the divan, with my dress flung over the top of me, giving me the old silent talking to down there, when who walks in but my cousin of all people and we have to swing right around and sit there like nothing is happening while I'm feeling like I'm sloshing around in a kiddy pool, and even after my friend wiped her mouth off, she had to keep her chin at this weird upturned angle so no one would see the Daisy run-off all over it. Her lips wouldn't stop fluttering, like she was still going at me. Why, our dresses must have looked like she had just blown me all over the house, because that's what had just happened.

But enough about my social life.

This is my first time using OkCupid, so I certainly hope that was enough information for a profile. If you're interested, do shoot me a message.

Please be wealthy, well spoken, well endowed, all the wells. Also, please do not be a weird ex-boyfriend who uses a fortune of illegally acquired funds to stalk me at my vacation home and spends evenings jerking off to colored lighting. Been down that road already, thank you.

Oh, speaking of roads, it's probably best if you drive on the date. I have a few points on my license.

Love,

Daisy Fay.

## "Nick Carraway" by Carolyn Ho

He reaches down and pulls out the enigmatic wonder of his smooth and clean-shaven testicles. Each one resembles a dark poached egg from which a lingering smell of pickles, groin sweat, and cheese inebriates me, a waft so thick I salivate and moan. I do not mean to moan, but for all my ability to remain aloof I cannot contain myself. My eyes roll back. And I faint. When I regain my senses, I am unable to move beneath my dear Gatsby's surprising paunch, a robust thing once restrained behind silken finery, now wild and flapping ecstatically upon me. Yes, my darlings, Gatsby is in fact flabby. Regardless, the world ends briefly now, in this moment, as I'm happily smothered by a wealthy millionaire; he collapses upon a bisexual, incest-loving, sardonic bondsman. And after a few seconds of rapid blinking, Gatsby's face hovers over mine. His lips tremble as he places his soft fingers on my hair, my neck. His fingers trail down to my ass and he calls my name with the urgency of someone calling another off a balcony, off a ledge, off a bridge. "Nick, Nick, oh, Nick, I'm bad. I've been such a bad, bad little boy."

I'm not ashamed of his sex talk, until a small dog comes close to the door, peers through the glass into the dim sitting room, and sits, watches diligently as I and the great Gatsby fuck as only gentlemen can, on the ground, slacks and boxers loose around the ankles, sock garters high on the calves. We collect our hair pomade and gather it generously around my buttocks. The dog, unblinking and unforgiving, seems to say, "Nick, old chap, what's happening?" I have no reply. I move my arms about as if shooing away a fly, but the dog sits, unflinching. It seems determined to stare, to be the voyeur. Eyes locked, we remain still, until it begins to yelp as only small dogs can, high-pitched and relentless. It even begins licking itself. Barks and then licks. And then more avidly bites its little groin as Gatsby increases his pace behind me. No matter how hard or fast, I cannot focus on Gatsby in the least, so we stop and resume outside into the ambiguity of the night.

And we do continue. On the beach he reaches down and once again pulls out his smooth, pungent balls, and I am both hungry and aroused and again cannot contain myself and come prematurely in my pants. And again, my eyes roll back. And again I faint.

After a few seconds I am awake. Gatsby stands upright and flicks off the sand lodged between his testicles and his anus and slaps my bare back as if congratulating me on a good game of tennis. "Good try, old sport." With almost all his clothes on, he offers his bejeweled hand to help me up. His every nail is manicured and smooth, his palms lotioned so softly, I instantly imagine the supple but firm penis that would be gloved by such a velvety grip and accept the gesture. We are, after all, more than men, but the quiet roar of the ocean, two great whales dancing, the sexing of water in the dark night, the sound of buttocks and balls clapping like the crashing shore around us, the thrashing and undulating slipperiness of a thousand phallic sea anemone reaching toward the surface of sky and opening. This is love. And I want more. I cannot stop touching myself.

We try again, and this time I can feel Gatsby's parts, their light knocking against my inner thigh as they tickle incessantly, balls tapping like impatient fingers. I cannot tell the difference between him and Daisy for a brief moment and almost call out her name. As if Gatsby's staccato engulfment of my anus and Daisy's strap-on dildo are one—a fluid transgression of time—and if Gatsby's dainty balls were not beating lightly upon my skin, I would have forgotten him altogether, lost in a memory. Gatsby's hips and hands are so like Daisy's, so familiar. I could almost see it now, that one summer vacation back home from Yale, visiting Daisy in the rear garden, her fingers twirling her hair and then tenderly stroking it. She had asked if I still remembered her, and I did. She placed her hand over my eyes, that delightful girl, and before I could ask further, she undid my belt and yanked my pants down with her other hand, and to my great surprise, managed to insert her new dildo with a swift and hard push, and giggled. But more so, I remembered her delicate, thin hands around her new wooden toy. Her hands were so smooth, so refined, like Gatsby's hands now, placed in mine, that the garden suddenly merges with the black beach side, a blurring of horizons. In one push of his pelvis, the past becomes the present and time becomes singular. I cannot tell you what happened next, other than I involuntarily whisper Daisy's name into Gatsby ear, and abruptly I hear the clear sound of water breaking as Gatsby's body stiffens. He coils away from me instantly, covers himself, and leaves without looking at me, without pausing, without a word.

I put on my clothes and find myself suddenly cold and more flaccid than I have ever been. My knees ache. I watch Gatsby's shadow return to the glow of his party. His outline grows smaller, sinks into the brightness. I follow him as one follows a broken heart, regrettably, and tragically still—my stained boxers are ruined and I am no longer hungry, for anything. With each step toward the spectacle of affluence and glittering excess of millionaires, I am more consumed by thoughts of how I could apologize, undo the damage of a name. I could send him hair pomade and attach a love note that reads, *This is as much for you as it is for me*. I fantasize chance encounters near the bathroom among his hand towels, miniature soaps, and gilded faucets. He would catch me grinding along on his laid-out tailored suits and shimmering ascots. Or perhaps the pool...yes, the pool, which was so like the ocean. Maybe I could swim naked, an elaborate backstroke with my penis floating left, then right, waving to him. I continue thinking of the pool and how the dramatics of the world required much maintenance, much plotting, and I was no exception to its tireless intricacies.

At some point, Jordan finds me engulfed by the view of the ocean

*The future seems orgasmic and stretched out like refractions of light from a place that could never be touched or held, and immediately I drink everything in one sip and ask for more champagne, endless champagne.*

from the balcony. She smiles as she hands me a flute of champagne and asks, "Finally having a gay time, are we?" And I am. Certainly. With thoughts of Gatsby, I feel every pubic hair stand straight up, stiff by the mere thought of his name. "Indeed," I say. The future seems orgasmic and stretched out like refractions of light from a place that could never be touched or held, and immediately I drink everything in one sip and ask for more champagne, endless champagne.

## "Myrtle Wilson" by Jacquelyn Landgraf

*ARE YOU GODDAMN KIDDING ME????!!* thought Myrtle Wilson in the split second of consciousness she had left after that hysterical wisp of a flapper twat plowed the car into her supple body, ripping off her gigantic left breast like some Amazonian sacrifice, ending with a final rimshot that dream deferred, raisin-in-the-goddamn-sun life of hers. She sucked in one last great gulp of the Valley of Ashes—also known more plainly as just the goddamn sorry-ass borough of Queens—and as her tremendous vitality mingled with the gravel of I-95 in the form of dark blood and vitriol, the three men who shaped her sad destiny flashed before her eyes.

Myrtle remembered all those nights bent over the gas pump. "You can't live forever; you can't live forever," she would moan in a stage whisper, her thick knuckles blanching as she desperately pumped herself again and again with the curved iron nozzle, the brute force of the hard cold pipe incrementally raising her internal odometer at increments of ten until she orgasmed angrily into the vast expanse of ashes, screaming bitterly, "America! America!"

This nightly habit began shortly after she married George Wilson. He had fucked her exactly one time: their wedding night. He had just barely managed to heave her ample body over the threshold of their garage when she overtook him and pinned him to the hood of the Ford

Model T he'd been repairing. Before he knew what hit him, Myrtle had bitten off and swallowed the three buttons of his borrowed wedding suit and was plunging his own astonished gearshift toward the back of her throat, where he felt not one but strangely several very muscular tonsils shoving the head of his penis in every direction, like bullies on a schoolyard. Next she had him on the ground, writhing in a puddle of grease, staring up the skirt of her wedding dress as the lips of her personal two-car garage opened hungrily and clamped back down on his unsuspecting emission hose. He tried to kiss her. She punched him in the nose.

Four hours later, without removing his cock from her muffler, Myrtle managed to carry George, his legs wrapped around her waist, into the twenty-four-hour diner next to the garage. The Greek who ran the joint turned away, nonplussed, as the Wilsons crashed into the kitchen. Myrtle instructed George to ram her from behind as she grilled herself a Monte Cristo and gulped down six Coca-Colas and a lime Rickey. She teasingly hid five hard-boiled eggs between her enormous heaving breasts for George. He could only find one. It was all he had eaten that day.

At hour thirteen they were back in the garage and George felt momentarily revitalized when Myrtle turned the hose of the air pump toward his face, but then, raising an eyebrow in curiosity, she inserted the hose into herself. He felt the head of his beleaguered pecker curve downward slightly and soldier on, like a determined migrant worker forging forward through the Dust Bowl. Which had not yet even occurred. A pair of rusty alligator clamps were chomping steadily at either end of their nipples in a bloody game of tug-of-war when, at the twenty-hour mark, out of sheer boredom, Myrtle stuck a wrench up her ass and tried to unscrew something. But it wasn't until the final minutes of their first and only consummation when Myrtle at last felt the stirrings of something akin to satisfaction. With great ceremony, she locked eyes with the billboard of Dr. T. J. Eckleburg, spilled a can of motor oil onto her genitals with one hand, huffed a gasoline-soaked cloth with the other, and came with a barbaric yawp heard over the rooftops of Flushing. George, sobbing with relief, ejaculated a small hiccup of ashen-colored semen and promptly slipped into a coma for a week. Myrtle Wilson had fucked her husband for twenty-one hours straight, and in those twenty-one hours he had given her all there was of his manhood, all he had in him, forever.

*Tom Buchanan could get it up, that's for sure,* thought Myrtle as the dust that the careening car left in its wake settled on her exposed heart cavity. The mere thought of polo mallets, New Haven, white supremacy, or his own body sent Tom's pocket rocket pummeling forward like the Wabash Cannonball, and thus he had a constant, aggressive erection. Myrtle would sit alone in the train car covertly humping her portable gas can, sighing over the enormous trunk of dresses she was forced to bring anytime she went into New York City to fornicate with Tom. Tom's spooj could fill the Hoover Dam. Myrtle would turn on some Scott Joplin hymns, climb aboard his cock, get fucked hard and dirty for five minutes flat, at which point Tom would bellow into her knockers, "I AM THAT YANKEE DOODLE BOY!!!" and promptly break Myrtle's nose. She would double back as his semen hurled at gale force into her East and West Eggs, beat a hasty retreat, and spewed ecstatically back out of her vaginal maw, peopling every object within a three-yard radius with the excessive seed of Tom Buchanan. "I love him," she confided softly to her puppy as she cleaned the cum out of its fur, bandaged her nose, changed her dress, and prepared to go at it again.

But she loved Tom the way she loved taking a gulp of battery acid on a hot day in the Valley of Ashes: It was a quick reprieve from the existential crisis of her life as a plot device in the Great American Novel. She realized this as black bile began to trickle slowly out of her mouth.

Her thoughts turned to her one great love, that wild wag of an oculist, Dr. T. J. Eckleburg. At age sixteen, Myrtle wandered into an Astoria optometrist's office, a budding virgin who just recently had developed X-ray vision. Teej found her astonishing. They spent an entire chaste summer at each other's side. It was Myrtle's idea to put up the billboard above the highway announcing his new practice. They stood, hands entwined, beneath the fresh paint that immortalized the spectacles that only had eyes for Myrtle. That very night she gave herself to him, and it was then, sitting on T. J.'s face, that Myrtle realized the tremendous power of her own vitality. As the eye doctor licked, sucked, bit, and gnawed his way through her velvet curtains, electricity powerful enough to light all the skyscrapers in Manhattan surged through Myrtle's body. She bore down harder and harder as she came into herself, into this country, into her Manifest Destiny—and especially, into the face of Dr. T. J. Eckleburg. She finished triumphantly, unfastened her mountainous thighs from around his beautiful head, and...let out a desperate wail. She looked down at her lover's lifeless body, suffocated by the power of her ambition.

So it was with one final effort, as she lay mangled on that gravel road, that Myrtle lifted her skirt to place one hand over the lush forest of pubic hair that concealed the secret homage to her love—a tattoo of an eye chart, the tiniest letters readable only by a man who dared to place his face directly on her clitoris...which after T.J., no one ever had...

Myrtle Wilson took one last look at the sorry-ass borough of Queens, stared longingly at the eyes of her beloved Dr. T. J. Eckleburg, and goddamn died.

# GREAT EXPECTATIONS

## "Miss Havisham" by Lauren Traetto

Get this: You and your partner are on a European tour of banging each other—hashtag *eat pray fuck*. The blue-green moor has sprawled around you for hours, so you reach the rusty gate of your English Airbnb rental as the sun sets and not a minute too soon. You're both randy—you haven't done sex in, like, twelve hours.

You drive past rank gardens and park your Prius behind a decrepit manor. Definitely not as described. Your partner pulls up the listing titled "Rustic Bohemian Getaway Amidst English Gardens! Complimentary Cake Included" and rates it one star.

"Are you ready to get boinked like you've never been boinked before?" you ask. Rooks gather as you read the Airbnb instructions, which just say, *Strike the brass bell with the hammer, then proceed down the darkened passage.*

Inside, finding yourselves alone, you guys start seriously making out with each other. You know, you're doing Frenching and nipple play and everything, when you hear heavy breathing and the echo of footsteps. You freeze. "Who's there?" your partner says, trembling. The only response is silence...and then a wild cry. Do you:

* Follow the noise to find out what's going on? (Go to 1)

OR

* Run like hell back toward the exit? (Go to 2)

(1)

You follow the noise of the footsteps. In the dim passage, you are startled by a pale man with shitty teeth—the porter. "Room's upstairs on the right," he cackles, handing you the key. You pull up the collar of your North Face jacket and follow his instructions. (Go to 3)

(2)

You tear back through the dim passage. When you've almost reached the exit, you smack into a figure that appears out of nowhere— the porter, a pale man with shitty teeth. "Room's upstairs on the right," he cackles, handing you the key. You pull up the collar of your North Face jacket and obey his instructions. (Go to 3)

(3)

The stairway is draped with a fine lace. Dust glimmers above it, and green velvet coats the steps. Your partner slips, and you realize it's not velvet but a living carpet of moss and mold, and what you took for lace is just layers and layers of cobwebs. Something faster than anything human scrabbles down the walls and disappears.

Under the flickering sconces, you come to a door crawling with large black beetles, which scatter as it creaks open. A mist floats through the room, revealing a banquet table laid with cobwebs, a great rotting cake, and a stack of fresh guest linens, like the pins on your "conscious clutter" Pinterest board. There's a fire roaring in the hearth. "OMG, I love their staging," your partner says, taking off their limited-edition Toms. "Now let's do sex together on all the furniture that will bear our weight."

You schtupp furiously. You're enjoying each other so vividly that you almost don't notice a new shadow joining yours on the floor. You hear low laughter and look up to see the veiled specter of a woman, with hair indistinguishable from the cobwebs towering above you. A silk bridal gown hangs from her body like tattered cathedral banners.

"Well don't mind me," she says in a grimly playful manner. "I'd like to watch you play." The woman steps closer to you, one foot clad in a decaying stocking, a little white shoe on the other. Do you:

* Let her watch, because YOLO! (Go to 4)

OR

* Stop immediately because facing your own mortality is kind of a mood-kill? (Go to 5)

(4)

You and your partner continue fornicating, while your host watches. You're naked and writhing in the cobwebs and your own wetness like horny little houseflies. After about a minute, your host walks over to the vanity and starts drawing on her eyeliner like a boss. Is she bored by your hot yuppie sex? (Go to 6)

(5)

You stop noodling each other and watch as your host walks over to the decaying vanity and starts drawing on her eyeliner like a boss. (Go to 6)

(6)

You put your clothes on and cautiously walk over. "Who are you?" you ask.

"Give me your hand," she says, and places it on her chest. "What do you feel?"

"Your heart?" you guess.

"No. It's my boob," she says. "And it's still firm and great, and it bears no resemblance whatsoever to wax or a skeleton, because I'm only in my forties. I keep my shit tight with an exercise routine I call 'walking in circles around the banquet table.'"

She turns away from the mirror, wearing fabulous theater-style eyeliner. Her dress is torn open to the navel, revealing her powdered breasts. A faint bolero plays. "You may call me Miss Havisham," she says. "I'll let you commoners in on a little secret," she continues, rising from her rotting chair. "My whole life was ripped away from me once, by the two idiots I trusted most in the world. So I did what anyone would do."

"You hired a good therapist?" you ask.

She cackles. "No. I adopted a little girl. I thought, I'll be damned if I let the patriarchy use her as human property. So I taught her to play the game. And she's damn good at it." She picks up her crutch-headed cane and runs her fingers along its smooth, knobbed end.

"Of course, when Estella left, I found other ways to occupy my time." She absentmindedly lifts her skirt, revealing a shredded pair of silk panties. You could call them crotchless.

"That's when the orgies began," she continued, caressing the silk. "My pleasure, on my terms—the most liberating type of healing." She puts the tip of her cane to her mouth and runs her tongue along it. You can feel your face flushing as you look at Havisham's bare nipples.

She sees your hungry eyes on her. "I'm an unchaperoned woman with power and property," she says. "People around here literally don't know what to do with me. But I bet you do." She beckons you both to her black velvet couch and taps it with her cane. "Now you know where to take your stations to come feast on me."

"So, we're invited to the orgy?" your partner asks.

"It's optional for our Airbnb customers," she replies. "It starts at twenty minutes to nine. The other guests are arriving now. Cake is free either way."

Just then, there's a sound like beating wings outside the window, and you watch in horror as a pale, bluish hand touches the glass, frost etching its way outward from the fingerprints. The sound gets stronger, and through the haze you think you see white wings flapping. A burst of cold blows in, revealing a pale blue bearded face.

"A BRIDE!" he exclaims. "It must be my lucky day!"

"Oh for God's sake, go around back." Havisham closes the window on him. The cold has tightened her nipples. You look at your partner. Do you:

&ast; Stay and participate in the orgy? (Go to 7)

&ast; Pass for tonight and take your chances on the moor? (Go to 8)

(7)

The guests begin to file in, in various states of undress, and as the couplings begin, among the ethereal moans and supernatural pleasures, Miss Havisham begins to sing an old blacksmith's song in her low, growling tone. "Old Clem," she sings, keeping the rhythm for the guests. "Beat it out, beat it out—Old Clem. Blow the fire, blow the fire—Old Clem."

And the fire in the hearth rages through the night, casting your pulsing shadows on the fog. (The End)

(8)

"I think we're going to pass," you say. "Group sex isn't really something we are comfortable with yet."

"That's cool," Havisham says. "You can stay in one of the other rooms."

You decide to take a walk. Just outside the house, you hear Havisham singing an old blacksmith's song in her low, gravelly tone, keeping the rhythm for her guests. The hearth rages, casting pulsating shadows on the fog. Farther out on the moor, you look back to see what appears to be flames engulfing the estate, and then... nothing.


# "200 Pages of Exposition and Chill" by Joe Wadlington


Mr. Wopsle checked his pocket watch and realized he'd been banging on the gate for four pages.

"WOP-SUUUUUUUUL! WOP-SULLLLLLLLL!" he yelled, shaking the gate. Estella appeared out of the gray. Disdain was painted all over her pretty fucking face.

"Shit! Okay," Estella said, unlocking the gate. She closed it behind Mr. Wopsle before another white character could be introduced.

She drifted ahead without pleasantries, stopping only to adorn a flickering candle. He followed Estella through the labyrinth of passageways—which felt like a metaphor but never followed through. Eventually, they came to an open door. Estella flipped him off and disappeared.

"You can do it, Wopsle!" he said to himself, and entered. Miss Havisham was so reclusive it made Boo Radley look like a Kardashian.

She was wearing a yellowed wedding gown. Her veil connected to the floor, mimicking the cobwebs around her. On the dusty table was a mold-covered sheet cake with *Congrats, bitch!* written in pink icing.

"I'm Mr. Wopsle." He bowed.

"Ah, how neutral." Miss Havisham remained seated, weary from being the only interesting character. She began monologuing.

"I spend most of my days frowning at Estella in different levels of darkness. Other times I just gaze upon myself in the mirror and jack off onto one of my old save-the-dates." She nodded wearily. "My time is my own. I can take thirty pages to describe how greasy my walls are and the reader just has to fucking sit through it. But, Mr. Wopsle, I have enough characters who don't further the plot hanging around. Why are you here?"

Mr. Wopsle balled his fists and played at courage. "I'm merely a clerk at the church. But I practice sermon on my own accord—always improving my volume. It's important for the people in the back to hear you," he said.

"Well, God isn't listening, so it's proper they can," Miss Havisham said.

Mr. Wopsle felt his face casting to blush. "But unless the church is thrown open I will never serve as priest. I am boarding in my aunt's upstairs room, but my dream is to serve the theater," he said.

"You're living in your aunt's attic until your acting career takes off? How LA!"

"Please! You gave Pip Great Expectations? I'm hopeful you'd bestow the same generosity on me," he said.

"What the fuck are Great Expectations?" she asked.

"It's like inheritance," he said.

"Then why don't people just say 'inheritance'? 'Great Expectations' doesn't even sound like what you mean it to mean. Anyway, I haven't the theory why Pip carries on that way. I didn't give him Great Expectations. I just co-signed his student loans. That shit will be fucking him for the rest of his life," Miss Havisham said.

"Can you help me?" Mr. Wopsle's wheezing had found him. And he was sweaty in each of his personal corners. Miss Havisham rose and touched his cheek with tenderness.

"Oh, Wopsle, I won't start repenting for four hundred more pages. I'm sorry...this just isn't your chapter." She slapped him gently. "But this visit needn't fall to waste." She smiled with teeth like welcoming tombstones.

"It is in my service to visit a lonesome spinster."

She slapped him less gently. "Lonely? Baby, I never put the cake away because I didn't want the party to stop! I never wanted to get married. I just wanted to make Pinterest boards. But then I got 'tragically jilted.' That fuckboi gave me my freedom AND I have an excuse to ignore bridesmaid invites for the rest of my life! Do you understand how impossible it is for a woman to be free?!" She grabbed her ivory cane and hobbled to the head of the table. "This dress cost more than your church makes in a year and I don't even take it off to shit. I just pull it over my head like I'm a silk tulip."

Mr. Wopsle found himself flustered and pursued the woman. "The church doesn't make money," he said. "It's all donation based."

"Oh, I love Kickstarter!" Miss Havisham sat on the edge of the table. "But shouldn't your funding window be closed by now? I mean, it's been a while."

Mr. Wopsle couldn't accommodate his anger justly and it spilled into yells. "The church is not a fund. It's a community where I hope to preach! Which I shouldn't have to explain to the town's shriveled oddity!" he said.

"I await your apologies, Clerk! My oddity is the liveliest thing about my condition! My strangeness makes me virile!"

Their faces grew close, shaking with anger.

"You are GRAVE, depressing—a withered leaf," Mr. Wopsle said.

"The only thing the grave and I have in common is we're both irresistible." Miss Havisham stared at him powerfully and he shivered. She blew a long, dusty breath into Mr. Wopsle's mouth and he felt his blood switch organs.

"Wopsle, would you like to touch my genitals?" she said.

He looked at his feet. "Shouldn't we foreplay?" he asked.

"It took two hundred pages of exposition to get here. If this were the *Canterbury Tales*, I'd already be peeing you out!" She pulled her feet onto the table.

"I am a man of honor!" he said.

"No, you're an actor," she reclined.

"Yes, but if only the church were thrown open, I...I COULD serve."

The skirt made soft cracking noises as she pulled it upward, revealing her full, personal treasure. She pointed at her labia with the cane.

"Then here is the church," she whispered. She tapped at her clit gently. "Here is the steeple." Her knees parted. "Throw open the doors...and take a nice mouthful!"

The cane acquainted Mr. Wopsle's head and led him to dinner. His wheezing returned, filling Miss Havisham with vibrations.

"More nose!" she yelled.

Mr. Wopsle retreated a few inches and let his Roman nose slap great pleasure into her private fortune. His hands grabbed the gown's hem and broke it with a crunch. He grabbed more. Crunch! More crunch! The dress crumbled in sections, littering the table.

"Preach!" she yelled. Mr. Wopsle spoke Revelation into Miss Havisham, bass tones so low they shook dust from the walls.

She was so light and frail, the pulsing from Wopsle's tongue pushed her body away. He climbed onto the table to continue the occasion. With each glide forward, more of the dress broke off and crunched loudly like dry leaves.

"THIS IS MY FAVORITE PART OF FALL!" Wopsle yelled, stomping with his knees. He never broke rhythm, wheezing into her with quick falsettos and Great Exhalations. Miss Havisham hit the cake and started making an icing snow angel. She was so close! She started yodeling "Great Exclamations!" Her flailing arms knocked over the candles. They immediately caught on the dry dress fabric covering the table. Mr. Wopsle's head engulfed in flame. She was even closer!

"I DOOOOOOOOO!" Miss Havisham screamed. Great Ejaculations covered the table, extinguishing the fire and saving Mr. Wopsle's life.

He looked up. He had stars in his eyes and addressed her with dreams in his voice.

"M'lady! You...you goddess!" he said. Burns acquainted his face.

"I still got about four hundred pages before I'm nice," she said. "Buuuuut the Uber pool I called when you walked in is only a block away now—so there's that."

"Corpse bride," he mumbled, walking out.

Miss Havisham gazed at her rings and saw her smile reflected in each facet, feeling the joy of being tragically alone.

# PRIDE AND PREJUDICE

"Pride and Prejudice: A Novel of Manners"
by Alan Leggitt

### *The Unedited Edition*
by Jane Austen
Volume III
Chapter XIV
### *Historian's note:*

*Surely anyone who has read Jane Austen's* Pride and Prejudice *will never forget the iconic scene where Lady Catherine de Bourgh confronts Elizabeth Bennet, accusing her of intending to marry Mr. Darcy to climb the social ladder. Many consider this scene to be the climax of the class tension expressed throughout the book. Few readers, however, know that this scene was heavily edited before publication. Though seemingly innocent to the contemporary reader, the original text was considered far too explicit at the turn of the nineteenth century. It is this historian's hope that the reader will find this unedited edition just as climactic and a truer embodiment of Austen's literary genius.*

—Dr. Reginald Farnsworth III, PhD

*As soon as I see that little slut, I'm gonna kick her in the snatch!* thought Lady Catherine de Bourgh as she gazed out the window of her exquisite

carriage. Whenever the Lady of Rosings was vexed, she would draw a
deep breath and try to take in the scenery, but as she looked upon the
countryside of Hertfordshire, she could not help but think, *I'd sooner roll
in all the horse shit in Rosings than visit this cum dumpster again.*

When at last her long journey came to an end, her dutiful driver helped
her out. When she first saw the Bennet residence, she turned to her humble
servant and said, "This hovel? I wouldn't take a shit here with your ass!"

"Yes, m'lady," the driver said with a bow.

As the noble lady approached the house, the Bennets' faithful servant Wilfred opened the front door. "My lady—" he started.

Lady Catherine raised a lace-gloved hand and said, "The cloth rubbing against my twat is worth more than you'll make in a lifetime. Get
the fuck out of my way."

The esteemed lady entered the drawing room of the Bennet residence,
where the family sat drinking tea. Elizabeth Bennet stood, surprised to
receive such an honored guest. "Lady Catherine?" she exclaimed.

The rest of the family immediately stood. Mrs. Bennet cried, "Lady
Catherine de Bourgh? Of Rosings? To what do we owe this enormous
pleasure?"

"Stuff a cock in it, peasant," the venerable lady replied. She turned
to Ms. Elizabeth Bennet with the posture and poise becoming a lady of
her station and said, "Outside, bitch! Just you and me."

The Bennet family complied with the wishes of the esteemed and
respected lady. Elizabeth escorted Lady Catherine to the garden, while
the rest of the family returned to their tea.

When the two ladies were alone, Lady Catherine turned to Ms. Bennet and inquired, "You're fucking my nephew, aren't you?"

"Excuse me?" replied the young Ms. Bennet.

Lady Catherine promptly repeated. "You're fucking my nephew,"
and added, "You waved your smelly little gold digger pussy around my
nephew's face, and now you're fucking him."

Elizabeth Bennet was not as skilled in the art of conversation as the
Widow de Bourgh and was unsure of the most appropriate response.
She settled for a simple, "Bitch, I might be!"

Lady Catherine was quite taken aback. She had grown used to the ladies and gentlemen around her heeding her pearls of wisdom with quiet and respectful contemplation. This Ms. Bennet had most certainly committed a terrible impropriety, and it was the duty of the renowned Lady to educate the young girl.

"I have two friends I like to introduce to hussies like you," Lady Catherine said, raising her gloved fists. "I call them Pride and Prejudice!"

With the grace of a dancer, Lady Catherine swung the fist she called Pride, deftly striking Elizabeth Bennet about the face.

As she fell to the ground, Ms. Bennet felt aware of her inferior breeding. She suspected that the Lady of Rosings had more experience with this particular waltz. Elizabeth resolved to bridge the gap of familiarity with cunning. Observing that the ground was still wet from the morning's rain, she grasped a handful of mud and flung it quite expertly at Lady Catherine's face.

The soiled projectile struck the lady in the eyes, a development that she found most displeasing. She was further disappointed when the young Ms. Bennet barreled into her in quite an unladylike fashion, sending them both splashing into a nearby mud puddle.

Lady Catherine was now quite vexed by the young Ms. Bennet. She had traveled all this way to Hertfordshire to confront the girl about her improprieties and instruct her in the manners more becoming of a lady, yet Ms. Bennet remained obstinate.

What ensued was a veritable flurry of mud and women's clothing. When the ladies could not land blows, they resorted to stripping the other of their dignity. Elizabeth's high-waisted frock was torn at the neckline, followed by her chemise, followed by her corset, until her young breasts were exposed to the mud. Lady Catherine's garb proved a harder egg to crack. She wore a dress with a high neckline, followed by a chemise, followed by a petticoat, followed by a tightly laced corset. Yet Elizabeth persisted, swinging and slapping and tearing with veracity, until Lady Catherine was similarly exposed.

Despite her dislike for the headstrong girl, Lady Catherine began to feel a stirring in her Netherfield, not unlike the feeling she often

*What ensued was a veritable flurry of mud and women's clothing. When the ladies could not land blows, they resorted to stripping the other of their dignity.*

experienced when she and her late husband were first wed. This dance that she and Elizabeth were engaged in began to feel more like a sport.

Elizabeth was engaged in a similar line of reasoning. She felt no love for the Lady of Rosings, who represented the very social structure that encouraged the wealthy to look down on those less situated and resigned women to aspire only to marriage. Yet in the midst of their present activities, she could not help but regard the lady as a strong woman who had played the game and succeeded in finding some measure of independence.

This newfound regard was put to the test when Lady Catherine mounted the young Bennet and cried, "Eat my pussy, strumpet!"

Although astonished by this sudden command, Elizabeth was often titillated by acts that were unbecoming of a lady. Thus, she began to lick the finely aged pussy, which was coated in a layer of mud.

Lady Catherine expressed her approval with a resounding, "Yeah, you like that, slut!" Although the Widow de Bourgh had only ever ridden sidesaddle, she began to understand the merits of riding astride one's mount.

In no time at all, Lady Catherine began to feel a climax coming on. She was ashamed to admit that even she did not know the proper small talk for this occasion, so she settled for a simple yet elegant, "Fuck... yeah...fucking...slut!"

Afterward, the Lady of Rosings stood and gathered her things, leaving the young Ms. Bennet panting and touching herself. Perhaps it was the heat of the moment speaking, but the distinguished lady felt a pang of generosity. She turned to Elizabeth and said, "Marry Darcy, bitch. But only 'cause I said so."

# "The Sisters Lucas" by Na'amen Gobert Tilahun

Maria Lucas was for all intents and purposes invisible. It had taken her most of her eighteen years to perfect this skill. She'd tried to teach it to Mary Bennet, who seemed a perfect candidate; everyone wanted to ignore her and did so almost automatically. Unfortunately, the Bennet sisters had all followed the example of their sister Lizzie in some way, shape, or form. They wanted to be loud; they wanted attention paid to them; they wanted to be known. They did not understand the power in silence.

Not that Maria did not adore Lizzie; she was Charlotte's best friend and so many years spent at their feet could not help but foster affection between them. Though Maria suspected that Lizzie's affection was more of the kind one would feel toward a beloved pet. Maria did not mind; underestimation was a lady's greatest weapon.

When people underestimated you, they did not notice you taking control.

Now with Lizzie married off, as she had always wanted, no matter her vehement denials, and with Charlotte living with her husband, Maria had decided it was time to make her way in the world. She wrote to Charlotte asking to come for a visit. The invitation that arrived days later was not a surprise.

And so she packed her bags and said goodbye to her parents for what she knew would be the last time.

On her first night in her sister's house, she was awoken by the sound of leather hitting flesh. A sound she was intimately familiar with. Maria rose from the bed, not bothering with a sleep robe, as the weather had been unseasonably warm. Her stockinged feet slid down the hallway, past all the horrible decorations that Lady Catherine had gifted to her pet vicar.

"What is my name?!" Charlotte's voice rang out, forceful and angry. Maria had never heard her sister sound like that even when she'd spilled ink on Charlotte's favorite ribbon. The bedroom door was open a crack.

"Charlotte?" Her husband's voice was muffled.

"Are"—*smack*—"you"—*smack*—"asking me?" *Smack.* "Or"—*smack*— "are you"—*smack*—"answering"—*smack*—"me?"

Maria put her face gently to the crack.

Her brother-in-law was tied to the bedposts, his gnobbly troll body naked. His backside red and glowing in the firelight. Maria's hand slipped down the front of her thin nightgown. Her eyes darted over to Charlotte, taking in her nude upper body and stocking- and panty-covered lower half. Maria looked back at the doughy man on the bed.

Her fingers slipped under her gown and into herself.

She caught a glimpse of her brother-in-law's face in the mirror—red cheeks covered in tears, his upper lip covered in mucus. Maria bit back a moan and added two more fingers. This was what she wanted. The breaking of those who thought themselves powerful, the degradation, the shame. In those moments she felt a power denied to the women; she felt a hundred feet tall; she felt numerous and monstrous; she felt wet and tight.

"Charlotte," he sobbed forcefully.

There were more smacks, and he whimpered and shook as they landed.

"That is right. My name is Charlotte. Not Catherine!" There was a loud crack and Mr. Collins howled in pain. "Silent, fool. Do you want my sister to hear? To come in here and see you like this? You shameful excuse for a man."

"No, no, no, no," Mr. Collins sobbed.

The shame and terror in his voice caused Maria to writhe and thrust her fingers deeper.

Her thumb rubbed against her button and she bit her lip as another wet sob escaped Mr. Collins. His pain, his being stripped down to his core, was the most beautiful thing she had seen in so very long.

Maria was no stranger to the erotic arts but the orgasm that took her was quite a surprise. She tightened so hard, she worried her fingers would be pulled from her very hand and even then it would be worth it. She gushed, she poured her midnight joy down her legs and into the carpet.

"You think you are worthy of Lady Catherine?"

Charlotte had her hand buried in Mr. Collins's hair, pulling his head back so far it must have been painful.

"No." The word was grunted, strained with pain. He sounded like a little pig. Maria tightened around her fingers again as another wave of pleasure burst through her at the thought of Mr. Collins, naked, wallowing in mud.

"That's right. She knows you are nothing but a worm, a filthy worm."

"Uh-oh."

Even as he came, the most natural of acts, Mr. Collins sounded like something dying in its own filth. She watched as he flopped about, pulling at the restraints that bound him, pale clammy skin turning an unbecoming pink. He flopped and frenzied and her sister stood back, giving him a look of disgust mixed liberally with satisfaction.

Maria pulled her hand from under her gown, too sensitive to stand it any longer, and snuck back to her own room. She lay awake as a plan coalesced where before there had only been hints.

The next day the sisters Lucas sat in the solarium, warmth and companionable silence filling the room.

"Sister, I would ask you a favor."

"Of course, Maria. If it is within my power, it is yours."

"I wish to join Lady Catherine's household."

Charlotte placed her embroidery on the table while Maria continued her work.

"Why, Maria? That woman is horrid."

Maria giggled and smiled at her big sister. "Oh, Charlotte, I know. I shall take her in hand and train her, as you have Mr. Collins."

Charlotte jerked in surprise and then met her eyes. They stared at one another in silent communication for a few moments and then they both burst into giggles and leaned their heads together as they had when they were young girls.

"Oh, Maria, it is so wonderful. To be the center of someone's world in such a way."

"I know, Charlotte. But I want more. You are settled here and happy in your position for now. I wish to find my place and I believe Lady Catherine is my first step."

Charlotte nodded with a slight smirk.

"I will speak to Mr. Collins of it this evening, after we retire."

Maria smiled and nodded. That night she was awakened by howls and sobbing cries; they echoed down through the small house along with the smacks of wood and leather. She lay in bed, her fingers inside of herself, imagining Mr. Collins, crying and broken at her feet. It was the sweetest sleep she had ever had.

Only a week later, Lady Catherine had generously decided to take Maria in, thanks no doubt to her sister's influence over the officious toad she had married. She was to be one of Lady Catherine's maids and she made sure to be the one to help her into her baths, to dress her. She made sure to see Lady Catherine nude as much as possible.

It was a subtle display of dominance to always be clothed while she was naked. Lady Catherine did not acknowledge it consciously but began to respond automatically, allowing Maria to make small suggestions of change to house and wardrobe. Even looking to Maria to decide another servant's punishment. That is when Maria began to be rougher in her attentions, washing and massaging her lady. Lady Catherine loved it, moving into the feeling, the verge of pain.

She pinched Lady Catherine's nipples with the tips of her nails when washing her. They creased like old cheese under her keratin.

Maria apologized profusely, of course, pleading exhaustion and Lady Catherine had waved the apology off but Maria had seen the way the old woman had reacted, the way her back had arched, how all the loose skin of her face had slid backward.

The next evening, Lady Catherine asked for Maria specifically to draw her bath. She kept her touch gentle and teasing until she could see the tension building in Lady Catherine's back.

The

an...

ti......

ci.........

pa............

tion of waiting for something that might never come. She dried the old woman and helped her to bed, the whole time as gentle as a lamb. As she helped Lady Catherine into bed, she could read the disappointment and resignation in the wrinkles around her mouth and eyes and nose and neck and, really, just the mass of wrinkles that was her face.

"You may go, Ms. Lucas."

"As you wish, mum."

Maria picked up the last candle to carry with her from the room. As she passed Lady Catherine, she allowed the candle to tip ever so slightly so that the wax slipped down and dripped across Lady Catherine's exposed thigh.

"Unf." The moan was cut off and Maria looked up to see that Lady Catherine was staring at her, eyes wide and wet at the corners, her lizardlike point of a tongue slipping out to wet her lips.

"I am so sorry, my lady."

"No"—a deep breath—"no, my dear. No apologies necessary." She stared at Maria for a long moment and Maria wondered if the lady's legendary iron self-possession was about to break. Would Lady Catherine give in to her desires so easily?

"You may go."

Maria nodded, hiding her grin in the movement. The lady was not truly a challenge, but to break so easily would have undermined any respect Maria had for the harridan.

In all, it took a little over a week for the woman to surrender and invite Maria into her bed. Another week for her to admit to the power she wanted to give up, the vulnerability of giving herself over to another's power.

She bought silks for Maria to bind her to the bed, paddles of the finest woods and phalluses of the finest, softest wrapped leather. It was a month before Lady Catherine suggested that she present Maria and her sister—"Of course, Maria. Of course"—to the royal court. Maria smiled and nodded as if the idea had truly been Lady Catherine's.

Lizzie Darcy and her husband came to visit them not long before they were to be presented to court by Lady Catherine.

"That hussy, that strumpet, that miserable ingrate. To come here to my home!"

Maria soaped the woman's back, ignoring the way the flesh moved as if not connected to muscle at all.

"Did you not invite Mr. Darcy?" A week ago Maria would not have dared to speak to the lady in such a way but their relationship was steady. The lady already appreciated the rough touch of Maria's hands and knew that if she yelled or snapped at Maria, she would be as gentle as possible. Lady Catherine did not want this but was still too proud to ask for what she did want when the candles were bright and her face visible.

"Well, yes, but I thought he would come alone."

Maria only hummed as she smoothed her hands around Lady Catherine's ribs to cup her breasts.

"Well, I . . . I suppose that would be a foolish hope."

"Mmm." Maria bit at Lady Catherine's shoulders, wrenching a moan out of the woman.

"Let us go to bed, my girl, and dim the lights."

Maria bit down hard and pressed the older woman's nipples between her fingers hard enough to wrench a gasp of pain from her.

"What was that?"

"I meant . . ." The lady's voice dropped and Maria leaned forward to hear her better. "May we go to bed and dim the lights?"

"Good."

Maria rose and retrieved a towel for her mistress, who refused to meet her gaze, whose cheeks were pink with excitement, whose fingers kept drifting toward her nether regions.

When they arrived in Lady Catherine's bedroom, Maria snuffed out most of the candles while Lady Catherine took off her robe and lay naked and spread on the bed. Maria took the ropes of silk and tied her ankles first, then her wrists. Lady Catherine let out a moan.

Maria brought out two of the smaller phalluses in their collection. The smallest slid easily into Lady Catherine's quim; she found the grease and slicked up the black leather one, a bit thicker than the red one, whose end she could still see as Lady Catherine twitched and moaned in her bonds. It slid into her arse with very little resistance. For a few moments Maria just admired her mistress, stuffed full of phallus rather than hot air. She tapped on the bases of the phalluses and it was as if she played Lady Catherine like an instrument. Tap the red base and she went limp; tap the black base and her body arched and pushed back for more.

It was a game.

*Tap, tap*

*Tap, tap, tap…TAP, TAP*

A muffled scream.

"Do not bite the bedding, my dear. You know it creases it and also I enjoy the sounds you make."

She spent the next hour tapping out rhythms on the phalluses in Lady Catherine, eventually trading them for larger ones that made the lady scream and faint in pleasure.

The visit the next day was very uncomfortable. Lady Catherine refused to acknowledge Lizzie, Anne refused to leave her room, Mr. Collins refused to shut up, and Mr. Darcy refused to sit down. It was tense and Charlotte and Maria both were thankful of their ability to fade into the background and avoid being dragged into any of the conflicts.

Finally Lizzie, Charlotte, and Maria went for a walk in the gardens to talk amongst themselves.

"I honestly do not see how the two of you can be happy here," were the first words from Lizzie's mouth.

The two sisters met each other's eyes over Lizzie's back as she bent to smell a patch of roses. The sisters Lucas smirked at each other. Lizzie believed herself very worldly and in many ways she was but in many ways she was also naive, blinded by her beliefs. She could only understand her own path; everyone else's was a mystery to her.

"We enjoy it. As I told you, Lizzie dear, I do not desire much in life. What I want, I have here," Charlotte answered, putting on the sad, lonely spinster face.

"And it is a nice place for me to decide where I wish to go next." Maria tried on her own naive, young fool expression.

Lizzie looked at them both with a sad turn of her mouth and a widening of her bovine eyes. She was sad for them. Maria found it cute.

Poor Lizzie would never understand the Lucas's way to power. The power to be invisible in public and someone's leader in private, but she was happy in her world and perhaps that was all anyone could hope for.

As for Maria, well, she had an appointment to meet the queen next week. Her next step was in her grasp and she would reach for it with both hands.

# "The Lost Epilogue" by Maggie Tokuda Hall

Historians may never come to a consensus on the veracity of the following epilogue. It was not found within Jane Austen's estate, but rather, within a collection of papers discarded amidst her maid Lizzie Wallace's diaries. It is possibly the first known "fanfiction." And while most historians agree that while the characters are familiar, the language and the situations therein are certainly not canonical.

*Pride and Prejudice: The Found Epilogue.*

It is a truth universally acknowledged that while monogamy is an easy and good arrangement to make, it is a tedious and difficult one to keep. So it was that Mrs. Elizabeth Darcy, the new Lady of Pemberley, found herself in want of extramarital sexual attention.

It was not that she did not love Fitzwilliam; of course she did. But she learned on her wedding night that his stiffness in manner and countenance translated equally and proportionately to his behavior in their bedroom. While his poetry about her was fervent with desire, his actions between the sheets? Less so. Coitus with him typically consisted of a few impatient and silent thrusts, a deep exhalation, and his underclothes back on within the minute.

Flicking the bean to make up for the difference just would not cut it anymore.

Eliza needed cock. Real, sturdy cock. Thick, long, and hungry cock. It was all she could think of, starved for it as she was. It was with acute disappointment that she evaluated the staff, the entirety of it—from the footmen to the stable boy—and found not a single fuckable dude in the entire joint.

Eliza sighed, the deep and despondent sigh of a woman in dire need of a raucous hump. Resigned to another day of disappointment, she lay back on her fainting couch and opened the well-worn pages of *A Midsummer Night's Dream.* It had become her habit, when in need of sexual inspiration, to visit the library and open the pages of the play to Oberon's might and anger—to imagine the Fairy King, vast and muscled, upon her, his hands tearing through her clothes, her lips upon her neck.

Her hand found home between her legs as she imagined, and she moaned.

No sooner had the sound escaped her lips than she heard a *SNAP*, like someone cracking a crop against a horse's flank. For a brief and delirious moment, she thought, she prayed, she hoped, that the Fairy King had become manifest, that he would stand before her in all his glory, poised to fuck her face off.

She was close, but not correct.

Before her stood a satyr, his goaty tail flicking with excitement.

"My lady," he said with a bow. His bow was low and lovely, the kind of bow one did before royalty. Eliza felt her pussy quicken.

"Oh, sweet satyr, please, please tell me you are here to give me the rutting I so desperately need!"

The satyr blinked, all confusion. "Ma'am? I'm, uh, here to grant—"

"My desire to fuck, yes, yes! I hear all you little fellows have the most splendidly gargantuan of wieners—that's what all the books say. You will show me, won't you?" She couldn't help it; her voice was a rush of anticipation, an unstoppable flow. She'd already pulled her underthings to the floor and flung them across the room, where they rested, unceremoniously, across the marble bust of her husband. "I hear you're hung like the Tower of London."

Gathering his wits, the satyr straightened. "I, my lady, am that merry wanderer of the night, the forest spirit, Puck. I came to grant your dearest wish... I just thought it'd be, like, your husband's affection or like a new pianoforte, not—"

"What? No! Don't be a frivolous idiot. What I need. Is. Cock."

Puck shrugged, a lascivious grin growing across his face. "You're really jumpin' for a humpin'—"

But before he could finish, Eliza had torn off all her clothes and stood before him, her pink nipples pinched between her fingers.

"Jesus," the forest spirit said. This lady was forward, and Puck had fucked forest nymphs.

To her unending delight, Puck pulled his penis from his furry loins. It was no impressive thing, and perhaps her face showed it, for Puck smiled his goaty smile and said: "Be patient, lady. It's a grower, not a shower."

And in this, the satyr was all truth. For as she watched, his penis grew, first thicker, so it was the width of her wrist, then her ankle. Then it grew longer. And longer. Past his fuzzy navel. Past his protuberant nipples. Past his sly mouth and mischievous eyes. Clear past the top of his horned head.

The Lady of Pemberley gasped, her mind a whir of horny delight. So the Greek fertility pottery was real, she realized, an actual account of the most magnificent organ meat she had ever beheld.

Just as she bent over the mahogany side table to receive his blessed meat, just at the absolute most incriminating moment, her pussy lips spread between her fingers, wet with anticipation of that elephantine peen, her husband, Mr. Fitzwilliam Darcy, strode into the library.

He blinked. He stepped out, then back in again. His eyes drifted to his marble bust, where his wife's underthings hung. Eliza and Puck stood frozen, in shock.

"What the—my Elizabeth," he sputtered. "Are you... fucking live-stock?"

"Hey!" Puck shouted. "Racist."

"Little man," Darcy hissed. "If it walks like a goat, and fucks like a fucking goat, then for fuck's sake, it's a fucking—"

"Fucking your wife you—" Puck interjected.

"Enough!" Eliza cried. She stood and approached her husband, her hand pressed gently against his chest. She knew she must intervene before his good opinion was irrevocably lost. "This is the forest spirit, Puck. He came and kindly obliged my desire to have my poonanie plundered." She smiled generously at Puck. "It was my dearest wish."

"But...but that's my job!" Darcy whined. "Not the job of farm animals!"

"Wouldn't need a farm animal if you could give your wife a good plow," Puck spat back.

"Boys!" Eliza yelled. They both stilled at her sternness. "Let us not be blinded by our pride." Here, she reached out and laid a consolatory hand upon Puck's cheek. "Or our prejudice." She touched her husband's cheek, lovingly, gently. "Let us instead sample the sexy strange we all know we really want."

"She's right," said Puck.

Darcy smiled, one of his rare smiles. "She always is."

Darcy made up for his questionable comments almost immediately by taking the satyr's cock in his mouth and sucking it as if the cure for consumption lay within it. As he did so, Eliza spread her husband's butt cheeks apart and licked his tight little butthole, causing him to moan, wetly, around Puck's dingle.

The satyr brought something out in her husband, something alive and wanting, something gross. Eliza was all about it.

Perhaps her husband was not all stiffness, after all, Eliza reflected, but stiff only where it counted, which was to say his penis, which she now took in her own butthole, which she made loose and prepared for such intrusion by sodomizing herself with a candle while her lovers had furiously made out. Her anus was an abiding thing, and Darcy pumped madly in and out of it.

Meanwhile, with much careful positioning, Puck situated his goat legs such that his nearly three-foot-long cock, still wet with Darcy's spit, could reach Eliza's lady cave. She moaned with transcendent happiness as it finally entered her, filling her in the way that she had craved so fervently for all her life.

Yes, having a butthole full of Darcy and a pussy full of Puck, this was it. This was the happiest moment of Mrs. Darcy's life. She relished the way Puck's furry goat legs brushed against her inner thighs now and again and the way that Darcy's fingers felt as they stroked her nipples.

They all came together, magnificently, in unison, as though in the crescendo of some marvelous dance. Eliza felt Darcy's cum, hot and wet, fill her poop chute as Puck pulled his wiener out and came all over Eliza's tits and just a little on her chin. She was amused and pleased to learn that night that she was a squirter, though less pleased that her cum had laid waste to her well-loved copy of *A Midsummer Night's Dream*.

"Oh, Mrs. Darcy," Mr. Darcy said.

"Oh, Mr. Darcy," Mrs. Darcy said.

The postcoital mess, the semen and spray, the sweat and goat pellets, were not their problem, after all. That was for the servants to clean. Such was the great joy of being rich.

# MOBY DICK

## "Gin and Molasses" by Alexander Chee

The innkeeper told me he was full but sold me his own bed. I didn't trust him, though, sure he meant to attack me in my sleep, and so thus did I spend part of the night prepared for murder, half asleep, half awake in torment, my harpoon in my hand by my bed, until the door opened, and in, with a lamp, came the one I would soon call Ishmael.

He blew out his lamp and, saying nothing at all, crawled, meek as a lamb and as sweet as one, into the bed.

My new bedmate smelled of gin and molasses—a sign he had no doubt been drinking downstairs with the rest of the seamen who filled this lopsided guesthouse. I assumed he was lost, and despite his seemingly harmless appearance and the relative quiet—he was asleep instantly—I knew, drunk as he was, he would not remember where he was come morning, and the sight of me might cause me trouble with him. So I stood, dressed myself such that I would not alarm any guests downstairs, and went to speak to my host.

"He was asleep on a bench!" the innkeeper explained in frustration. "Look at this!" He had shaved down the bench so it might be more comfortable for my new friend, only for the drunken young man to discover it was too short. "Do you really mind so much? It was my bed, after all. I'll be sleeping on that bench now. Or you can have this."

Well did I consider that it was a kind of luck that had brought me the young interloper upstairs and not this innkeeper as my bedmate. At the least, I knew I could handle him in a fight, provided he did not attack me in my sleep. I was still put out by the disturbance, however, and the late hour, despite the logic of this argument.

Worse, the innkeeper insisted on speaking to me in an insulting pidgin, despite my ability with his language. "You sabbee me?"

"Yes," I said. "I sabee."

I returned to the room. My invader slept still, deep under the covers, his hair the only visible sign the bed was not empty—he was a slight young man, still very young. Something of a Robin Goodfellow, despite the utter skilamalink surrounding his being there in my bed. He did not seem to have been to sea a day in his life, much less outdoors—his skin had that softness that comes from a life lived on land and mostly inside. I went to my bag, to be sure all was as I had left it, and nothing had been disturbed.

Thus reassured, I undressed again.

He didn't make a sound as I entered the bed, but I was sure he was awake, the silence then that exact noise a held breath makes at night. As I held up the coverlet, I could see he had gotten up in my absence, undressed, and now wore just a nightshirt. But his calves showed and glowed in the candlelight, as did the nape of his neck, and to my own surprise, the sight of these tender places on his body kindled me.

I had stripped naked, my own preference for sleep. I paused, uncertain if I should get into the bed or wait until my unexpected excitement had passed. I looked down at myself, to see the tattoo left by my last lover, the coil of a sea serpent that tangled up my leg to rest its head around my cock, within my own short hairs, almost a reproof. *I know I can't claim or keep you,* he had said, *but I want you to remember me, whoever else you're with.*

The memory of him, which he had thus ensured, was sufficient that the shadow of my member extended now to the bed, a dark arrow on the sheets.

I was too tired to wait much longer and climbed in. The bed was smallish but big enough for us both and clean, at least. Certainly, this young man was sweet smelling enough as I lay down. I turned on my side, away from him, to let myself calm, blew out the candle, and was nearly asleep when his heel gently brushed my own and an electric dart shot through me.

With that, I was awake again, hard again. He was awake, too, I was sure of it—was the touch of his foot then deliberate? An invitation? If so, I certainly wanted to accept—to turn around, pull the nightshirt up, lift him across me, take him any way I wanted. But instead I counseled patience to myself. It just might be an accident, and I did not want any violence now. So I waited, uncertain if I should move my foot away, or if I should let it stay—and the delightful agony of the indecision increased, which meant I let my foot stay, as did he. And so the dart soon became a current.

I wanted him to say something, anything, to make things clearer between us. Or was this delicate foot both his messenger and his message?

Our heels stayed together for how long I don't know, and then eventually, sleep snuffed me out.

When I woke, I was still hard. To my surprise, my arms were tightly around him, as if he were what I had left to hold on to after a shipwreck. I had slept that way with my old lover, back on our ship in the sea of Japan. He would smile to see me miss him so. My excitement had either returned or remained with me in the night and was now pressed fully against the small of his back—there was no hiding it from him now. His neck was almost against my mouth, and my left hand had even gripped his left wrist.

He had not leapt to his feet; he had not cried out. I still could not see his face. In fact, his feet rested atop my own, the smooth silk of the bottoms of his feet making me ache with lust. He remained still, as if asleep, except that I could feel his breath across the back of my hand, the back and forth almost like the regular stroke of an affection-ate finger.

The sure, regular breath of someone who was awake.

Was there a way to let go, to slowly smooth my hand down the front of him, to discover that way whether he was a yay or a nay? I needed both relief from this and yet I also was unsure how to let go. Or to go as far as I wanted, though how far that would be yet was also unknown to me.

I did not want to let go. I would not want to let go, in fact, for quite some time. That I would follow him, this bedtime invader, was not at all certain to me then. But it would be shortly. In the meantime, overcome and wanting some resolution, I pressed my mouth against his neck, ground my hips against him so he gasped, and knew my first answer. He was awake.

"Queequeg!" he said, and reached up to push against the hand on his wrist. I suppose the innkeeper had told him my name. I decided I would have a little fun, and did not immediately let go. "Queequeg," he said again, trying to turn to face me. The struggles he made up against me in the bed were too pleasurable to let go still. I faked a snore, as if still asleep, so as to linger a little longer. "Queequeg! In the name of goodness, Queequeg, wake!" At this I knew I needed to calm him, so I began to blink, as if I were just waking up and did not know where I was. He wriggled further, increasing my pleasure and the pressure of his bottom against my pike was enough to make me squeeze tighter. He kept saying my name, over and over, with various differences in emphasis and expostulation, all the while pushing against me.

It was heaven.

At last I let him go—I knew I had gone as far as I could with my lit-tle game, and if I was to go further, I needed to spare him any more for the time being. Also, my harpoon had fallen across us, and the point was dangerously near his smooth cheek. I sat upright, pushing it off us, staring about me as if confused. It was all I could do not to laugh, how-ever, as I was entirely erect as I sat there and we were both of us startled by it. No modesty could save me now.

I leapt from the bed. Sure enough, he could not take his eyes off me. Especially my manhood, which swayed with the effort. I gestured at the basin and water on the table. "I will bathe first," I said, sensing it would be sufficient to bring about what I desired.

He nodded.

I meant to turn away from him but saw he stared, shamelessly, at what I meant to hide.

I instead poured a bit of water into the basin and stepped into it, before pouring more across me and down my front. I took a bit of tallow soap and began to lather myself. He watched every journey the soap made. I felt as shameless as any whore, all the while astonished at how much I wanted him. I could scarcely believe the force of the desire in me. But I knew this bit of theater, this little carnival act I was performing for him, was bringing me closer and closer to my goal. He was shy, nervous, had not seen much of the world, but he had a great curiosity in him, this was clear. Especially for what was between my legs.

I made it bounce to tease him, and when I did, his eyes widened. I pretended not to notice and did it again. He blinked, flustered, but did not look away. It would bounce the more for him soon enough.

*Tip the innkeeper,* I thought to myself as I raised my head finally and Ishmael's eyes lifted up to mine.

# "Captain Ahab" by Nate Waggoner

And now, a recently discovered deleted chapter from *Moby Dick* entitled "Every Time Captain Ahab Had Sex."

In the interest of the reader's full edification, I feel I must take it upon myself to detail the woefully limited and unusual carnal aspect of the great monomaniac's existence. Those of us strong of Christian faith and innocent of the stranger varieties of intimate contact will turn away in horror and disgust—but what is human life but a series of unspeakable interactions, what then the purpose of the written word but to articulate that which is too gruesome, too sublimely pleasurable, for public discussion? Surely no one shall gather in the future to hear these words performed; surely no one shall ever applaud these vile acts in any kind of respectable company.

Precisely one year after Ahab was wed, our devil captain's sweet and resigned wife, Muriel, had an uncharacteristic moment of impudence, driven by that mad desire with which kings and sailors and beasts alike must reckon. She asked, quite sweetly and resignedly, for her husband to please, for the first time ever, perform his husbandly duties. In such a resigned and sweet manner as to make one think he was hearing the voice of the Christ child himself, our windblown Penelope mewled thusly: "Gimme that big-ass whale bone, my dude. Take your bitch to the South Seas, if you know what I mean. Sink your harpoon hella deep in my shit. Plow your big boat all up in my salty ocean. Lemme see that white whale, bro. Ya girl is tryna get straight bathed in sperm, son. I'm grindin' on that wood, grind-grindin' on that wood. Eat me by my own light, dawg. Dive into those depths, you big ambiguous-metaphor chasing hunk of hubris."

Fearing this day would come and knowing the only desire he felt was for revenge against the white whale and that the only true romance he would ever know was one of mutual hate between himself and a beast, Ahab formulated a plan. He found within their humble bed quarters a sheet of white fabric, great in size and thickness, of inexpensive material, specifically of the type manufactured in the Orient during—

So at this point it goes into really long-winded detail about this piece of white fabric that Ahab has. And then there's several pages about the history of fabric manufacturing in general, and it's really beautifully written but completely extraneous so I'm just gonna skip it for the sake of time.

He wrapped sweet and resigned Muriel in this fabric. He then drew a bath and in it placed several fresh cod, a few tuna, and some seaweed. Confused but still wild with anticipation, Muriel acquiesced to Ahab's

*He wrapped sweet and resigned Muriel in this fabric. He then drew a bath and in it placed several fresh cod, a few tuna, and some seaweed. Confused but still wild with anticipation, Muriel acquiesced to Ahab's request that she enter the bath whilst covered in white cloth and make a kind of lowing, crooning sound.*

request that she enter the bath whilst covered in white cloth and make a kind of lowing, crooning sound. Our ungodly madman of a captain then mounted his sweet and resigned wife and performed the marital act in as wild and ecstatic a frenzy as may occur in any Nantucket house of ill repute.

In the months that followed, Ahab remained ashore, insatiable. Scarcely did a moment go by without sweet, resigned Muriel turning to face a freshly impassioned captain-husband—the two lovers missed meals, let daily chores go neglected. Dishes piled higher than Babel. Bathtub fish rotted away. Finally, the effervescent bride's enthusiasm did wane for our obsessive captain's bizarre requests.

One night, as the couple entered into what had become a nightly— nay, hourly!—ritual, Muriel in her crude whale costume, descending into the tub, adorned with seafaring sundry, proposed an escalation of variety in their congress: First, she endeavored to apply metal clamps to the nipples of our whale-fixated captain, pinching and twisting and turning, now fast, now slow, causing the old salt to howl with infernal delight. The clamps she procured from a clamp-manufacturing concern, whose—

So again, Melville here spends around four pages just talking about the type of metal used in making the nipple clamps and the process of forging the metal. It's rich with wonderful description, allusion, and symbolic meaning, but I'm gonna skip ahead again.

The kindly young bride then pushed her nubile, whale-suit-clad form several inches heavenward and let loose a torrent of liquid waste upon Ahab, as though he were a commode in the form of a man! The warm liquid spilled across his chest and over his face and into his mouth, and he cried out in joy.

For her finale, the unassuming maiden wrenched forth Ahab's mutilated leg and unscrewed his ivory appendage. A smell as if from the very depths of Hades blasted forth, but Muriel could not be deterred. She strapped the leg to her nether regions and commenced to use it as a kind of artificial phallus, pegging it forth into Ahab's most absolutely ungodly orifice. It is a gift to humanity, a rare hint of providence, that the captain's pleasure-mad utterances were never recorded.

In time, Ahab would inevitably ship out and go mad with thoughts of revenge against the white beast. But even now, in his defiant final steps to his watery grave, he remains ever haunted by Muriel's perfectly ladylike, obedient utterings of, "Aww, fuck yeah, my dude. You better take this pussy to the damn boiler room! Fuckin' put it in my Marianas Trench, Papi! I'm tryin' to learn some marine sexology! Pirate this fat ass, my man! Now entering Port of Pound Town, population you!"

## "Fedallah" by Ryan Britt

Call me Fedallah. Seriously. Do it. It turns me on soooo much. I know it's not for everybody but what can I say? I guess I like thinking of myself as the kind of person who will remain a muffled mystery to the last. I know a lot of you DickHeads get turned on by thinking of yourself as the whale and I totally get that because we've all been through that phase and who doesn't love acting like the Dick?

But if you're the Dick, you've only got one move, really—total domination. Sure, being the Dick lets you flirt with your beloved, be the elusive thing beneath the depths of their desire. Being the Dick is like swiping left on Tinder, but somehow asking that rejected person out on Tinder anyway. It's aggressive and hot as fuck to be sure, but what kind of variety of moves do you really have in the bedroom if you're the whale? Plus, if your partner is Ahab, that dom/sub situation gets pretty boring pretty fast, amiright? I mean, how many times has someone's safety word been *Pequod* or *Stubb* or *Hey, I don't want to be Ahab anymore*? Plus—and I know my fellow DickHeads will agree—being the whale means group sex gets super boring. Too many harpoons and not enough boats!

Because I've been a DickHead since like way before there were like a million podcasts (the Carpet-Bag was the first and best y'all), I've already imagined every permutation of becoming the whale and fucking Ahab or becoming Starbuck and fucking the whale while Ahab rides him, or transforming into Starbuck from that old TV show *Battlestar Galactica* while fucking Starbuck from the canon. By the canon I mean, the only book that matters and if you're not a DickHead and you're reading this it's a little weird, but maybe you'll get turned on and want to become a DickHead. Also, I'm totally into the idea of being Fedallah and fucking Starbuck from the canon while he's in a cannon.

Anyway. As you can probably tell I've got a really bad case of FOMOOFS. If you're unfamiliar, I actually feel a little sorry for you. But just in case: FOMOOFS is "fear of missing out on fictional sex." And a lot of us DickHeads have it. But other fetish groups have it, too, I guess. I'm friends with a guy who is in the Baker Street Irregulars, which I'm sure you've heard is a big Sherlock Holmes fan group. Uh-huh. Well, the "Irregulars" might think they're kinky but honestly how many times can you say, "Oh, now you put on the hat. Let me smoke the pipe," etc. Plus, I was at one of those parties one time and these two guys were just whispering "elementary" to each other over and over and even though it was kind of sweet, it wasn't hot. As DickHeads, we've got a little more going for us.

Dugan was the guy who introduced me to all of this way back in college, way before everyone claimed to be a swinging DickHead. He'd switched from being an Irregular to being an OliverTwister, which are people who only play as Oliver Twist characters, which is great, but there's way too much singing at those parties. Like, the second you put your keys in the bowl at one of those, someone is on their way out with "Cheerio and Be Back Soon," which is a massive turnoff. To me, anyway.

Anyway Dugan is TOTALLY the one who taught me to play as Fedallah because it's all about power dynamics. We were in his dorm room eating Pop Rocks and I was complaining about how I was always the one who paid when we went out for grilled cheese sandwiches—and the Pop Rocks, for that matter—and he was like, "You're my Fedallah, bitch!" And I was like "What?" And he was like, "I'm Ahab, and you're my little Fedallah." It was hot enough then but later, when "I got it," it was even hotter.

Suddenly Dugan was on top of me—he was wearing a Phoenix Sun's jersey, I think Charles Barkley, but it might have been KJ—and he started quoting from the canon. I think he was doing it to get himself hot and you know, it was hot.

"All ready there, Fedallah?"

"Ready?" was my half-hissed-sort-of-crackly reply. The Pop Rocks were working, too!

"Lower away, then, d'ye hear!" Such was the thunder of his voice, that in spite of my amazement, I came like in two seconds. Then a bunch of Dugan's friends busted into the dorm room! There were like three of them, and they leapt goatlike, rolling down my side and on my front and there was a lot of tossing. Dugan had hardly pulled out from under me when one of his buddies (I'd later think of him as a "Starbuck") rolled up on my windward side and started like rubbing his hands on my shoulder like he was rowing me. He and Dugan were rowing me. I felt like an old man. It was heaven.

I came again and again, each time in a mannerly fashion, but I felt a sort of an unaccountable tie as to why I was linked to Dugan and his "sailors." Later, when the others left and I was lying on my starboard side with Dugan and looking up at the ceiling while running my fingers in little whirlpools on his Phoenix Suns jersey, did he explain it to me thus:

"Fedallah," he said to me, cooing like someone who really should stop smoking or at least switch to menthols, "You are linked to my peculiar fortunes; nay, you have some sort of half-hinted influence. Heaven knows, but you might even have authority over me. But none of the others can know."

Fedallah! Of course. I paid for everything and no one knew it. Which means even though it seemed like I was subordinate to Dugan, the reverse was true. He was my bitch. I secretly paid for the grilled cheese, paid for the Pop Rocks, ran the ship. I was the elder statesman (or woman?) of this party, but I was slick about it. Among DickHeads now, everyone knows me as one of the best Fedallahs. When I walk on the deck, someone will drop an ore, a harpoon, or peg leg in amazement and lust.

Because when you're a Fedallah, no one can sustain an indifferent air concerning you. You can call out in the air, "Spread wide, boys! Spread wide! Down! Down! Down! BLOOOW!" But you don't have to, if you don't want to, because it's, you know, implied. When you're a Fedallah, you are a creature of sexual civilization, seen only in the dreams of those who now and then glide among the unalterable countries, which, even in these modern days consort with the daughters of men and whales and also...of devils...

## "The Whale" by Danielle Henderson

The least imaginative always start with the blowhole.

Here I am, twenty-eight yards of slick, white wetness eager to feel those calloused nubs glide over my silky smooth fins, and you keep throwing yourselves bodily into my breath hole without even so much as an "Amen!" I like a good suck fest as much as the next girl, but you may as well be throwing a hot dog down a hallway for all the pleasure it brings. I'm eighty-five feet long and a third of my body is a head made almost entirely of jizz—you're going to have to work a little harder than that to get me off, honey.

My top hole might seem like a steamy pleasure pocket to you, but it's certainly not as thrilling as the way you swim lithely along my underbelly or caress the flat ends of my fins. I fuck sailors for fun but I still appreciate a little romance, you know? The complicated process of blowing you idiots back out of me is made easier by the way your hair tickles the sides of my slippery passage, but my insurance company simply won't cover it anymore, not after the Ahab Incident.

Did he tell you I bit his leg off in a fit of whaleish rage? He's just saving face—I'm a docile motherfucker! He couldn't admit that he broke his leg at the knee in three places being shot out of the blowhole of a sexually aroused leviathan and still maintain the respect of his crew. When he looked down and saw the ragged shards where his knee used to be, the dirty bastard asked me to chew it off so he'd have a good story, and being the kindhearted girl I am, I obliged. I was completely okay being a patsy, but I drew the line when he used my cousin Glenda's jaw to fashion a new leg for himself, after those French Bouton de Rose bastards offed her in a snuff film. That's a bridge too goddamn far, Ahab—a bridge too goddamn far.

Before I broke it off, we really were in love. Our little game of hide-and-seek did wonders for building sexual tension. I'd echolocate until he found me, clicking away in anticipation, and then he'd sneak away on his little boat for a night of wanton concupiscence. We did all the moves—the Lofty Pulpit, the Impregnable Quebec, the Connecticut Diddler, the Queequeg Quickstep, the Starbuck and Stubb, the Kokovoko Stinger. The man hadn't set foot on dry land in forty years and it showed! There was one night my craggy libertine and I shared night after night of orgiastic passion so strong we once flooded a seaside village, chuckling as children screamed on hilltops while the limp bodies of their lifeless parents washed out to sea. There were good moments, you know? We had a time, we really did.

He couldn't tell his crew that they were the unwitting passengers on a sex cruise, so Ahab snuck away those first few nights to rendezvous with me far out in the ocean where no one would see. That nosy new guy, the one who never shuts up and talks in monologues almost exclusively? Ishmael? He almost blew our cover once but didn't know what he was looking at as Ahab slid his unctuous legs between my phonic lips to caress my distal sac. It's hard to see with the naked eye, but trust me when I say I felt the titillating reverberations from head. To. Toe. He was a man of few words and many, many caresses.

I broke it off with Ahab after I saw him stumping around on what used to be Glenda's mouth. I slipped farther away into the abyss, but he kept following me to an obsessive degree. I guess the old adage is true—once you give over to the salacious advances of a raunchy whale, you never go back.

I admit my anger got the better of me that fateful day. He finally caught up with me; I was trying to get over him and just wanted to be alone, but when I saw him hopping around on the same jaw Glenda used to gobble up squid, I lost it. And to hear him! Screaming, over and over, "There she blows! There she blows!" Like the bard says— we found love in a hopeless place, Ahab, and you reduce me to sport? What am I, a common gutter whale?

The last straw was the harpoon. I'd only ever had one rule: I don't fuck with harpoons. You can strap me down with all the hemp rope your little hands can carry, but the minute you pierce my skin with a harpoon is the very moment I tell you to pack your bags and take that S&M shit somewhere else! Try that den of iniquity act on the octopi, buddy! The moment his rod hit my skin, I knew that it was either him or me. When I reared up and crashed his boat in half, I knew that dragging him to his death would be my only chance to be free.

What? No, I'm fine. I didn't even realize I was crying.

Anyway, thanks for listening to the code of conduct and rules of consent, guys. You boys sign those release forms, keep your cocks away from my blowhole, and we'll be on our way to Fuck City!

## "Thar She Blows" by Maya Rodale

It was a dark and stormy Sunday morning. In church. And God was watching. Father Mapple rose and made his way to the unusual pulpit. This, and so much of the décor, was a throwback to the priest's days spent as a sailor among the seamen and the wet, salty seas.

This particular pulpit was crafted like the bow of a ship with dark wood, soft to the touch, weathered from the elements having their way with it: salty ocean waves pounding hard against it and the craftsmen lovingly rubbing it with a slick and pungent oil from a sperm whale.

Father Mapple displayed a reverential dexterity as he mounted the rope ladder, such as one finds on a ship, with shaking hand over shaking hand as he climbed. Did anyone in the congregation notice that their clergyman was taut and trembling with anticipation of what lay ahead? Under his robes, his cock was already half aroused at what would happen next.

Upon reaching the pulpit, Father Mapple climbed onto it. He saw perplexed faces in the crowd as they wondered why he was pulling the rope up after him. Did he really think anyone would dare to climb up and interrupt him as he gave his sermon? No. The truth was between him and God and Mary Sue, a delectable widow tucked on her knees, snug in the crook of this pulpit, which blessedly provided just enough space and just enough cover for her lithe little body so she could do wicked things to a man of God.

No one in the congregation could see anything remiss. However... a painting hung behind the pulpit, and Father Mapple glanced back at it: a dark ship thrusting into the dark heaving waves, each capped with white froth. An angel gazed down at the ship...or maybe the two sinners in the pulpit. Hastily, he turned away.

In a mild voice of unassuming authority, he ordered the scattered people to condense. "Starboard gangway, there! Side away to larboard, larboard gangway to starboard! Midships! Midships!"

There was a low rumbling of heavy sea boots among the benches and a still slighter shuffling of women's shoes. There was a rumble of thunder outside. He drummed his fingertips on the hard wood of the pulpit, impatient, especially when he felt a rustle of his robes as Mary Sue's soft little hands skimmed up his legs higher and higher, skimming through the rough wiry hair on his legs. As she lifted his robes, he felt a rush of cool air on his arousal. "Good God, woman!" he yelped, and then, correcting himself somberly, addressed the congregants. "Good women of God. And gentlemen."

Mary Sue ducked underneath his robes and let them fall over her head.

He paused a little. Folded his large brown hands across his chest. He uplifted his closed eyes and offered a prayer so deeply devout that he seemed to be kneeling and praying at the bottom of the sea. In truth, he was thanking the Lord God his savior that the rain outside drummed out the sharp hiss of his breath as Mary Sue's tongue teased circles around the tip of his cock. It was now hard. Throbbing.

He opened his mouth to speak just as Mary Sue took him in her mouth. "Ahhh..." and "Mmmm" and in such, uh, reverential tones he commenced reading the following hymn:

"The ribs and terrors in the whale," he began as her hot little mouth closed around him. Alas, just the tip. Damnation!

"Arched over me in a...a..." He arched himself, thrusting forward, forcing more of himself down Mary Sue's blessed throat...dismal gloom.

Somehow the words poured forth. Even though he was...distracted.

"While all God's sunlit waves rolled by, and lift me...deepening down..." Sure as hell, Mary Sue was deepening down. She took the hot, hard length of his cock deep down in the back of her throat. "...to doom. Mmmm.

"I saw the opening maw of...oh hell," he swore as her nimble little fingers kept busy, rubbing the sensitive flesh between, well, never mind what it was between, and inching back toward...

His manner changed toward the concluding stanzas as Mary Sue grasped his cock and bobbed her head to the rhythm of the hymn, moving her mouth in and out. In and out. In and out.

His voice burst forth with a truly, truly genuine pealing exultation and joy and—

"With endless pains and sorrows there; Which none but they that feel can tell—oh, Oh, OH I was plunging to, uh, ah..."

Plunging indeed. Mary Sue was taking him in deep down to the depths of her throat and then pulling back to suck in a deep breath of air. Deep down and out his throbbing cock moved in her moist mouth.

"In black distress, I called my..." He forgot the words entirely as Mary Sue did something downright wicked with her tongue. And her fingers. In the darkest nether regions of his body. At the same time. "My God... OH MY GOD!" he bellowed. He glanced down at the damn Bible, the hymnal, whatever the hell had the words he was supposed to being saying. Singing. Ah there..."Nearly all joined in singing this hymn, thank the Lord Baby Jesus, which swelled high above the howling of the storm, drowning out his own desperate cries to the Lord God for salvation and mercy from this erotic frenzy seething and churning within on the verge of explosion and then the crash, like massive, powerful waves pounding down, sending a salty spray over everything in the vicinity."

A brief pause ensued at the end of the hymn; the preacher fumbled with the pages of the Bible and at last found the proper page and said in a hoarse voice: "Beloved shipmates, clinch the last verse of the first chapter of Jonah. "'And God had prepared a great fish to'"—he gulped, and so did Mary Sue—"'swallow up Jonah.'"

In the back row of the church, Louise murmured to her friend with whom she'd been sitting for the duration of the service, "Father Mapple seems very...inspired today."

"Indeed," said Mary Sue with a wicked smile.

# "Ishmael" by Maris Kreizman

Call me Fuckboy.

Call me whatever you want.

Call me whatever you're able to pronounce.

Some years ago—never mind the exact time or place, just trust me, bro—I got real bored. I yearned to escape the drudgery of day-to-day post-collegiate life by taking to the sea. I decided to participate in the age-old tradition of packing up one's old carpetbag and embarking on a philosophically uplifting ocean voyage. I would become a sailor on a whaling boat and exercise my mind and my body. I would go cruising for Dick.

Perhaps a hunky old sea captain would order me to do menial tasks such as sweep the decks at the butt crack of dawn or shine his shoes or cut his meat, and I would handle such degradation with grace. Yes, I was a privileged white guy, but aren't we all slaves, in the grander scheme of things? In fact, don't all of us mortals exist to serve the Fates? Aren't we all subject to the whippings and thrashings of the gods, their treacherous ass-slappings and their tender mercies? Perhaps spending some time slumming as hired help would broaden my horizons.

Little did I know that my seafaring adventure would begin well before I climbed aboard a ship. In fact, it began in a motel called the Spouter Inn, a hole-in-the-wall whose "No Vacancy" sign was flashing in neon when I arrived, weary and cold and hungry, at the check-in desk. Alas, it seemed that the motel was completely full of seamen.

"Sir, I'm afraid I cannot offer you a room," said the proprietor. "This motel is covered wall to wall with seamen."

However, he must have noticed my despair, for he added, "But if you'd be down for this kind of thing, I can let you share a room with another guest."

My curiosity was aroused.

"There's this dude staying with us," he continued. "He's got a real weird name that's hard for me to pronounce without butchering so I won't bother trying, but let's just say he's a real intense and exotic guy, his abs are super tight, and he's got a couple of sick face tattoos. He's out peddling his wares right now, so I can't introduce you at the moment. But it just so happens that the heater in his room is broken, so I'm sure he'd be okay if you wanted to hop into bed with him for the sake of keeping each other warm."

*Here it is,* I thought. *My chance to learn from and be inspired by someone really different from me!*

How could I refuse? The sea gods had clearly ordained it.

That evening I had a few drinks with some fellow guests and we gossiped the way one does when a few shots of Fireball have loosened one's tongue.

"Oh man, I hear you've gotta shack up with that religious freak with the weird accent tonight," said a dude whose name I didn't catch.

"The one who carries the tomahawk around with him all the time?" asked a fellow imbiber. "I hear he likes his meat really, really rare."

"Yeah, he seems like the kind of guy who might chop you up and eat you," said this guy Brad. "But I mean, he does have a bunch of pretty dope tribal tattoos."

That night, I lay awake awaiting my bedmate's arrival, feeling equal parts terror and excitement. I must have drowsed, for I was startled by the appearance of a menacing yet undeniably beautiful beast of a man. We tried to make small talk, but we became so tired that the only sensible thing we could do was cuddle each other to sleep. We did not exchange many words, but the heat from his Big Spoon warmed up my Little Spoon almost instantly.

When I awoke the next morning, I knew that my life had changed forever. "Queequeg," I purred, "I feel like we are so firmly bound to each other, we could be man and wife. We are such a cozy, loving pair and I am ready to learn all about your pagan religion and your life philosophy.

"I want to fetishize your otherness for all of eternity," I said, looking to my noble savage for a response.

"Hey, Ishmael, shut the fuck up and suck-ee me cock."

I complied.

# LITTLE WOMEN

## "Felt" by John William

The Beth March Hospital for Neglected Dolls was a hatbox on a trash heap behind the burning barrel. Dark smoke befouled the air with the soot of shit and corncobs, which the March family, like most Civil War–era Americans, used for toilet paper. You can Google it.

Blacker than the corncob soot was the mood of the dolls that day. There were six dolls, five of them cast-offs from the older March sisters. Lavender Lawrence had once just been Lavender, until a butter-churning accident tore her skirt. Respecting the fluidity of gender, Beth cut the doll's hair and sewed the skirt into a pair of purple culottes any dandy would envy. Uneven Pete lost a leg to a rabid cat, so Beth replaced it with a matchstick and made him talk like a pirate. Sally No-Face had no face, and Gretta's Skin had lost her stuffing entirely. Only one doll, Joanna, was completely intact, so Beth declared her a paralytic. She built a toothpick wheelchair and piled it high with blanket scraps to keep Joanna comfortable. The sixth doll was the finger bone of a dead Gypsy.

Beth fed and clothed her dolls daily, nursed them and sang to them, made certain no act of neglect would ever sadden their hearts. When it rained, she fashioned them tiny umbrellas; when the sun shone, she took them tea in the garden. Once, during a manic episode, Jesus

commanded Beth to sew nipples on the dolls, which she did with packing twine dipped in her own blood before crying herself to sleep while
masturbating.

Then Beth became ill, and the hospital was thrown out.

"Why have we been tossed on the trash heap?" fretted Sally
No-Face. "Surely Beth will come for us now that she's recovered!"

"Yarrr," said Uneven Pete. "Haven't ye read *The Velveteen Rabbit*, ye
ghost-faced harpy? Don't ye know what happens to toys when children
get the scarlet fever?"

"I can't read! I have no eyes!"

"They're cast into the flames, along with all the sheets and clothes.
Like a buncha dirty corncobs."

"Wait a minute," said Joanna. "I've read it. The velveteen rabbit
cries a single tear of love, and a flower grows right where it lands, and
then a fairy turns him into a real rabbit."

"I can't cry either!" moaned Sally No-Face. And she banged her
featureless head against the side of the hatbox.

"Have any a ye toothless cunt rags ever shed a single tear?" asked
Uneven Pete.

The dolls looked at each other, but nobody spoke.

"Beth cries all the time," offered Joanna. "At cloudy days, or math,
or corduroy…"

"Aye," said Uneven Pete. "I once heard her blubberin' when she
burned herself on the stove."

"No burning!" the other dolls said in unison.

"Humphashiflumbinalamphlemuff," mumbled Gretta's Skin, which
had been lying motionless on the floor, like always.

"What's that?" asked Lavender Lawrence.

"Humphashiflumbinalamphlemuff."

"She says Jo once cried when mother March spanked her."

"That's it!" exclaimed Sally No-Face. "Spanking! Spanking will
save us all!"

There was a soft, cottony commotion as the dolls considered this.

"Bend me over your knee," Joanna said to Lavender Lawrence. "The rest of you gather around me and spank until somebody cries."

Lavender Lawrence raised his arm and brought it firmly down upon Joanna's pillowy mound.

"Oooh," she said.

"Are you crying yet?"

"No, but do it again."

He spanked her a second time, his yarny hands playing her ass like a dead girl's piano. A long, tremulous moan poured from her lips.

"Yes!" she howled. "Spank me! Spank me!"

The other dolls could stand it no longer. With the fury of a raging storm, their hands descended upon Joanna's backside. With each landing blow, she writhed and wailed in ecstatic exultation. Sally No-Face tweaked her twine-y nipples while Lavender Lawrence stroked the seam where her ass crack should have been. And then Uneven Pete struck something hard.

"Yarrr," he said. "What be this here?"

The dolls peered into a small, fur-lined pocket between Joanna's legs, where the nubby end of a snap button had been affixed with spirit gum.

"Shiverin' sea dogs!" he exclaimed. "The wench is full 'o buried treasure!"

"That's my clitoris," Joanna said proudly. "Beth gave it to me the day she discovered her own."

The dolls marveled and cooed at Joanna's clitoris.

"Beth called it Satan's pimple," she continued. "She said I must never touch it. But I do, I do touch it." She guided Lawrence's hand to the shiny rivet. "Like this," she said, coaching his fingers in slow circles.

Lawrence teased her metal clit while Sally toyed with Joanna's nipples and Pete continued to spank her mercilessly. So engrossed were they in this carnival of discovery and desire that all thoughts of tears and burning barrels slipped their minds completely, even as the rags and sheets piled around the hospital were fed, one by one, to the cleansing flames.

Then, something miraculous happened: Joanna arched her back and let out such a gasp of joy as none of the dolls had ever heard. In the pocket between her legs, a single drop of shimmering liquid was forming. It swelled and plumped until it was so full, so pendulous, that it fell to the bottom of the garbage pile, where a flower sprouted and unfurled its petals to reveal a tiny, winged woman.

Sally No-Face gasped. "It's the fairy!"

"Yes," said the little woman. "I am the Cum Fairy. You have summoned me with your lady spoo, and now I shall bestow my magical gift upon you all." At the wave of her wand, torrents of pleasure washed over the dolls. They rolled and rollicked over each other, all control having left their bodies.

"Are we going to become real people now?" Joanna asked.

The Cum Fairy nervously tucked a golden lock behind her ear. "Oh...uh," she said. "That's not really my thing. I'm the Cum Fairy, and you just came. So...tada!"

"But the fire!" Joanna protested.

"I can give you another one?" offered the fairy. "One of those long, rolling Os that starts at your feet and moves all the way up your spine and back down again. Total rubber sheet job. I call it Brunch with Sting."

"I don't want another orgasm!" said Joanna.

"Yarrr, I do," said Uneven Pete.

"I want to live!" Joanna begged. "I want to be real!"

The Cum Fairy hovered closer and put her hand on Joanna's shoulder. "Look," she said, "you're five inches tall and made of yarn. Real was never in the cards for you. But you did just bust a really good nut, and that's gotta count for something."

Joanna thought of all the real, human things she would never get a chance to do—running through a field, falling in love, wiping her ass with a corncob—and a cloud of despair closed over her tiny doll heart, which was actually just a cottonseed nestled in her stuffing. Then, with a wink, the Cum Fairy disappeared. Joanna felt wetness on her cheek that she hoped might be a tear, but it was only a drop of kerosene that had somehow fallen from the sky.

# "Little Assholes: I Read This Book for All of You" by Lauren Parker

Meg March had once been the prettiest of the March girls. She had hoped her beauty would serve her in marriage. She strived to be good and proper in order to achieve her castles in the sky—a large mansion with many servants to wait on her hand and foot. She looked on the situation of Sallie Gardner with envy, pining for fine clothes and good, rich food. As the only character with dreams that satisfy the antiques porn and food porn quotient of the book reader, Meg was not edited out for marketing purposes but had all the character dimension of a fine tapestry rug that was mentioned offhand in a scene. Meg March was for the *Downton Abbey* audience, but Louisa May Alcott was just ahead of her time.

Meg had married humbly, however. John Brook had been sweet, deferring, and pleasing. While he did not have large coffers, he did have a grand capacity to endure her wrath. A strong back is sometimes just as gratifying as fine furs. Her home was filled with hours of her hard labor—the curtains made of fine, tight, identical stitches, the gardens overflowing with flowers and clean rows of vegetables, and a small pillow that read *Bless this Mess* on John's armchair.

Meg scrubbed the kitchen table and it gleamed. She kept a very clean home and took pride in it. She had sewn the dress she was wearing, a fine blue thing that accentuated her shape, but not too much. She was very proper, after all. While considering herself the epitome of a good Protestant woman, she did not think of this as pride. Pride was a sin. Meg didn't sin. Therefore this wasn't pride.

John came into the kitchen, his waistcoat showing off the slimness of his frame. John was not considered traditionally handsome but Meg admired his beauty. She favored the long, lean paleness of John, stretched across their bed like a week's worth of laundry. His hair was getting long and gently grazed the top of his ear.

Meg stirred a spoon in a jar of last year's currant jam with the careful demureness of an Easter bonnet. Her long blue dress brought out
the sparkle of her eyes and the honey glow of her cheeks. She was proud
that while age and children had certainly changed her body, she was
still a great beauty with a glossy coat and a warm wet nose.

"Whatever do you need, my darling," she asked, sucking the pad of
her finger to get the sticky jam off it.

"Oh nothing, my dear. You needn't fuss on my account," John said.
Meg loved it when he talked decently. It gave her a stirring of feelings
in her baby door. She rose from her chair, which possessed intricately
carved legs mirroring the spindly and useless nature of her own, but
Meg and John were very poor, so of course it wasn't as nice as Sallie
Gardner's chairs, which had thistles and roses carved into the legs. But
Meg wasn't in any way jealous even because she was a little woman, full
of Protestant goodness who did not experience avarice or jealousy or
independent thought. The handle of the spoon was green and not black
and gold as she had envisioned in her dream home but these things
aren't relevant to the plot but I'm going to catalog them here anyway
along with the delicate pattern painted on the teacup that perched near
her right elbow. The pattern was reminiscent of the French countryside
but since neither Meg nor John had been there, the painter needn't
have bothered to capture that particular essence. No, this has nothing
to do with the plot and it will never be mentioned again.

John looked up at Meg, basking in her demureness. "I hate to trouble you with my needs. For they might put you out and you already
work so hard."

"Sweet John," she said, brushing his hair back from his face.

"It would make me so happy if we could have some pleasure today,"
he whispered, "but I certainly don't want to interrupt your day." Meg
and John's marriage was the epitome of convention in every respect but
one—the thing that really got fair Meg's blood sewer boiling was sewing
her name in fine, tight stitches across his ribs in cheerful pink thread.

"But of course, my dear husband. It's no trouble at all."

John brought out Meg's sewing kit and she placed her pincushion on the table. "Would you be ever so kind as to put your hands on the table and not move them until I tell you to?" Meg said, extracting long pins from a tiny stuffed pillow. John unfastened his pants, dropping them to his ankles. His skin was already glowing with the anticipation of thread skating through the flesh on his flanks.

Meg pulled open John's shirt, a white silk thing that had been a gift for their anniversary, and ran her fingers over the repeated scarring of her stitched initials—MB.

Meg began to slip the long sewing pins into the softness of John's inner thigh, drawing a little blood as she carefully went higher up toward his taint. The pins had been a gift from Marmee and had little daisy-shaped heads on them. If only she hadn't misplaced so many of them she could line the entirety of John's inseam, but no matter now.

"Now, John, would it put you out entirely if I stick some needles into your cock?" Meg asked brightly. John turned, presenting his upright reverend to her. Meg clasped her hands together and made quick work, sliding pins into the trunk of his member. He mewed like a kitten as the sharp pins made a ladder up his shaft, getting closer and closer to his frenulum.

"My darling, Margaret, today does seem like an excellent day for buggery. The weather is ideal for it," John gasped, gazing outside at the sunshine.

"I couldn't agree more, John." She looked across the kitchen for a tool suitable for the task. Amy had visited early that day and had brought three lovely limes that now sat on the butcher's block. They had shared a chuckle at the little joke from Book One. Nothing is quite so precious as a citrus-based anecdote with no purpose. Meg picked up the biggest of the round fruits and brought it over to John.

Meg coated the lime with the red currant jam, giving it a thick protective layer, before placing herself behind John's shapely ass. His hands were on the table and his heart was fluttering with excitement. Carefully, Meg pried open John's asshole and slipped the lime into his back pantry. He howled as the lime's navel pressed against his prostate, the rough skin of the fruit pushed tightly against the velveteen of his anal crypt. The lime was colder than the rest of him and it chilled him to his very core.

"Is this all right, darling? I wouldn't want you to be overwhelmed."

"Oh, don't trouble yourself about me. You emotionally abused me for a fair amount of the original text, so please proceed, dear."

Meg gripped a wooden spoon and brought it down repeatedly on John's backside. His skin was dappled with sweat and he moaned loudly, his cries of ecstasy almost drowning out the monotony of his character arc. Meg was getting wet. John's declarations of love and his impeccable manners (such a good boy to keep saying "please" over and over again), left her rosebud glistening with the dew of desire. She snaked her hands into John's hair, pulling harshly at the roots as his back arched and his moans grew louder.

"You're more virtuous than Helen Keller!" he shouted euphorically. "You only speak when spoken to and often not even then!"

John's sphincter rippled over the firmness of the lime. As the fruit began to thrust farther inside him, he felt its skin begin to give. Meg reached for a delicately etched cocktail glass that Amy had given her for Christmas and splashed gin into it. She held the goblet under John's rabbit hole.

"John, if it isn't too much trouble, aim into the glass." Meg reached around, grabbed the head of John's quivering cock (is it really erotica if *quiver* isn't used at least once?) and worked it like a champagne cork. John's cries of pain and pleasure could surely be heard for miles. Songbirds dashed from the trees as his contracting canal finally pushed the lime's skin to its breaking point and juice flooded out of his anus like a citrus geyser, landing in Meg's glass, running down his thighs and soaking his socks.

Meg leaned over and plucked a pin from John's cock. She swirled the gin and juice in her glass before dropping the pin in and taking a dainty sip. "My favorite cocktail has always been the Ass Gimlet," she declared with delight.

# GONE WITH THE WIND

## "Scarlett O'Hara" by Maggie Tokuda-Hall

Dear Miss Mitchell,

Thank you for sending me more pages from your novel. Generally, I think it's coming along nicely, and your prose is lovely.

However, before we move forward I would encourage you to reexamine the direction you've moved in this chapter. I worry it will severely limit your readership, not to mention the fact that as it stands, it's pretty gross. We may also want to discuss cutting down or altogether eliminating the gratuitous masturbation sequences.

To put it as gently as I can, you really jumped the fucking shark here.

I've left a few notes, but mostly I'm at a loss. Let's rethink.

Thanks,
Editor in chief James E. Newcom

## Chapter 6: The Original Cut

Scarlett was three fingers deep into what promised to be a satisfying, sticky diversion when she heard the commotion. At first she thought the thumping was merely that of her own heart, hammering as it was—in her mind's eye, Ashley Wilkes's cock stood tall and perfect, like a knight's lance—but as it grew more persistent, she realized it was, in fact, from an external source. Scarlett had been hoping to get in a good wank before the party started, but it seemed that fate would not allow it—the ruckus was too much for her to ignore.

*Editor's note: Ms. Mitchell, does "a good wank" really fit with this narrative? I beg you to reconsider.*

On her nightstand, a glass of water shook.

"I declare," Scarlett huffed. She pulled her skirts back down and scurried to the window. Down the tree-lined lane that led to Tara strode a stranger Scarlett had never seen before—he was powerfully built, and dark. Despite herself, and her undying love for Ashley Wilkes, she felt a flutter in her chest that was matched, wetly, by a flutter in her womanhood.

She tried her best to ignore it, but for the entire day she could feel her eyes drifting back, unbidden, to the tall (very tall), dark, and handsome stranger. To her delight and distraction, he ceaselessly returned her gaze, hungrily.

"Who is that?" she asked her friend Cathleen.

"Who?"

"That imposing stranger, looking at us and smiling. The nasty dark one."

"My dear, you don't know?" Cathleen clucked, and fanned herself more vigorously. "That's Tyrannosaurus Rhett. He's from Charleston. He has a most terrible reputation, and also he's a dinosaur."

*Editor's note: I love that he's from Charleston, but does he HAVE to be a dinosaur? I'm not sure I see what you're getting at here. This is exactly where I think we're starting to lose focus.*

"He looks as if...as if he wants to eat me alive," Scarlett breathed.

Cathleen giggled. Scarlett excused herself to the library. It was always quiet in there, and perhaps, she figured, she could finish what she had started earlier in the day.

In the dark of the library, with the curtains drawn, Scarlett pressed herself against her father's many leather-bound volumes. There, she fiddled beneath her layered skirts, aching to put the thick, red candle she'd pilfered from the dining room betwixt her thighs. Though she boasted a seventeen-inch waist, she had been delighted to find that she could, with little preamble, insert phallic objects of considerable girth into her covetous lady-pocket to great and pleasurable effect.

*Editor's note: Now really, Margaret, is this appropriate? Additionally, the nomenclature used here is not nearly the prose I've come to expect from you. On a side note, do ladies of the upper class often use domestic objects of a phallic shape for self-pleasure? It does raise some salacious if emasculating follow-up questions about my wife's relationship with her summer cucumber garden.*

Today's candle was a perfect fit. As she slid it in and out, in and out, luxuriating in it, in herself, she did not notice the stranger who entered the library.

"That's no way for a lady to act," T-Rhett growled.

Scarlett, shocked to be caught, froze, mid-candle thrust.

Tyrannosaurus Rhett blinked, confused. His vision, which was sensitive only to movement, had lost all track of the beautiful young lady, but he played off his temporary blindness as rakish indifference.

"Oh my, Mr. Tyrannosaurus Rhett," Scarlett purred. This afternoon was working out even more to her favor than she would have dared to dream. She cocked her head coquettishly. "I'm afraid you've caught me."

"I AM quite hungry, Ms. O'Hara. Perhaps you can be of some assistance?" He stepped toward her, his eyes full of fierce, feral desire.

Scarlett felt herself go as wet as October. "Take me in your tiny, tiny arms, you big silly lizard!" she cried.

*Editor's note: The rest of the editorial staff is curious, is that really how a woman's desire functions? Does she simply GO WET? I mean, my wife does when we copulate, but that hasn't been the rest of the team's experience, and I promised I'd*

*ask because THEY were all curious and they didn't believe me. Also they asked me
to ask you: where is the clitoris?*

The lust-filled dinosaur did his best to wrap his diminutive, scaly
arms around Scarlett, and he kissed her to the best of his ability, his
enormous tongue lapping against her face in long, slimy strokes. Nothing had ever been too much or too big for Scarlett O'Hara, and she
celebrated T-Rhett's enormity.

As T-Rhett used his enormous claws to tear her dress from her
heaving bosom, Scarlett, who was never one to be shy with her desires,
removed the candle from her scarlet gash and pushed it, not gently, up
T-Rhett's quivering cloaca.

"I'm going to fuck you into extinction," she whispered to the dinosaur.
He roared his enormous roar with delight. Outside, the trees of Tara shook.

*Editor's note: I must admit I am curious about this anal stimulation scene.
While it certainly doesn't have a place in this narrative, I wonder, how does one
coerce one's wife to partake of such activities? It seems a very sensitive topic to broach
without inadvertently raising questions about one's sexual orientation, IF one were
interested in such things, which I'M NOT.*

However, before T-Rhett had the chance to reveal what Scarlett
hoped would be the largest cock she'd ever seen, they were interrupted.
Ashley Wilkes stood at the door, looking dumbfounded by the scene
that played out before him.

"My sister said you were fast," he murmured. "But I had no idea you
were nasty." He took a step toward the pair, a filthy smile spreading
across his face. "Fuck Melanie Hamilton," he declared, to Scarlett's
infinite happiness. "Now let's get weird." T-Rhett grinned his toothy
grin. Scarlett sighed with delight.

And getting weird was just what the three of them did.

*Final editor's note: I think perhaps you and I should sit down to discuss the
direction of this novel, and also to clarify some of the finer points about coitus as are
represented in this chapter. I would also love to invite you to join me and Mrs. Newcom at our home so that you may perhaps impart some friendly, womanly advice to
her on the matter of lovemaking.*

*But really, this dinosaur stuff can't stay in. It's complete shit.*

*"Take me in your tiny, tiny arms, you big, silly lizard!"*

# "Sylvia Unchained" by Ivan Hernandez

Sylvia idled her 1998 Toyota Corolla at the Atlanta mansion's gates, wrought iron encircling a painted Confederate flag. This symbol of the oppression of her people and its legacy of hatred and bile was the final obstacle between her and a fifteen-hundred-dollar craigslist gig playing a waitress/slave at a *Gone with the Wind*-themed party for the world's shittiest white people.

It was a hard decision, and she'd weighed the consequences. On one hand, she could potentially disrespect her ancestors while reinforcing outdated stereotypes perpetuated by institutionalized racism. And on the other hand, fifteen hundred dollars. It was a life of compromises, being a black actress in Atlanta who wasn't willing to shake her ass in a parking lot for a daytime rap video, nor pretend that Tyler Perry is straight.

Her friend Tonya had worked the event in years previous. "Eh, it's an okay gig, considering they're the world's shittiest white people," she said. "Some of them get too into character, but they'll back off if you whisper 'Django Unchained.' My advice: don't go to the second floor, and whatever you do, stay away from Miss Pittypat."

They asked performers to familiarize themselves with the source material, but the movie was too long, and reading is for nerds. She'd watched ninety minutes of crackers in histrionics when her boyfriend, Marcus, demanded she shut it off before they kick him out of the Nation of Islam. "Baby, I just got my bow tie pressed," he pleaded.

And here she was, milling about the crowd of well-to-do turkeys while hoisting a tray of mint juleps. This was the first time in her decades of living in the South that she'd ever heard someone with a Southern accent ask for a mint julep and had lightly pooped herself from stifling laughter. You just had to smile and accept their choices; it was like living inside a community theater production where everybody was the director's nephew.

The event was boring more than anything, an excuse for the moderately wealthy and minimally literate to indulge in an era that had never truly existed. And then came the presentation. A man who looked like Clark Gable with an extra chromosome took to a makeshift stage holding a stand with a cloth draped over it.

"Ladies and gentlemen, welcome to the thirty-fifth Annual Never Be Hungry Again Dinner and Ball. There'll be a sla—a servant girl passing out carrots shortly. But in the meantime, we have another fine addition to the many antiques and collectibles we've presented over the years. From Leslie Howard's jawbone, to Clark Gable's penis pump, to half of Vivian Leigh's original eyebrows, we've had it all. And I am proud to present, tonight, Hattie McDaniel's Academy Award."

Sylvia stared at the statue, mouth agape. Rumor had placed the award somewhere in a box at Howard University's drama department, yet here it stood. The first Oscar awarded to an African American, the first act of recognition and acceptance by an industry that had shunned her people.

"We'll be displaying this piece upstairs, in a somewhat more...intimate exhibit."

Sylvia watched as the man took the statue and marched up a staircase. She grabbed one of the other waitresses by the arm.

"What's on the second floor?" she asked. "What are they doing up there?"

"They fuckin'," said the woman, "like, greasy, all holes, no exits fuckin'. I'd go up there, but pink dick makes me vomit."

Sylvia had no such compunction against pink dick. If this, one of the great relics of African American culture, was held captive by these people, the purpose could only be nefarious. She marched up to the man guarding the staircase.

"Guests only," he said. "Servants have to go through the back entrance."

"Oh, I'll go through the back entrance all right," she said, and spun the man around, pantsed him, and grabbed a carrot from a nearby table. She lodged the vegetable in his asshole and thrust with all the collected outrage of her forbearers in her wrist, until the root's orange skin turned brown. Sylvia picked a piece of corn from under her fingernails and ran up the stairs. Paintings of characters in increasingly slashier pairings surrounded her, Rhett Butler gnoshing on Gerald O'Hara's dong, Scarlett snapping a Yankee's neck with her Kegel muscles, Prissy and Mammy performing analingus in such a way as to form the shape of the African continent.

A pair of guards stood watch at the top of the stairway, and Sylvia pounced upon them. She worked their cocks from the trousers that contained them and delivered a double hand job so sublime, it was like she put three points into dual wielding. She burst through the doors into a banquet hall and was blinded by the sheer amount of colorless flesh on display. The orgy was nearing its dread climax, and, above it all, there was its ringleader.

She sat on the dais like a garbage bag full of wet ground beef. Makeup stained her drooping face and attendants crowded around her undulating form, the golden curls atop her head soaked in more jizz than hair product.

"PITTYPAT HORNY," the creature bellowed. "PITTYPAT WANT STATUE NOW!"

A vintage 1800s cannon stood near the leviathan, and one of the servant boys lugged out a bucket of bacon fat. He dunked the statue in the grease and shoved it into the cannon, Pittypat presenting her anal cavity like a gift nobody asked for. In that moment of staring into this white woman's death hole, Sylvia realized their plan.

"Oh my God," she said, "they're going to shoot Hattie McDaniel's Oscar into that lady's asshole!"

She tore through the piles of writhing flesh; each dick punched a victory for civil rights, and each testicle kicked an assault on Jim Crow himself. The cannon's fuse was lit, and Sylvia knew there was only one hope left. She jerked the nearest ghostly pale cock to completion and balled the cum up in her hand. She uttered a silent prayer to the patron saint of black actresses, Anna Deavere Smith, and flicked the ball of jizz with all her might. It sailed through the air, spinning like a wet bolo, and found its mark true, extinguishing the fuse's flame.

Sylvia jumped onto the dais and grabbed the Oscar, holding it aloft like a cum-stained Excalibur. Only when it was in her hands did she notice the proportions were off, the weight too light. It was foam, a fake.

"What are you doing?" the former Pittypat demanded, breaking character.

"Oh, ah, I thought you were going to shoot a culturally significant piece of Americana up your butt. My bad?"

"You've ruined my party, made a useless spectacle, and assaulted some of the finest genitalia in Atlanta society. What do you have to say for yourself?"

"In my defense, you guys are the world's shittiest white people. I'll just take my fifteen hundred dollars and leave."

"No."

"Fair enough."

And later, as she drove away in her Toyota Corolla, Sylvia came to the same decision as everyone else who grandly embarrasses themselves or otherwise flunks out of living in most every other American city.

"Fuck this, I'm moving to San Francisco."


## "The Velvet Drapes" by Carolyn Ho


Few people have felt Rhett's ass, let alone sat between his ass cheeks for several sweaty and strenuous minutes as I have. I am the green drapes of Tara. "Velvet" if I can formally introduce myself, or "V" for short. The things I could share with you, like the firmness of Rhett's robust anus as he thrusts over and over, his balls laden upon me, or perhaps how once his fists raised to the sky in climax as he cried out, "Ashley, Ashley!!" and wept into his cum.

On difficult days, Rhett makes love to me twice, as only Southern men with a full head of hair can. He speaks to Scarlett with his body pressed against me; he argues with her while his large hands play with my piles, stroking me, teasing my softest parts between his fingers. I'm sure he feels a twinge of guilt, but he deserves better than that husband-killing Scarlett, that dramatic hussy. Friends, in truth it is I who hold all of Rhett Butler's affections. His heart is too epic for merely women or men, or livestock for that matter; indeed, he loves inanimate objects more. Tables, chairs, the occasional ceramic candy bowl, but his proclivity, my friends, is for a good strong window covering, such as myself, and during our relations he tells me he loves me, that I need to be fucked, and fucked good and often, by someone who knows how, and rips me down from the window rod for the best two minutes of my life. Oh my word yes. Yes. Rhett. Yes.

Whenever he comes to Tara, he locks himself in my sitting room and fondles whole panels of me, slapping himself with my gold cords, sliding me between his damp ass cleft, raising the heft of his buttocks and letting them bounce gleefully upon my chartreuse lining.

I think of him often like this, bent over, farmed and rubbing his scent along my hand-stitched cotton lining, letting the room fill with his animal musk; I can see him with his slacks down, his coattails raised, and his lips quivering, and in those briefest moments I do declare, I can see the true valley of Rhett Butler's deep and earthen heart, his dark anus puckering open and closed, a dirty rose smelling of fresh tilled land, calling out to me, telling me that the land is the only thing that matters, and here is such a piece of land in that space between Rhett's anus and shaft, a warm place for me to call home.

Oh the tragedy of not being able to prod him back with my engorged tassel tiebacks, to be his anal beads or a gag. If only I could bind him at my leisure or whip him as he begs, or choke him as he violently comes while I faint right off the rod into his arms. The want to love him as he ought to be loved, and deeply.

Some days when I'm just hanging about, I daydream Rhett runs away with me and carries me up the grand staircases of hotels and summer homes. He spreads me on the floor and rolls me open onto every inch of our love nest. I imagine he fucks me with an orgy of random furniture, naughty bits of carpet, some antique decanters, maybe a funeral urn. My beau would press his large endowments over every inch of my velvety rolls until the room and I glisten with his throbbing manhood. This, ladies and gentlemen, is a dream I share only with you. Even now as I look down, his ass streaks are all over me like little brown kisses from long ago. I cling to him as he to me, in tiny clumps of a distant memory.

One night exactly like this one, Scarlett mentioned "Ashley Wilkes," and as usual nothing but the wide dimming of the Southern dusk is alive between Rhett and that whore, a light so faded it appears bloody and swallowed in the darkness of approaching night. In this wasted night, Rhett comes to me, slams the door to the drawing room, and rushes into my folds. He does to me what he wishes Scarlett would do to Ashley, finally, and as he begins removing his slacks, I part myself slightly, fluttering in anticipation, letting patches of the sunset glow and a Southern humid breeze queef between my cracks and wait. Rhett pours himself a glass of brandy and fingers me, my threading, cups my knots and sighs. Somewhere between his unbuttoned collar and his fifth glass, he finds himself massaging a rose-colored armchair with one hand and the other prodding himself with a white parasol. Lightly he opens and rests the tip inside his anus, while his semi-erect penis stirs a pitcher of iced tea, making a delicate sound, as a tea bag hitting a ceramic bowl does. Thick and wet, he stirs himself, beating gently his triumph over and over. He continues this one-man orgy, until Scarlett opens the door and screams. Her wails match a fevered glare. Their eyes meet. He openly touches my pert tassels in response. Scarlett, unable to run, or speak, or faint, grows hoarse, then silent. He continues on, rubbing everything. The more obvious her immobility the more feverish his thrusts. He runs his moist hands into my velvet parts, into the fields and fields of green laid open to him, and tells her, with the quickness of a man whose heart cannot be broken twice by a common whore, that frankly he doesn't give a damn and comes wildly and thickly over me.

"Sweetheart. V," Rhett croons, ignoring Scarlett's quiet shrieking, the sound of her heels growing fainter down the hall as he pulls me down, fully dismantled from the rod, and molds me into a gigantic orifice, gathers all of me from each window, and engineers a giant vaginal/anal mound on the carpet, where he envelopes all of himself: his face, his penis, his feet, all parts of him absorbed into one hole, until he resembles a large green caterpillar, wrapped and writhing on the floor, a cocoon ploughing the air, moaning with abandon. "I love you more than I have ever loved anything."

But that was the end. Sadly, I'll confess, I never saw Rhett again, except once in jail, when I was an ugly dress. He hardly recognized me. After the incident, I was stowed away, like a guest hand towel in the back of a closet. The vastness of each day and night indistinguishable, in the dimness of eternity left waiting for him, his well-defined calves, his smoothed hair, his swift wet hands taking every fiber of my being.

Tomorrow, he'll come for me. Tomorrow. But tomorrow was over a hundred years ago, and still my lovely friends, I wait. Tomorrow is an ailment only the luckiest of us recover from. I fall apart, seam by seam, yearning through the centuries, living from stuffy mansions to historical houses to cold museums. I fall apart knowing I have been loved and loved well by a man whose brown streaks are faded but forever stained along my hem, in a richness still stinking sweetly of Tara, of tomorrow and at the center of an unyielding heart that never dies.

# ANIMAL FARM

## "The Cat" by Gabriel Cubbage

Mr. Jones, of the Manor Farm, had been too drunk to remember to shut the barn door. He lurched across the moonlit yard and stumbled through the front door of the house to his favorite easy chair.

But the chair was already occupied. "Get off, you!" barked Jones. The cat, nestled comfortably in the crook between the cushion and the chair back, ignored him. "I said GIT!" Gripping her by the scruff of the neck, Jones hauled the cat outside and dropped her onto the wet grass.

*"Hsssssss!"* she protested, scratching at the air behind him as he went back inside.

"And *that*," observed a grizzled voice nearby, "is a perfect example of how the private appropriation of surplus value by the bourgeoisie compounds the disenfranchisement of the proletariat."

"I hate politics," said the cat.

"Nay, cat. I speak not of politics, but revolution!" She barely looked at him. It was Old Major. Twelve years old, the wise boar was the most respected animal on the farm. "Come to the barn tonight, where I shall tell of a dream I have had. A dream of a time when we, the oppressed, will rise up against tyranny, and the likes of Farmer Jones and his cohorts will be banished or killed."

But the chair was already occupied. "Get off, you!" barked Jones. The cat, nestled comfortably in the crook between the cushion and the chair back, ignored him. "I said GIT!" Gripping her by the scruff of the neck, Jones hauled the cat outside and dropped her onto the wet grass.

"Killed, you say?" The cat was intrigued. "Tonight?"

"I cannot say exactly when. Certainly not in my lifetime."

"Oh no," said the cat. "That's much too long. Couldn't you...speed it up?" She flicked her tail flirtatiously.

The boar turned to leave. "No, I'm afraid the ponderous, churning wheels of social progress are not subject to the whims of mere—"

"I could make it worth your while," she purred.

"I beg your pardon?"

The cat rolled onto her back and spread her legs wide. "Ever seen anyone do this?" She began licking herself, slowly at first, then with more fervor. "It feels *sooooo* good."

Old Major was transfixed now. "I've...uh...*ahem*. I've never been able to reach."

"First time I ever saw a pussy lick itself!" called out Squealer the pig from across the yard.

The cat sighed and ceased her ministrations. "Well, now that we've got *that* one out of the way..." Before Major could protest, she was slinking between his haunches, drawing a sensual figure eight around his hind legs and tickling his underbelly with her fur. He shivered from snout to tail. "Let's focus on this...*uprising* of yours..."

The speech Old Major gave in the barn that night—twenty minutes later than scheduled—was very different from the one he'd planned. Sex between a cat and a boar was considered a great crime. Yet the forbidden pleasures the cat had shown him had felt so...*right*, he found himself championing an entirely new cause.

"Comrades!" he intoned to the assembled pigs, horses, donkeys, goats, dogs, rats, rabbits, sheep, and other metaphors. "Tonight, I fucked a cat. And it was sublime!"

There were gasps of disbelief and cries of "Blasphemy!"

Major continued. "Among the wise and benevolent humans, there is a notion called 'sexual liberty between consenting adults.' It means that if a cat and a boar or a mule and a turkey want to make sweet love, then no one has the right to stop them!"

A few animals looked doubtful—particularly the sheep, who never get any respect in literature. The rest were stirred by Old Major's words. Partly out of deference, but mostly because they could all think of at least one other species they secretly found sexually attractive.

Sensing his audience was primed for his pièce de résistance, Old Major cleared his throat and began to sing.

### *[To the tune of "Clementine"]*

*Beasts of England, beasts of Ireland,*
*Beasts of every sex and size,*
*Shed your inhibitions*
*And prepare to feel alive.*
*Where's it written that a cart horse*
*And a she-dog can't entwine?*
*Is their love so very wrong just*
*Because his shaft won't fit inside?*
*Soon or late the night is coming,*
*When we all shall surely bone.*
*And no longer shall the ugly*
*Be forced to masturbate alone.*
*Let your morals and your values*
*Be subsumed by baser needs.*
*Drop down upon your haunches*
*And accept your neighbor's seed.*
*Ecstasy so sweet and dangerous,*
*Could be yours this very night.*
*Farmer Jones has gone to bed and*
*Now the moon is shining bright.*
*Dogs and horses, rats and ducklings,*
*Bears, penguins, whales and African elephants,*
*Let your preference for other species*
*Be no mandate to remain celibate.*
*Beasts of England, beasts of Ireland,*
*Beasts of eeeeeeeeevery kink and cry,*

*You've been naked since your birthday,*
*TIME TO LET YOUR FREAK FLAG FLYYYYYYY!*

As the song ended, the barn erupted with cheers and a thunderous stomping of hooves. Old Major's words had awakened a need for bestial carnality the animals had all been afraid to embrace until now. The ducks were already openly masturbating, and the sheep were chanting "Freak fla-a-a-a-g, freak fla-a-a-a-g" in lusty unison.

"I know this all sounds radical today, and it may be years before it's socially acceptable for animals of different species to—"

"BARNYARD ORGY!" The cat's voice, scattered by the rafters where she was hiding above the mob, seemed to come from everywhere at once.

A complete literary account of what happened next would surely be banned in any civilized nation. Suffice to say that the grunting, braying, neighing, rooting, pecking, snorting, squeaking, humping, honking, crowing, quacking, barking, growling, bleating, wheezing, and squealing that ensued was more than enough to wake Farmer Jones from his drunken slumber.

Shotgun in hand, he stormed into the barn, bellowing, "What in the Jumping Jesus Joseph Stalin is going on?!" The moon outside had been bright, and it took a moment for his eyes to adjust. When they did, the shotgun slipped from his grasp and clattered onto the floor.

"My God...," he choked. "Benjamin! What are you doing?!"

The donkey was on his back, legs in the air. But instead of hooves, he had...sheep. Four prize ewes, each filled to the cervix, and all "B-A-A-A-A!"ing with ecstasy. Perched along Benjamin's massive erection were three chickens and a rooster, all pecking furiously at him as he rocked back and forth in pain and pleasure.

Old Major was eyeball-deep in Mollie the mare, who had a pink silk ribbon in her mouth, with which she was whipping one of the dogs. It was hard to tell *which* dog, since he or she was being aggressively straddled and suffocated (happily, the wagging tail suggested) by Clover the horse.

Not to be outdone, the pigs (always the cleverest of the animals) had constructed a great, wooden dildo on wheels. A battering ram of sorts, which they were driving repeatedly into Boxer's anus. "Harder!" whinnied the great cart horse as he braced himself for the next assault. "You must work H-A-A-A-A-RDER!"

The rest was almost vanilla by comparison. The ducks were still masturbating. The geese were watching. And the goats were milking the cows. With their mouths. Onto the rats.

It wasn't long before Farmer Jones was doing some milking of his own. With his pants around his ankles, he worked himself furiously, like a rusty water pump, as tears of shame ran down his cheeks.

This was the moment the cat had been waiting for. She darted between the farmer's legs, out of the barn, and flicked her tail up at the release lever for the counterweighted sliding door. It slammed shut behind her, sealing Jones inside with his insurgent livestock.

As the sun rose on Manor Farm the next day, and every day thereafter, the first of its rays found their way across the unplowed fields, between the unpicked apple trees, through the windows of the farmhouse, and bathed the cat with light and warmth as she slept contentedly in her favorite chair.

## "Raven Rebooted" by Nathaniel Waggoner

Moses the raven thought, *If Sugarcandy Mountain is real, how could Lord Licorice allow animals to live in such pitiful squalor?* After the other birds in his youth group had flown off to lay eggs in other towns, there hadn't even been another outward sign of the idea of his religion save for Napoleon's and Snowball's virulent condemnation of it . . . until now. A scrap of parchment fell from the sky, hitting the roof just in front of him.

"EMERGENCY DISPATCH FROM LORD LICORICE: Because of your loyalty and devotion to spreading the gospel of Sugarcandy Mountain amongst the heathens, we have some special duties for you to perform, duties that will necessitate a brief and forgivable transgression from your Sugarcandian values. You must take down Napoleon and Squealer. In order to gain knowledge of the inner workings of the manor, your best option is to seduce and get information out of Napoleon's mistress, known as Pigathius. So in addition to murder, we are giving you permission to fuck. You have to fuck this pig, Moses. It is democracy's only hope." Moses's heart swelled. He knew he could do it.

At four p.m. every day, certain animals were allowed to line up near the stables, where they'd be given a gill of beer. Moses was one of them, and so was Pigathius. Moses sidled up behind her in line and said, "Excuse me, miss."

"Hmmf?" she muttered. "Hey, watch it, Buster!"

She turned around, and Moses was stunned to see the most beautiful animal he'd ever laid eyes on: She had long blond hair and bright blue eyes with lashes that poked out like butterflies had landed on her face. She wore a pearl necklace, purple gloves, a leopard-print jacket, and heels.

Moses's shock lasted only a moment. Soon, he was laying on all kinds of slick moves. Complimenting her cleverly but not in too needy or obvious of a way. Just really saying some of the most classy, intriguing shit, I swear to God. If you heard what he was saying there in that beer line, you'd be like, *Fuck, I am horned up as heck now. I want desperately to make out with that bird.*

He took her gloved hand (it seemed to be more of a hand than a hoof) and kissed it (it was more of a peck than a kiss).

"Moses," he said.

"Piggy," she replied, batting her eyes. Soon they were getting it on all kinds of ways. Missionary, doggy style, the others. The cowgirl one. The sex they did was so hot, you wouldn't even believe it. They thrusted sexfully upon each other like nobody's business. Then they did that some more.

I'm sorry, I'm sorry. I know the point of this is to write sexy stuff. It's just that I don't really have much experience with that kind of thing. Sex, that is. Actual sex in real life. And by "I," I mean me, the person writing this. I'm sitting in one of these chairs right now. Somebody

asked me to do this fanfiction contest, and I love *Animal Farm* and I've
written pages and pages of fanfiction, but honestly, now I'm uncomfortable with the whole thing. My experience with erotic contact with
another person is limited to the time Jenny Chambers let me sniff her
T-shirt at guitar camp. I thought she was my girlfriend for three years
after that. It's not easy for a person like me to get dates. I can tell you all
about allegory, metaphor, farming, politics, and the English language,
the rise and fall of Communism in Russia, the entire Muppets oeuvre,
the life of Jim Henson, but how to stop talking about those things? How
to just smoothly go with it, let the other person talk but then think of
casual, non-creepy jokes in response, then open up about myself? Let
alone the other steps.

Anyways, Moses and Miss Piggy panted and heaved and stared into
each others' eyes. For a moment, Moses almost forgot his mission—but
he knew what he had to do. They talked all night, and she told him not
only of her dreams of becoming a star of Animalist propaganda films,
but also of her affair with Napoleon, the many promises he'd made to
her. More importantly, she detailed his daily routine, his weaknesses, his
fears. A brilliant plan began to form in Moses's mind, when suddenly:
"Hiya!"

Moses pitched backward and hit the floor. He looked up, dazed, to
see Miss Piggy pointing old Mr. Jones's huge rifle at him.

"Fly, bird," she said.

"But why?"

"Because soon the animals of the world will rise up to end Napoleon's insanity—only they'll do a shitty job, and for a while Napoleon
will have the same weapons as everybody else, and they'll just keep racing to get more weapons instead of trying to find a real solution. Finally
one of you, some Sugarcandy-worshipping bird from another, much
richer farm, perhaps himself a star of that farm's propaganda films,
will get Napoleon's successor to concede.

"Except everyone here will be heartbroken and miserable and
drunk for years as a result, until finally another awful pig will lie to

them enough about how they should have pride in being animals, and he'll treat them just the same as Napoleon did and start taking over other farms and threatening still more.

"But you Sugarcandians will be around forever. You'll always have it easy. Not like me, Buster. Fabulous female pigs will be getting a tough break for decades after Manor Farm is destroyed, here and everywhere. Fabulous animals, females, entertainers, anyone different from those in power. Frogs, bears, whatever Gonzo is, the lovers, the dreamers, virginal fanfiction writers . . . all destined to struggle forever, to various degrees. Imagine a hoof stamping on a face forever. You think you're so important, coming here and seducing me, obviously after something else? You know nothing, Moses Crow. Now get the fuck out of here."

So he did. He flew up and up and up and just kept flying until his heart heaved and he couldn't breathe anymore, and he couldn't keep his eyes open anymore, and suddenly everything was bright, and more colorful, and he could smell the caramel in the breeze.

# "Muriel Stages a Coup" by Camden Avery

For months, now, Mr. Jones of Manor Farm had come home stinking drunk, too tired even for a titty nuzzle or a 2:00 a.m. rollover fuck. What was he doing instead? Touching up the chicken coop, he said. Raking out the stables. Bathing the cows, he said.

Mrs. Jones of the Manor Farm was being driven mad by degrees.

Mrs. Jones had grown progressively more desperate and found she had developed, in balance, an alarming obsession with household cleaning. She spent her days polishing the silver obsessively; she mopped the kitchen by the hour. In the wee hours of the morning, unsleeping, she peeled off her nightgown and scrubbed the bathroom floor naked on hands and knees, making sure the tender folds of her cunt brushed drowsily against the plunger handle in the corner or the edge of the cabinet. She teased the soapy sponge with the tip of her tongue. She developed unimagined uses for rubber kitchen gloves.

"Men," she would say to herself meanwhile, cursing Mr. Jones, "men are the only animal that consume without producing!"

It had become too much. Mrs. Jones yearned for a new allegiance.

Tonight, upstairs at the Manor House, Mrs. Jones thumbed her nipple in lazy circles beneath the bedclothes, listening to the clock tick off the minutes. Mr. Jones finally flopped over on the bed and began to snore through a heavy fog of beer.

Mrs. Jones put out the light and had a glass of brandy. Down in the farm buildings there was a stirring, a fluttering.

"Mrs. Jones," it said. "Mrs. Jones is coming, hurry! Hurry!"

Certain after a time that Mr. Jones was out for the night, Mrs. Jones slipped out of bed in her calico nightdress, the good one with the lace Peter Pan collar and the satin trim. She crept down the back stairs through the kitchen and pulled on her Wellingtons, bunched the hem of her nightdress up round her waist, and marched down the back steps toward the barn. She was beginning to glow with the brandy.

Inside the barn, bathed dimly in the warm light of a single lantern hung from a rafter, presided Muriel the white goat. From a raised platform at one end of the barn she shouted imperiously, "Quickly! There isn't much time!"

The piglets were constructing a theatrical manger in the half-light.

Across the dark yard under the moon, Mrs. Jones trudged steadily, nightdress hiked high, the crisp midnight air flirting playfully with her soapy pink squealer. In a dizzy euphoria of anticipation, she approached the barn door and knocked, quelling her excitement.

"Four legs good," she whispered, "two legs bad."

Muriel nosed open the door and admitted Mrs. Jones. At the door, Mrs. Jones accepted the customary horse tranquilizer from the bottle.

In one sweep Mrs. Jones whipped the nightdress over her head and tossed it to the piglets, who carried it away into the corner.

"Get it good and dirty," she crowed.

Boxer, the horse, ambled over and brought one of his feedbags, which Mrs. Jones obediently put over her head so that she could not see.

As the tranqs took hold, Mrs. Jones began to have an expanding, extraordinary sense of community. She was among her own kind. All need not be strife.

"Four legs good, two legs bad," Boxer said.

"Four legs good, two legs bad," was her muffled reply. She felt her equilibrium start to swim.

Muriel led blind Mrs. Jones up a rickety milking stool to the platform at the end of the barn, transformed now by the manger and some artfully arranged hay into a life-sized nativity. In the center, on a haphazard nest of straw, Mrs. Jones was pushed onto hands and knees. Mrs. Jones was getting into the spirit of things. She swung her tits around.

Muriel mounted the scene, leather riding crop clenched in her square teeth. "Four legs good!" cried Muriel, and with one forehoof drove Mrs. Jones tits-first into the hay. "Two legs bad! Seize her and fuck her!"

The animals in the barn were in a frenzy. Mrs. Jones on all fours waved around her piggy-pink cunt like a faded suede catcher's mitt. The animals went wild, squealing, braying, calling out.

"Oink!" screamed Mrs. Jones from the depths of the feedbag. "Oink, oink!"

In a moment the piglets were upon her, nuzzling, pushing, grunting.

"Here, piggy!" she cried. "Piggy, piggy, oh! Oh, piggy!" Soon she was pushing and sliding her way among the pigs and their slop-caked bellies.

Meanwhile, Muriel, at the head of the platform, braced her hooves and towered over the scene, her shining rectangular pupils dilated. In the darker corners of the barn the shyer animals were playing out elaborate, interspecies fantasies on the sidelines.

A sheepdog bounded across the stage and removed the feedbag from Mrs. Jones's head. Muriel, quivering, backed her haunches over Mrs. Jones's face.

Muriel mounted the scene, leather riding crop clenched in her square teeth. "Four legs good!" cried Muriel, and with one forehoof drove Mrs. Jones tits-first into the hay. "Two legs bad! Seize her and fuck her!"

"Oh!" cried Mrs. Jones. "You smelly goat bitch, fuck my face! Fuck my face!"

Nearby the hens had left a basket of their eggs. Gasping for air between mouthfuls of goat hair, Mrs. Jones swung out an arm and grabbed a handful of the eggs. She crushed them between her tits and spread the runny mess down between her thighs. Chaff and animal hair matted to her body.

"Yes!" she screamed. "Yes, yes!"

It was exactly then that under Muriel's orders Snowball and Napoleon, working for once in unison, pushed a slop trough, brimming with vegetable scraps and rotten feed corn, across the platform.

"Oink!" squealed Mrs. Jones. "Oh, oink!"

Snowball tipped over the trough and Mrs. Jones flipped and flopped in the mess.

"I feel so dirty!" she shrieked. "I'm filthy! I'm filthy!"

Then, from the back of the barn, came the creak of a door hinge, barely audible in the chaos. The hens, perched by the back door for a better view of the stage, rustled their wings and began to chatter, afraid.

The frenzy on the platform at the head of the barn took no notice, Mrs. Jones being now up to her shoulder inside Bess the dairy cow and pulling on two teats at once, but slowly, dazed, in walked Mr. Pilkington, of Foxwood Farm, a curious expression on his face. Mr. Pilkington wore a thick rubber butcher's apron.

He stepped into the ring of light and saw where Mrs. Jones was squealing in the muck. The sheep let out a cry of alarm, and Old Major shouldered toward Pilkington aggressively.

"No," said Mr. Pilkington. "Stop!" He put up his hands. "Let's face it: our lives are drudgery and short. Four legs good, two legs bad!"

And in a gesture of goodwill he got on hands and knees so that they could see that he wore nothing but his butcher's apron. He spread his exposed thighs toward the Major in an offering of peace and swung his balls purposefully, for all to see.

With that, Napoleon, who wasn't much inclined to talk but was accustomed to getting his own way, charged at Mr. Pilkington's winking pink rectum and thrust himself inside.

"What is this?!" bellowed Mr. Jones from the front door, having wandered down to understand the source of the feral screams he'd heard, fearing a fox had found its way into the chicken coop.

The scene that met his eye was nothing he had ever imagined: his wife driving a young piglet's snout into her cunt, his respectable neighbor swinging his dick around and screaming, "Get it! Get my bacon!" All manner of animals cavorting, feathers and hay floating in the steamy light. The scene was anarchy.

"Get up! Get up!" he cried to Mrs. Jones. "On your feet!"

He flung at her the rumpled calico nightdress, now sodden with pig shit.

"Get dressed!" he shouted.

Mrs. Jones let the dress lay where it fell at her feet. Breasts heaving, she swept the hair and hay from her eyes, spat out some cow hair. She pulled the handle of a garden trowel from between her legs and pointed it at him.

"You horrible bastard," she said. "Can you not see that liberty is worth more than a few ribbons?"

"Charge!" screamed Muriel, and Mr. Jones was trampled in an instant.

# THE PICTURE OF DORIAN GRAY

## "Sibyl Vane" by Alan Leggitt

"Have you heard the news, Basil?" said Lord Henry one evening as Basil Hallward was shown into the aristocrat's opulent study. "Dorian Gray is engaged to be married."

Hallward swooned and flung himself onto the nearest velour fainting couch. "Dorian engaged to be married!" he cried. "To whom?"

"To a stripper."

Basil turned pale and pulled his smelling salts from his breast pocket. "This is all your fault, Harry," he cried. "Dorian was supposed to be my twink, but you've ruined him with your ten-page lecture on hedonism."

"Dorian is blossoming into his own twink now, Basil," Lord Henry replied, sniffing a nearby carnation. "And I get a creepy, paternal hard-on from watching him step on his own dick."

"But think of Dorian's birth, and position, and wealth," Basil whined. "It would be absurd for him to marry so far beneath him."

"The dullest marriages are for all the right reasons," Lord Henry quipped.

"I hope the girl is good, Harry. I don't want to see Dorian tied to some gold-digging skank."

"Oh, she is better than good—she is beautiful," murmured Lord Henry, sipping a glass of vermouth and orange bitters. "Dorian says she has tits like fresh watermelons, and he is not often wrong about such things. After all, hanging out with us has taught him misogyny of a kind to rival the upskirt subreddit."

"But do you approve of the marriage, Harry?"

"If Dorian Gray proposes to wed a beautiful girl who can put both legs behind her head, it is not my job to air my moral prejudices. My only concern is that he looks good doing it. But here is Dorian himself; he will tell you more than I can."

"My dear Harry, my dear Basil, you must both congratulate me!" said the lad, throwing off his evening cape with its satin-lined wings and shaking each of his friends by the hand. "I have never been so happy. Of course, it is all so sudden—all really delightful things are. Yet it also seems that I've always dreamt of having a magnificent trophy wife to call my own." He was flushed with excitement and pleasure and looked simply irresistible to the two older men.

"I hope you will always be very happy, Dorian," said Hallward.

"Come, have a seat on my lap," Lord Henry broke in, "and then you will tell us how it all came about."

"There is really not much to tell," cried Dorian as he snuggled up to Lord Henry on the sofa. "One evening about seven o'clock, I determined to go out in search of some adventure. I felt that this gray monstrous London of ours, with its myriad people, 'its sordid sinners and its splendid sins,' as you once phrased it, must have something in store for me. In short, I wanted to get Dirrty. About half past eight, I happened upon an absurd little theater, with gaudy posters of naked women and a sign that read 'ALL NUDE CABARET.' I simply couldn't resist going in.

"The innards of the theater were even more ostentatious than I imagined. A veritable rainbow of lights illuminated a black runway stage, surrounded by drunken ruffians. Serving girls roamed the floor, clad in neon bikinis and grotesque amounts of rouge. In the far corner, a lecherous DJ presided over an enormous phonograph. As I arrived, a completely nude woman was onstage wiping down a shiny pole with a dirty rag. The whole place smelled of brass polish and Lycra.

"I nearly walked out, but I remembered what you once told me, Harry—stick your dick in every dirty hole you see before you become old and can't get it up anymore. So I took a seat near the stage and ordered an appletini. Just then, the house lights dimmed, and music began playing. I believe the tune was 'Flawless' by Beyoncé. The DJ announced that Sibyl Vane was to take the stage.

"The pearly gates of heaven must've been concealed behind those dingy curtains, for out walked an angel, clad in a white corset, a short ruffled skirt, white fishnet stockings, and a pair of enormous transparent platform heels. Across her collarbone was a tattoo that read 'MANEATER.' The way she moved was hypnotic. Her body was petite, yet she commanded the entirety of the stage with her divine presence.

"The music wailed through the tinny phonograph, while Sibyl Vane climbed, twirled, crawled, and twerked her way into my heart. As Beyoncé sang,

♫ Bow down bitches ♫

"…she tore open her corset and let the girls loose. Her breasts were two perfect bouncing cherubs. Her nipples stared at me, like the shining eyes of a tiger in the darkness, captivating yet deadly. I was drawn to the edge of the stage, where I emptied my pockets of shilling after shilling, while Sibyl gracefully gathered her spoils into her various orifices.

"After the performance was over, I returned to my seat, quite exhausted. To my delight, Sibyl returned to the stage to clean up. We made eye contact, and she held my gaze as she ran the filthy rag up and down the length of the girthy brass poll. I stared back and could practically feel that rag rubbing my cock down with brass polish.

"When she finished, Sibyl, completely naked, save her plastic heels, hopped off the stage and walked straight to my table. It was as if the Mona Lisa herself had stepped through her frame to greet me in the flesh. 'Hey, big spender, want a lap dance?' she asked. Her eyes held a look that was either barely contained lust or abject contempt. I'm gonna go with lust.

"Before I knew it, she had me by the hand and led me into the private booths. The wallpaper was dreadful, the floor smelled of vomit, and the door was guarded by a terrifying man. I was in heaven all the same. In a dim corner, she sat me down across from a sign that read 'NO SEX IN THE CHAMPAGNE ROOM' and stood before me. Then, the music began.

♫ My milkshake brings all the boys to the yard ♫

"She began to gyrate with the rhythm as she leaned slowly, sensually toward me. Her tongue nearly touched my ear as she whispered, 'Let me make you more comfortable.' She began to undo my necktie... with her mouth. The aroma of cigarettes was on her breath and I grew quite light-headed. After removing my tie, she let it fall onto the growing bulge in my trousers. With bewilderment, I watched as she lowered her hips onto my lap and picked up the silk tie with her Kegel muscles. She ordered me to hold out my hand, then spun around, bent forward, and dropped the tie into my palm. It was warm and moist. As I held the fabric to my face to smell her essence, she began to grind her backside against my pants.

♫ La La—La Laa La. Warm it up ♫

"Her hips moved like the waves of the ocean, while her powerful buns crashed against the beachhead of my loins.

♫ La La—La Laa La. The boys are waiting ♫

"She turned back around and mounted me, her angelic tits smothering my face. I could feel the fire of her cunt against my Dorian Jr., and in a matter of seconds, my milkshake... was all over my pants.

"I feel that I should not tell you all this, but I can't help it. Of course, our engagement is a dead secret. My guardians are sure to be furious, but I don't care. I'm young and rich and white and I'll do whatever I want."

Lord Henry sipped his cocktail in a meditative manner. "At what particular point did you mention the word *marriage*, Dorian? And what did she say in answer? Perhaps you forgot all about it."

"My dear Harry, I didn't treat it as a business transaction, and I didn't make a formal proposal. After I creamed myself, I told her that I loved her and she said, 'NO TOUCHING!' But as I wrote her a cheque for the lap dance, her eyes held a look that was either unadulterated love or wretched pity. I'm gonna go with true love."

## "Dorian Gray" by Samuel Rye

Dorian Gray lay draped upon his fainting couch, as limp as a stole around the neck of an elderly dowager. Having woken up too late to be useful but too early to be social, he had locked himself away for hours rereading a well-worn copy of a certain yellow book. Just as his fingers unconsciously began tracing circles across the protuberance in his trousers, a faint creak alerted him to the opening chamber door, and the dour face of his servant appeared, just like his conscience—unwelcome.

"Lord Henry pays a visit, sir," said the man.

*How predictable,* Dorian thought, petulant at the loss of both his reverie and his erection.

Descending to the parlor, he found Lord Henry Wotton smoking a gold-tipped cigarette, held in a hand of upraised but disaffected posture.

"Hello, Harry," Dorian said. "My apologies. Have you waited long?"

"Oh, I have been here some time, but I've amused myself with your etchings. I didn't think you actually had any when you said it. Anyway, I have a gift for you! Your indiscretions with the Rostov siblings have even the Trappists talking. Your reputation as a scoundrel has surpassed my own, and it calls for a trophy."

"Oh, Harry, surely you shouldn't have. Besides, you've seen my collection; you know my tastes are very...singular."

"Ah, but this is different." With a flourish, Henry unrolled a tapestry as long as two footmen are tall.

*Dorian was fascinated at once; a delicate woven scene of Bedouin pleasures, orgiastic clusters of men, women, and eunuchs performing perplexing acts of fornication in clustered contortions of carnal delight.*

Dorian was fascinated at once; a delicate woven scene of Bedouin pleasures, orgiastic clusters of men, women, and eunuchs performing perplexing acts of fornication in clustered contortions of carnal delight. The beautiful and the grotesque spread bare, interpenetrating and unashamed. For a man with no gag reflex, he was shocked to feel his breath caught in his throat. "This is truly unique!" he sputtered.

"I thought you might fancy it. It's finely wrought, yet tastelessly salacious. I've never seen such deep blues and midnight blacks."

"Harry, you are the best of fellows, but such a contrarian," Dorian said, laughing. "To call that black and blue when it is so clearly gold and white. I must thank you!"

"You needn't thank me. Excessive gratitude betrays an abundance of tact and good behavior. I know how a gentleman misbehaves, and I can see you are a perfect gentleman."

Dorian did not hear this, driven to distraction by the graphic patterns, recollections of his earlier reading stoking a fire in his loins.

"This is a wonderful gift, but I am afraid I feel unwell today, quite flush. I should retire, but you may stay as long as you wish."

Harry stamped out his cigarette on something priceless and foreign. "No, I ought visit Gwendolyn before tonight's performance. I will see you at the opera, in my sister's box?"

They made their plans and parted, Lord Henry leaving and Dorian commanding his servant to bring the gift to his private collection.

Dismissing the man as soon as he could, Dorian wasted no time. Consumed by the spirit of the book he wished to exceed, he closely studied the silk threads. There had been one figure he had noted earlier, and he scanned for it again. Satyrs dancing about drunkenly, naked virgins, men and women in myriad combinations, lost in the throes of passion. This was a truly transcendent display of perversion, and there! One satyr in particular jumped out at him, a gnarled and bewarted creature who was sodomizing a milkmaid, who in turn was milking a bull. The eyes of the satyr bore into the girl, demanding everything. Something so depraved and ugly having its way with something so pure reminded him of every day, and it was hot. He frantically shed his fine clothes, his pristine young cock springing from his trousers. Eyes flicked from figure to figure, hands tugging at himself until he was sore of palm.

He thought back on Sibyl, the first disappointing lines .of her fateful performance echoing in his head: "Good pilgrim, you do wrong your hand too much" indeed. Her tragedy marked the beginning of his descent and brought the painting to the forefront of his mind, along with a wicked idea.

Plundering his collections, he grabbed an assortment of suggestive items, rolled up the tapestry, and ran them to the schoolroom. Nearly breaking down the door in excitement, he dumped the tapestry into the middle of the dusty room and tore the covering from the painting. The weathered image glowered at him, and he exulted in it. Today he would play the milkmaid to the painting's satyr.

Dorian first bent down on all fours and reached for a black lacquered bamboo flute from distant Japan. Taking it into his mouth first, eyes locked on his painted countenance, he inserted the flute into his eager asshole with a gasp and began to stroke himself once more. Satisfying, but after a few minutes he was unable to manipulate himself and the instrument fast enough. Tossing the flute aside, he balanced on the small of his back, legs spread as he reached for a bag of jewels.

He started with a pillow-cut ruby. Placing it between his boylike cheeks and with a gentle push of his forefinger, he inserted it up his ass—*bloop!* Gone, but then followed by a sapphire, a lapis, some first-century Roman coins, and three strings of pearls. With two fingers deep inside, he flexed his finely trained sphincter muscle, removing each ring, one by one. The heavy, queasy feeling of fullness began to overwhelm; his tender rectum stretched to accommodate the fortune within his bowels. Lastly was a rare Russian Fabergé egg, the insertion of which was so delicate as to almost be as artful as the object itself.

With this he began to stroke away with manic intensity. He gripped at the length of his cock and pounded, growing closer to climax but willingly delaying it. Dorian knew that pleasure was a passion of the flesh but ecstasy a passion of the mind. His tremulous fingers grasped the mirror that he always kept near the painting.

Holding it level, he alternated his gaze between the painting and the mirror. He thrust back and forth between two bodies; the scarlet pout, then the waxen lips; his smooth unmarred brow, then the crinkled forehead, his spun-gold locks, and the wispy, graying hair. The agony of the painting and the ecstasy of the mirror, of his body and soul wrenching him as he was wrenching himself, ever faster, locking eyes with himself in the mirror, yanking up and down andandand!

"Oh! Yes! Ohhhhhhohohhhhohhoh, Dorian!" Dorian cried, firing a torrent of semen. Streaming across the woven scene, spilling on the floor, splashing on the painting itself. As it landed on the chin of his image, he could almost feel its warmth, taste the salty tang on his own tongue. Sputtering to a stop, he felt all the tension let out of him at once, jewels and pearls falling from his thrumming ass and scattering in a heap beneath him. He slipped to the ground, licking his lips and thinking he knew what Narcissus truly drowned in.

Stunned by the sensations he had unleashed on himself, he lay still, delaying the pleasure of what was next to come. At last, he gazed up at the portrait.

It had changed again! The soul of Dorian Gray was laid bare, the ravaged figure still a map of his sins but cast in a different light. Now the buttons of his coat were undone, his tie unslung, his trousers greasy and stained with a telltale crust. The sinister gleam in his eye and cruel hook of his mouth had transformed into a vile leer, leaning toward the viewer with an eager thirst. Its poise was less cruel and more lecherous, penetrating. And his hands! The bloodstains were mixed with a pearly white substance, copious strands dripping from his fingers.

He grinned and looked at the mirror again, admiring his fair face and exulting in the evidence of his perversion dripping off the canvas. To Dorian, still naked and wallowing in his own ejaculate, body throbbing with self-abuse, it was this transformation that was the height of art and pleasure. He knew for the rest of the day, he'd be quite useless.

# "The Joy of Painting" by John William

The Picture stood on the bridge, that kind of Japanese-looking one with the shitty water lilies. Just clumps of white and green pigment, really. You've seen it. He liked to go there and stare at his reflection, smudgy and ill defined, amongst the shitty water lilies.

The Picture had gotten used to living a life of someone else's syphilis, the way you get used to anything. Dorian Gray went to a party; the Picture woke up with a strange rash. Dorian took a lover; it burned when the Picture peed. Dorian killed a prostitute; the Picture's face was creased with guilt until it looked like a damn catcher's mitt. It wasn't a good life, but it was a masterfully rendered one, every brushstroke of his being a tiny smear of genius. How delicately the shadows had danced across the pits of his cold sores; how playfully the sunlight had kissed each fleshy, nubbly, genital wart...

But all of that was gone now. Dorian Gray was dead and the Picture restored, made whole and beautiful again, except for his new shame, his terrible secret, which he hid beneath layers and layers of creepy Victorian garments. Cravats and waistcoats or doublets or whatever. Probably some velvet in there, lots of buttons.

All of this he pondered, wistfully imagining that his featureless reflection was still that of a dehydrated sex criminal.

But then, across the shitty pond, he spied such a stunning figure as he had never beheld, a pure distillation of form and motion and boobs. How enchanting she was! How mysterious and dreamlike! His heart quickened as she approached, and he pulled his vest or jerkin or whatever shut.

"My lady," he said to her, "how you enchant me! How each delicate fiber of my nature quivers to look at you!"

"I'm a Cubist Nude," she growled, all throaty and Kim Cattrall-like. "I've got boobs in places you've never dreamed." The Picture flushed at her boldness.

Beside the Cubist Nude stood the waist-high outline of a cock and balls someone had drawn on the door of a bathroom stall. It had been given two little jellybean feet and a pair of tiny wings.

"We're going to a sex party at the Christmas Cottage," Cock and Balls said in its helium voice. "You should come." It talked through its pee hole, in case you're wondering.

"Everyone will be there," added the Cubist Nude. "Tom of Finland, the Sabine Women, Whistler's Mother."

"More like Whistler's MILF," said Cock and Balls. "Amiright?" The Picture guessed that Cock and Balls wanted to high-five just then but couldn't, on account of not having arms.

"Are you coming?" asked the Nude.

"I...I can't," said the Picture. "I have a..." But he couldn't bring himself to say it.

"Suit yourself," she said with a shrug. She turned and walked from the bridge, though the positioning of her ass made it hard to tell if she was facing him or not. How the Picture wanted to follow her! How he longed to go where she was going, to debase himself in the kind of debauched wantonness and depravity he had always paid the price for but never experienced. After a moment's hesitation, he ran after her.

"Fair lady!" he called out. "Wait for me! I want to go to your sex party!"

Soon they were in a winter landscape, drifts of snow amassing on the pine trees and the cobbled path.

"Most of that is cocaine," said Cock and Balls. "People don't realize Thomas Kinkade had a massive blow habit." He snorted a passing flurry right up his pee hole.

The cottage was small and warm-looking from the outside, with a merry wisp of chimney smoke drifting up into the sky, but inside it was an Escheresque collection of hidden alcoves and dark corners. Figures of all schools and movements romped and cavorted, their naked bodies greased with sweat. A Paleolithic cave hunter had his way with an illustration from the Kama Sutra. The Blue Boy fucked a suggestive orchid. A quartet of Marilyn Monroes shoved soup cans in places that would make Roman pottery blush, while somewhere in the shadows, the silhouetted heads of state from several currencies took turns with *The Scream*'s mouth.

The Cubist Nude reclined on a couch and motioned for the Picture to join her. Hesitantly, he sat.

"Why don't you take off your overcoat?" she said.

The Picture fumbled with his lapels. He was about to get up and leave when she pulled the coat off for him. They both stared at the ragged gash running the length of his sternum.

"I was stabbed," he said quietly. "That's my stab hole."

The Cubist Nude's oddly articulated arms enfolded him. "Just relax," she said. She ran her weird, hoofy fingers across the shreds of his canvass. "Let it happen."

It hurt at first, but the pain faded into a throbbing ache of pleasure. She was teasing him, pulling the stab hole open, peeling back the flaps until he almost couldn't stand it, then letting them fall shut. The whole room could see his secret shame, but in the moment he didn't care. He lay back against her, his head between her breasts, a third breast kind of slapping against the top of his head. Onlookers gathered.

She wrapped her leg around his waist and unbuttoned his trousers with a foot that was maybe also a hand. The Picture's manhood sprang out, hard and almost inhumanly impressive, on account of having been painted by a pervy old closet case. The Cubist Nude moaned, and the Picture slid himself into the silky moistness of the back of her knee. Because it turns out that's where her vagina was.

He closed his eyes and let himself be explored. Exposed. Hands groped at him, more than he could count, and an army of tongues licked their way across his flesh. Someone put a finger in his butt. When the Picture opened his eyes again, George Washington was sucking his nuts and Cock and Balls was perched on his chest. It slid its basketball-sized head into his stab hole. The Picture groaned with ecstatic agony.

He could feel the stab hole stretching, opening up for love and acceptance and also a giant cock, but mostly the love and acceptance. Cock and Balls slid deeper, deeper, until the Picture couldn't take it anymore.

He erupted in an oily, multicolor gush. It spilled across his chest and the Nude and the couch, and Cock and Balls withdrew and shot its load all over the Picture's face. The three of them collapsed into each other, happy, safe, accepted.

# A CHRISTMAS CAROL

## "Mr. Fezziwig" by Heather Donahue

With a wave of his hand, Mr. Fezziwig laid aside his ledger and bid enter Miss Tuggensuckle to review the guest list for the Christmas Ball to be held that night.

"You've welcomed Jane Peggenoffen, I presume? I'm afraid only she will do for our poor Ebenezer." He rubbed the arms of his chair with great relish at the thought of some pleasurable respite for the hard-working Scrooge.

"I dare say, Fezzi, Dick Wilkins appears to have adopted the moniker Dick Milkins down there in their room. I'm not sure Miss Peggenoffen would be a gift they care to be given."

"No harm in building bridges, my pet. And Pegleg Jack? He will be joining, as is his custom, for our fete?"

"To be sure, my dearest Fezziwig. His family has already been presented with their ham hock."

"Their other ham hock, Miss Tuggensuckle!" Fezziwig jiggled from head to toe like finest aspic.

"And Heather Mills? You know I hate for there to be too much pressure on dear old Jack. A solitary amputee will not suffice!"

"Mistress Mills sends her regrets, dear Fezzi. She holds fast to the

sentiment that there are more contemporary and compassionate lubri-
cants than lard available, especially to a man of your means."

"Ah, 'tis a pity. A sublimer stump was never seen. More perfect with
a lardy sheen!"

"Yes, Fezzi, she did not hesitate to mention that your most excellent
verses also unnerved her."

"So they should, my dearest Tuggensuckle, so they should! Have
you tended to Mrs. Fezziwig, my sweet?"

"Thrice since noon. The holiday spirit is full upon her."

"I am most pleased to hear it."

Miss Tuggensuckle had been in Fezziwig's employ for nigh upon a
dozen years. Her exuberant worship at Eros's altar assured her a generous income and constant friendship with Mr. and Mrs. Fezziwig. Coming upon her thirty-sixth year, she continued to come upon much else
and to ever so generously have much else come upon her. Even her
hair was possessed of an easy laugh; her brown ringlets were the perfect
accent to her universal roundness. Press upon her and bear witness to a
depression short-lived. Only the solitary dimple in her chin seemed to
recede from the light; all the rest was resilience and good humor.

"Bring me those rosy cheeks this minute, my sweetest Tuggensuckle." Fezziwig reached out his hand while the Miss parried with a
laughing skip about the desk.

"You wish to see my rosy cheeks, do you?" she said, lifting her skirts
to reveal her bareness. Fezziwig clapped his hands and did a little jig. "I
daresay they are nearly blue with cold. If you wish to see them ruddy,
you shall need to bring the blood up."

Miss Tuggensuckle leaned over the desk and slid open the drawer in
which was kept the little paddle.

"Oh that all the lads had such daily merriments as you bring! Every
day a Christmas!" She was on her knees upon the desk dispensing with
his vest and suspenders as he kissed her on the mouth.

"Oh dearest Fezziwig, would that every lass could know such
unabashed hungers with skills well met." Miss Tuggensuckle opened
her chemise and lifted her breasts up under her chin where they pre-

sented like royal oranges. Fezziwig, glossy of eye and mouth, fell immediately upon them. He made a chanson of the la la la his tongue made
as it flicked her nipples to and fro. He nibbled until she moaned. He
sucked until she squealed. He fingerbanged until she squirted. Ah!
Such relief he felt as he buried his face between her breasts and spread
his open mouth betwixt them. She held fast his head until constella-
tions appeared behind his eyes from want of air. Upon the quick double tap of his foot, she released him. They had a language of symbols
between them, those mutual cartographers.

"I do adore helping you prepare for the party, my dear," he told her,
tugging off her sodden underskirt as he bent her back over the desk.
He lifted her dangling feet, the better to lick from the arches up the
entirety of her pale and solid legs. He buried his face in her lady's moss.
She liked the way his face looked, nostril deep in fur, with only the mer-
est indication of the thick fervor with which his tongue circled, sucked,
and licked.

As Fezziwig's tongue darted into her slit, Miss Ellen tried to grasp
it each time, impossible with such slickened lips. The loss was more
acutely delicious each time it slipped away.

"And what of my cheeks then?" she inquired. He lifted her legs into
the air with one large hand while the other meandered over the seam
of her, lingering trippingly across her pinks, dragging past the pucker
on its way to spread wide and warm between the dips in the small of
her back.

"A frosty rime there is upon them. We must remedy that anon."

"My ever-reliable Fezziwig!" Her legs butterflied upon the high
mahogany desk and Fezziwig dipped two stout fingers inside her.

"Yes, we must warm them up like this ripe delicacy here," he said,
pulling her fleshy red hood back with his thumb. He gave her clit a
long wet kiss. "Oh sweetest holly bush!" He passed his tongue along
the entirety of her openness, bottom to top until he landed to suck, but
not before speaking once more of her "Most admirable berry." Miss
Tuggensuckle made no attempt to grasp now. She simply took most
replenishing breaths, of the sort that filled her very toes. She offered up

the very essence of her softness. When the sound of her might drown the church bell striking six, Fezziwig removed his head from twixt her thighs.

"Belly down with you for trussing, my perfect swine!" said Fezziwig.

She flipped herself upon the desk and he gave a quick spank to her flank. He pulled the trussing scarves, of finest China silk, from the Drawer of Amusements, followed by a jewel box containing a truffle. He grated the fragrant fungus onto a little heap of lard from the bucket under his desk. Miss Ellen Tuggensuckle approximated the song of a sow and was rewarded for her jubilant efforts with a quick poke-and-press upon her back from all the forms of Fezziwig's girth and a smear of scented lard across her lips.

"Come now, my feral piglet! It's you who'll be trussed today!" Tuggensuckle slipped out from under him like a tiddly wink and bound dear Fezziwig's hands behind him. His happy exhortations did indeed suggest a juvenile boar. "Chair now. Sit." The scented fat did begin to slide down Miss Tuggensuckle's chin.

"I fear I'm in for a terrible basting," cried Fezziwig.

"Terrible," Miss Ellen said with a smile and a slash of lard across his violet turgidity.

"Hilli-ho!" cried Fezziwig as Ellen's skillful finger coaxed the pulse behind his sack. "Criminy!" shouted Fezziwig as Ellen's hands, not entirely wrapped around Fezzwig's considerable shaft, expunged his joyful brine with a shudder. Fezziwig came all over himself, from his shoes to his organ of benevolence and called out in a rich, fat, jovial, oily voice:

"Yo ho, there! Ebenezer! Dick!"

The two appeared at last, panting like racehorses, accompanied by the estimable Master Felcher. "Gentlemen, you might conserve coal, for there's a sheen of heat upon your brows!"

Mr. Scrooge suppressed a creamy belch. "'Tis the spirit of the season, my boys! Have at it! No more work tonight. Christmas Eve, Dick!" proclaimed Fezziwig, his sex now glistening low upon his thighs.

"Indeed!" said Ebenezer.

"Christmas, Ebenezer! Let's have the shutters up," cried old Fezziwig with a sharp clap of his hands, "before a man can say Jack Robinson!"

"'Tis the spirit of the season!" cried Dick and Felcher.

"'Tis the spirit!" echoed Ebenezer.

Then cried Tuggensuckle, with her radiant gloss, "May it bless us, everyone!"

# "How Cratchit Got His Groove Back" by Alan Leggitt

Bob and I haven't had a good fuck all year, thought Mrs. Cratchit as she wistfully scrubbed her pots in preparation for the morrow's Christmas feast. Before Old Mr. Scrooge had found Jesus or whatever and raised her husband's salary, Bob Cratchit had been an insatiable sex fiend. He would return home from toiling away for his abusive overlord, to a litter of needy children and seem utterly defeated. But when the candles went out, Bob would take Mrs. Cratchit like a drowning man takes breath, pounding her Queen Victoria and yelling "Humbug!" and "Surplus population!" Bob would fuck like it was the last salvation for his remaining scraps of manhood, and Mrs. Cratchit loved him for it.

But once Old Scrooge learned the true meaning of Christmas, the fire left the Cratchit bedroom. Bob was just so damned jolly all the time. Several times over the past year, Mrs. Cratchit had tried to get her husband in the mood, but all he wanted to do was cuddle and talk about how much happier he was at Scrooge and Marley's, and how thankful he was for their new standard of living. It was disgusting.

It was the old Scrooge that made Bob want to fuck, she realized. That old miser used to boil Bob's gravy. If I ever want a good hard screwing again, I need the old Scrooge back. But how?

An idea came to Mrs. Cratchit that she laughed away at first. But as the hours passed, she realized that this preposterous idea might be her only hope.

That evening, she slipped their eldest son a few shillings and convinced him to take the young Cratchits out caroling. "Don't come back until you've seen Santa Claus," she whispered harshly.

Once they were alone, Bob yawned. "I'd best be off to bed if I'm to make it to church on time tomorrow."

Mrs. Cratchit smiled coyly. "I've some mending to see to. You go on up without me, dear."

Nearly an hour later, Mrs. Cratchit opened the bedroom door. The candle was still lit, but Bob was fast asleep. As the door creaked, he stirred and opened his eyes. After one look at his wife, he nearly jumped out of bed, his face as white as a ghost.

Mrs. Cratchit leaned on an old black cane, clad in a heavy woolen suit, complete with top hat, but it was her face that caused Bob to gasp. From under the hat flowed thin cobwebs of white hair, shaggy white sideburns, and two bushy white eyebrows.

"Cratchit!" she yelled in a raspy voice she'd been practicing.

Bob was aghast. "Darling?"

"Let me hear another sound from you," she growled, "and you'll keep your Christmas by losing your . . . situation." She pointed the tip of her cane toward his loins.

Bob crossed his legs, speechless.

"Now, Cratchit, I have a small gift for you this Christmas Eve, though you scarcely deserve it." She approached the bed and produced a turkey baster from her pocket, filled with her famous Christmas pudding.

Flabbergasted, Bob reached for the baster, but Mrs. Cratchit rapped his knuckles with her cane. He gasped and withdrew his hand. Without another word, Mrs. Cratchit undid her belt and let the black woolen trousers drop to the floor. She inserted the tip of the baster into her womanly cavity and squeezed out every last drop of the festive dessert.

"Now, Cratchit, see that not a morsel goes to waste." When Bob did not move, she hooked the back of his neck with the head of her cane and pulled him off the bed. As he fell to his knees, she grabbed a handful of hair from his balding head and pressed his face against her fruity vagina.

Bob began to lap up the pudding with such vigor that Mrs. Cratchit pushed his head away. "Slowly, Cratchit! Or have you forgotten your table manners?" Before he could reply, she pulled his face back to the feast between her legs. Bob resumed, with more deliberate movements of his tongue. Mrs. Cratchit moaned in approval, moving her hips back and forth against his face. "Keep this up, Cratchit, or you'll find yourself in the workhouse!" After Bob had lapped up the last of the dessert, he opened his own trousers and began stroking his Christmas sausage. Mrs. Cratchit again rapped his knuckles with her cane. "I don't recall giving you permission to pull that out!" Before Bob could reply, she pulled his head back down to her wet cunt. Ever the dutiful clerk, Bob began scribbling on her clit with his tongue. She held him by the hair and rode his face, yelling, "Yes, yes, Humbug!" Harder and harder she rode, until she noticed Bob flailing his arms; he couldn't breathe. She was on the verge of coming and wasn't about to let Bob's need for oxygen spoil it. Bob grasped her hips and tried to pry them away. The tension sent her over the edge. She released his head just as she came, her ejaculate (and a little bit of pudding) squirting on Bob's face as he fell to the floor.

Mrs. Cratchit looked down at Bob. His dick was hard as a doornail. "I suppose you'll be wanting to get off."

Bob caught his breath and smiled. "If quite convenient, sir."

"Very well. On your hands and knees, Cratchit."

Cautiously, Bob did as he was told, and Mrs. Cratchit produced three spheres of polished coal from her pocket. They were chained together on a string of twine, in size order. Bob's eyes grew wide as she put the smallest one in her mouth and soaked it with her saliva. "First, let's start a proper fire."

She knelt behind him, spit in his tight bureaucrat asshole, pulled his cheeks apart, and firmly inserted the smallest piece of coal. Bob moaned as she rolled the coal back and forth with her thumb, fondling his Tale and Two Cities with her other hand.

"Would you like another coal in your fire, Cratchit?" she asked. Bob nodded eagerly. She spit on the next coal and pressed it through Bob's cellar door. As she rolled the larger coal back and forth, she cupped his jingle bells and rolled them around in her palm. After only a few seconds, Bob groaned, "Please!"

"Please what?" she growled.

"Please, sir, may I have some more!" Bob shouted.

Mrs. Cratchit pushed the third and final coal into Bob's rump, leaving a string of twine dangling out of him. Then she lay on the floor. "Now fuck me, Cratchit!"

Bob shoved his rock-hard yule log into her sopping wet pussy. She moaned and pushed his ass cheeks together to keep the coals from spilling out. He ripped at her shirt until her breasts fell out, then began licking and biting at her exposed nipples. His hands grabbed hold of her sideburns, and he used them for leverage as he plowed and suckled away. The hard floor at her back, the tug of hair on her face, Bob suckling on her tits, were all so much that she felt herself coming again. "Bah! Fucking! Humbug!" she cried. As she came again, Bob pulled out and ejaculated all over her chest, face, and eyebrows, then collapsed onto her cum-covered jugs.

"A merry Christmas, Bob!" said Mrs. Cratchit after a moment of silence. "A merrier Christmas, Bob, my good fellow, than I have given you for many a year!"

# "Most Fowl" by Ivan Hernandez

Ebenezer Scrooge sat at the head of the table that hosted his assembled family and friends and sighed contentedly as they neared the end of another prosperous, happy year. He closed his eyes a moment, sleepy from the night spent with his dearest Belle fucking in anticipation of the Lord's birth. His nephew Fred shook him awake.

"The bird, Uncle Scrooge!" he said. "It's the carving hour. This year's roast is a newfangled creation. The turkey is stuffed with a duck that is stuffed with a chicken that is stuffed with a pregnant mouse! The butcher tried to tell me its name, but I mostly heard screams!"

Scrooge thought the combination strange but decided to "just go with it," per his newfound agreeable manner. Fred's wife brought the ornate serving tray from the kitchen and deposited it in the center of the table. She pulled away the lid to reveal an orgiastic massacre of violated meat, a hole poked in the side of the turkey through which its contents were rent outward. A thin stream of clear liquid ran from the penetrative wound, its makeup equal parts grease and jizm.

"Sweet, white Jesus!" Bob Cratchit exclaimed. "Somebody fucked the Christmas turkey!"

Moments later, they gathered in the drawing room. All the possible suspects, all the post-pubescent males in attendance. Ebenezer paced the room.

"The case is clear, gentlemen," he began. "Our turkey has been ruined, in ways both physical and moral. We must ask '*Cui bono?*' Who benefits? Who would take the bird meant to nourish so many on so special a day and make it suffer as if a thriving African nation thrust under the sweaty, entitled bulk of colonialism?"

Jacob Marley clinked his chains.

"As a level two ectoplasmic entity incapable of effecting a corporeal manifestation, I would prefer to be left out of these proceedings."

"Come off it, Marley," said the Ghost of Christmas Present. "I've seen you corporeally manifest behind the scullery. Need we bring in that walking sore of a milkmaid to demonstrate?"

"You're one to talk," Marley retorted, chains clacking indignantly. "What with being patient zero for the afterlife's worst hepatitis outbreak since Saint Peter accidentally let in Caligula."

"Gentlemen!" said the Ghost of Christmas Past. "We gain nothing by the bandying about of epithets and accusations. There is a turkey-fucker in our midst, and we would do well to root him out. Future, have you any insight into the matter?"

The Ghost of Christmas Future shrugged in his long black robe, then returned to tuning his acoustic guitar.

"Thinks he's so cool because he's the physical manifestation of man's fear of the great unknown dimensions beyond life," muttered Present.

"I have surmised," Scrooge began, "that this predator would require motive, opportunity, and ability. In this, I can only accuse one man: my loyal employee with a cute butt, Bob Cratchit!"

Cratchit dropped his snifter of brandy and clenched the cheeks of his admittedly cute butt.

"You expressed dismay that you could not host this year's festivities, you excused yourself to the bathroom for oddly long intervals, and you are widely reputed to be one of the finest cocksmen in all of whatever era of London this is!"

"Why, I resent most of your accusations, Mr. Scrooge," Cratchit said. "While I have enjoyed accepting you all into the bosom of my home in the past, I took the time that would have been spent preparing last night and used it to bugger Mrs. Cratchit as she assembled the delicious mincemeat pies you have enjoyed today. The bathroom breaks have been in the service of a kidney stone that I, to my chagrin, have yet to pass. And though I shall not repudiate my reputation for cockery, nor shall I revel in it."

"Well," Nephew Fred said, "I've heard enough. He's guilty."

At once, lightning and thunder struck. And in that quick flash, Bob Cratchit was strung up naked from the chandelier, cute, dead butt agape to the heavens.

"Your conjecture now, Scrooge?" Past asked.

Ebenezer scratched his chin as his little gray cells worked. He turned to the Ghost of Christmas Present.

"You, with your bacchanalian undead lifestyle. This great bird would prove too tempting a prize to pass. What fetish would that satisfy, I wonder? That of the sexual liaise most foul, or most fowl?"

Present clapped slow in appreciation of the pun.

"Interesting theory," he guffawed. "You would prove more correct were I not of preference to eat food rather than fuck it. Though I'd accomplish both, given my druthers." Scrooge resolved never to accept the ghost's dinner invitations.

The thunder and lightning cracked conveniently. When it finished, the Ghost of Christmas Present appeared dead—that is to say, doubly dead, a sizable hambone what would never know the glory of making stock protruding from his anal cavity.

"Now, Scrooge?" Marley demanded. "What theories have you this time? Was it me who gamed the gamebird? Who even now picks us off one by one, as if the plot of a wildly problematically named Agatha Christie novel?"

The thunder and lightning returned, and Jacob Marley's ghost hung suspended from the rafters by his chains. His sputtering breath reached a climax as he did, a thick wad of ectoplasm shooting from his spectral cock and onto a portrait of the queen. The Ghosts of Christmas Past and Future took this as a cue to leave, disappearing in queef-like puffs. And then there were two.

"How could you, Fred?" Ebenezer said. "Your own turkey? I pray it was satisfying. Did it make you hard to take food out of your children's mouths and onto your cock?"

"Uncle, I would never! Sure, I put a blood sausage up me bum once. And there's not a man alive who hasn't teabagged a figgy pudding. But this is beyond me."

"Then who, dear nephew? Who?"

The thunder and lightning made their final appearance, and there the turkophiliac stood. Fred's body twitched in its death throes, a veiny, malformed limb shoved deep down his throat.

"Tim?"

"That's Big Tim to you, Scrooge."

He pulled what functioned as a cruel parody of a leg from Fred's jaw.

"What happened to you?" Scrooge asked.

The Tim formerly known as Tiny crept toward his former benefactor.

"The doctors, they said they could cure me. But the cures lay in deep, ancient knowledge, from forgotten cities eons past. From the sunken shores of Lemuria to the bedeviled scriptures of Abdul Alhazred and the demoniac oaths of the Great, Old Ones, I searched. There was a price to be paid, and only now does it make its cum-laden bargain known. Bear witness, Ebenezer Scrooge, for here is what your meddling has wrought!" He hoisted aloft the limb that once was crippled and weak, revealing a twisted, undulating tentacle that resembled a penis lined with rows of gnashing, serrated teeth.

"You've cursed me to this cockfoot, and now I curse you to hell!"

Tim leapt and pulled Scrooge to the floor. When the monstrous appendage was but inches from his face, Ebenezer felt his nephew prod his shoulder. He shook himself awake, again at the table.

"The bird, Uncle Scrooge," Fred said. "You simply must carve the turkey."

"Bird? Ah, yes. The bird," he said, looking over the creature for any malfeasance and finding none. The turkey was delicious, the company gregarious, the tidings good. All the same, Scrooge made Tiny Tim eat outside, behind the scullery.

# Genre

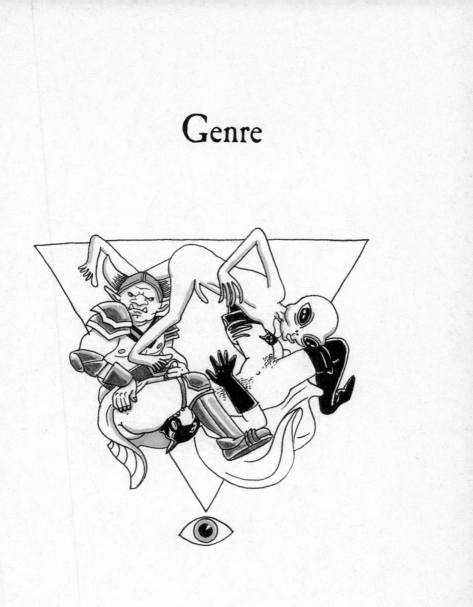

$\mathcal{W}$elcome to Genre. We've got a little bit of everything in here for you. There's some mystery, some sci-fi, some horror (of course, if you've made it this far, you know it's all horrible in its own special way), and even a graphic novel.

We love genre fiction. We've had some of the most fun with the books in this chapter. For *The Hitchhiker's Guide to the Galaxy*, someone in the audience held up a sign for the entire show that read, "INTERGA-LACTIC PARTY GIRLS NEED <3 TOO." For *The Maltese Falcon* (a San Francisco staple), we had a writer send a surrogate in their place, costumed in full femme fatale regalia.

Fandoms, Cons, and costumes aside, genre provides a unique para-dox that we wreckers of literature have a lot of fun exploiting (we only exploit paradoxes, never people). The books we chose for this section, with *maybe* the exception of *Hitchhiker's Guide to the Galaxy*, are stories that demand to be taken seriously while also demanding that you believe in a world of possessed demon cars, dinosaur theme parks, pseudoscien-tific monster workshops, and small towns hell-bent on sacrificing their denizens to a spiteful shark for a few summer tourist bucks. Where classics dealt in well-known, capital "b," capital "c," Big Characters and their baggage of deeply entrenched themes, genre is often already a commentary on the ridiculousness of the world, stripping character and environment to its barest essentials so as not to lose sight of the message. In other words, it's absurd long before we get our sticky fin-gerprints all over it.

As dizzying variety is a theme in this section, we may as well note that unlike Classics, several of the books to follow are represented by a single, solitary selection. Full disclosure: all *Shipwreck* shows are not created equal. Some books have such a narrow focus that many of the same themes appear throughout all of the stories. Other books fail to inspire writers to our lofty aims. Still others, lots of people just watched the movie. We're human is all. This simple truth aside, even when we opted to cut books as we sifted through our archives, there was sometimes that one piece that demanded inclusion. And whenever these special flowers pop up from here out, we'll take a brief moment to explain ourselves.

We'll kick things off with *Slaughterhouse-Five*, a novel wherein the main character is gifted with a porn bride young enough to be his granddaughter who's perfectly content to get nailed by him all day long as his reward for suffering the indignity of having been married to a (loyal, devoted) fat woman. Don't shed too many tears for Montana, though. She gets to raise their child in the solitude of her swanky mid-century space condo when the needs of the story take Billy home to alienate his older children and write letters to the editor.

Then we'll catch a ride with *The Hitchhiker's Guide to the Galaxy* for a quick check-in with Trillian, who gets saved from a space creeper at a space bar by her new space pal Ripley (yes, space Ripley). We promise there isn't a single joke about keeping a towel handy for sex purposes.

From there, we head to *Frankenstein*, which is a book about taking existing things and cobbling them together to make a new thing that eventually grows enormous and unwieldy, which we wouldn't know anything about. Also, did you guys know that Frankenstein is actually the name of the doctor who MADE the monster? Anyway, the monster knocks boots with Helen Keller.

After we've had our fill of artisanal, handcrafted monsters, we'll turn to the philosophical debate over GMOs with a fly-by of *Jurassic Park*. This is a novel whose plot relies heavily on dinosaur breeding and inscrutable #mathsplaining, so obviously it's perfect for us. Sure, it's a wonderful mess containing like one female character who isn't a fucking dinosaur and enough painstakingly explained '90s pseudo-science to make Johnny Mnemonic blush, but it's also well loved enough to inspire a grown man to wear a dinosaur costume to a bookstore in the middle of July on a Thursday night. That makes it all right in our book.

Then we get to Stephen King. When we first started *Shipwreck*, we joked about doing the Master of Horror every October until either we run out of books or the sun explodes. We follow through 100 percent on 100 percent of our jokes, so we've now done Stephen King every October for three years (maybe more, depending on what date it is when you are). King is magic for us. He's got so many books with imagery permanently cemented in the pop culture hive-mind, and most of them are already so bloated and over the top (not to mention casually racist and gleefully misogynistic) that *Shipwreck*ing them just seems like the natural next step. Every year we ask ourselves, "Can anything that happens tonight outdo the source material?" No. The answer is always no.

*Carrie* is one of his better-known yarns—the age-old tale of the misfit teen who gets pig's blood dumped on her at prom. It's a short story at best if you extract the anemic narrative from the surrounding filler of newspaper articles, interview transcripts, and excerpts from a minor character's future memoir. Carrie the Person only appears in about three scenes in the whole thing, and yet her scenes are so gripping that the image of her standing on that stage catching trichinosis from the raw pork in her eyeballs is permanently tattooed to our retinas. This is in part thanks to the movie and Sissy Spacek's haunted affect, but the reason so many of his books become movies is that he's an incredibly vivid and visual storyteller. Unfortunately, for all that action, a lot of the detail gets lost along the way. That's where we come in. Today we'll learn about Tommy's extracurricular activities and what the elusive and ineffectual Principal Grayle gets up to in his downtime.

Up next is a bracing dip with *Jaws*. We would like to go on record and recommend that no human ever read this book ever. *Time* magazine once called *Jaws* "a bathtub version of *Moby Dick*" and that's mostly true. But it's another one that manages to be resolutely racist and misogynistic throughout, despite ostensibly being about a fish. The book is so awful that when Spielberg got his hands on it, he basically changed all the characters and a lot of the plot. It contains gems like Ellen Brody standing naked in front of a mirror asking herself (and this is a quote), "Are the goods good enough?" to seduce the man she's having an affair with. After a lengthy examination of everything from the lines in her neck (???) to her pedicure, she decides (again, quote), "the goods are good enough." After a while we started to think that Peter Benchley's entire idea of What Women Are came from moisturizer commercials in the 1970s.

When next we see dry land, it's from the fog-drenched bay of Depression Era San Francisco with *The Maltese Falcon*—the only true noir mystery we've ever snuck into our lineup—where Wilmer Cook learns his proclivities aren't all that unnatural with the help of Inspector Gadget, Jessica Fletcher, and a bevy of anachronistic security cameras.

And in the end, we take on *Watchmen*, the quintessential Broody Superhero Comic for Dudes. How could we have a genre section without *Watchmen*? It's the superhero graphic novel for people who don't read superhero graphic novels. If you do read superhero graphic novels, it's the one you lend out to your friends so they come back strung out and begging for more recommendations. It's intense. It's beautiful. There's nothing like it, and it takes on everything from Pagliacci to Ptolemy. So join us, won't you, as we delve into the darker corners of Dr. Malcolm Long's diary.

Anyway, listen. Now's the time to limber up and come unstuck in time—refresh your drink, switch on the basement black light, settle into your reading futon—because this world might be a dumpster fire, but porn, uh, finds a way.

# SLAUGHTERHOUSE-FIVE

## "Eliot Rosewater" by Tara Marsden

Listen:

Eliot Rosewater was a volunteer firefighter, or at least that's what he wanted you to think. What he really was was bloody stinkin' rich. You'd know that if your AP English teacher had bothered to introduce you to any other books by Kurt Vonnegut besides *Slaughterhouse-Five*. Eliot Rosewater stars quite charmingly in a book called *God Bless You, Mr. Rosewater!* In *Slaughterhouse-Five*, he appears in just one chapter. So it goes.

Eliot Rosewater was asleep in his hospital bed. He was dreaming of fire. Not just fire. An enormous pile of money on fire. Not just any enormous pile of money. His family fortune. Dry, green kindling crackling with little *POP POP POPs*. In his dream, Eliot Rosewater had set the money on fire himself. He wasn't entirely sure why, but he thought it had something to do with Tolstoy, or maybe it was Dostoevsky; it was dream logic—it didn't really matter. Anyway, he had started the fire himself, with the intention of putting it out himself. Life is like that sometimes.

In his dream, Eliot Rosewater was no ordinary volunteer fireman. He had a very special hose. His hose was long and bulbous, bursting with the aggressive masculinity of a man whose only worthy enemy is fire. In his dream, his hose was not at all reminiscent of the chewed-up, plastic bendy straw that might belong to an aging nihilist alcoholic in a psych ward. No, this massive cylinder rose quickly and impressively in the presence of fire, aching to be put to use, to do its duty. Money was burning! God was dead! And Eliot Rosewater's hose was about to blast off like a ship to Tralfama-dore! Watching those poor little presidential faces melting like Nazis near the Ark of the Covenant, Eliot Rosewater's hose could hardly hold back the flood; hot ropes of viscous magma were ready to burst forth upon his piles and piles of money, to douse the fiery red tendrils and green fabric plumes of smoke with white-hot firefighting juices, sizzling and cooking the cash into a starchy stiff mass of US Treasury certified embers.

But suddenly he heard his name called softly, "Eliooooot?"

He looked down, bemused, at the sagging emerald face of Benjamin Franklin, wondering if this dream were about to get real weird, as he heard his name called again, more firmly, "Eeeeellllliottttt?"

Eliot Rosewater awoke to find he'd pitched a tent large enough to house all the Hoosiers in Indiana. And Billy Pilgrim staring at him intently from the hospital bed beside him.

"Yes, Billy?" said Eliot Rosewater, letting out a heaving, horny sigh. He felt too much misplaced goodwill toward mankind and their sorry condition, and particularly this man and particularly his sorry condi-tion, to ignore poor Billy Pilgrim, though he did nothing at all to hide his massive erection.

"I can't sleep. Would you read me a bedtime story?" said Billy Pilgrim.

Eliot Rosewater nodded solemnly. This had become a recurring routine for them, as it might for any two lonely men in a dismal, sol-itary corner of a psych ward. He reached under his thin mattress for two sticky, yellowing pulp novels hidden there, their well-worn cov-ers both emblazoned with enormous lizards and tits bursting from implausible space suits that certainly couldn't properly oxygenate the well-endowed earthling women who wore them. Both books were written by Kilgore Trout.

"Which would you prefer tonight, *The Naughty Space Nurse of Ooglabeepopa* or *The Second Coming of Christina*?"

"*The Naughty Space Nurse of Ooglabeepopa*, please," said Billy Pilgrim.

"All right." Eliot Rosewater solemnly began to read. "Cressida, the Space Nurse, was from a planet where females had vaginas on their heads and mouths between their legs."

"Would that really make much of a difference?" interjected Billy Pilgrim.

Eliot Rosewater turned to Billy Pilgrim with a frown. "What you just said is gross and casually sexist, but this takes place in 1969, so let's just ignore that and keep going, like readers in the future will."

"Um," said Billy Pilgrim.

"As I was saying..." Eliot Rosewater returned to reading. "Cressida, the Space Nurse, was from a planet where females had vaginas on their heads and mouths between their legs, yet inexplicably the preferred form of sexual interaction was the hand job."

"Mmmm," said Billy Pilgrim.

Both men reached for their stiff Midwestern poles, flags already flying at full-mast.

Eliot Rosewater read on, detailing the precise methodology with which Cressida, the Space Nurse, used her soft, small, perfectly manicured space hands to "examine" her space patients with tender love and care. At no point while he read did Eliot Rosewater consider how strange it was to read erotic fiction aloud to an audience and to get aroused while reading. Nor did his audience consider how strange it was to listen to erotic fiction be read aloud and to get aroused while listening. And because they were human, neither of them considered the possibility that from a Tralfamadorian's perspective, the reader, the audience, and the writer of the erotic fiction were all basically having an orgy together in the fourth dimension.

So they pressed on, each man in his bed, Billy Pilgrim imagining it was the hand of Cressida, the Space Nurse, that firmly and furiously

*"Which would you prefer tonight,* The Naughty Space Nurse of Ooglabee-popa *or* The Second Coming of Christina.*"*

tugged at his totem, and Eliot Rosewater imagining that the book he held was transformed into the pile of money in his dreams, burning with passion, ready to be wetly kissed into liquid submission by his tremendous hose. Barely two pages in, both men were grunting, in sync together in a sweaty rhythm, a perfectly matched pair, each incomplete without the other, like "best friends forever bracelets," only with dicks instead.

Just as Cressida the Space Nurse's patient was about to blow his load, Billy Pilgrim and Eliot Rosewater were ready to come unstuck in time, or really just come.

Billy Pilgrim wailed, "GOD. BLESS. YOU. MR. ROSEWATER!" as each man exploded into their hands and all over their bedsheets.

At that exact moment, Billy Pilgrim's mother, his most frequent visitor, walked into the room and surveyed the scene with the stunned puritanical horror of a mid-century housewife whose husband had never made her come.

"Billy, when I told you I wished you'd poke your head out from under the sheets more often when I visit, this was not what I had in mind!"

"Um," said Billy Pilgrim, looking over again to Eliot Rosewater. Both men let out groggy, satisfied sighs.


# "Slaughterhouse Fiiiiiine" by Harrison Boneron


All this happened, more or less. The butt stuff, anyway, is pretty much true.

After the bombs fell on Dresden, we emerged from the slaughterhouse basement to find the city transformed into the surface of the moon. Nothing but minerals, blasted and empty.

*Moon* is a word that means to expose one's buttocks. You get your hands around your belt and you drop your pants and you make excited, eager noises. Like this: "Geeeeeet it" (followed by eager, coquettish yelps). In the war, we had no belts and held our pants up with twine and sadness. Sometimes the pants fell down, and, struck by the memory of mooning, we would make noises like this: "Geeeeeeet it" (in a mournful voice).

Standing there on the surface of the moon, I made a pledge to myself, to no one in particular. Here is the pledge:

"When I write my famous erotic short story about Dresden, I will leave in all the butt stuff, and I will tell the truth about it. And I will never fake another orgasm as long as I live."

Well, I haven't kept the second half of that pledge, but I lived longer than I expected back on the surface of the moon, and there were a lot more opportunities to make mistakes. But this is my chance to be honest about the butt stuff, and I can't afford to pass it up.

Sometimes I try to call up old boyfriends on the telephone late at night, after my wife has put a plaster model of the Eiffel tower up her ass and gone to bed. (Always use a flared base, kids.) "Operator, I wonder if you could give me the number of a Mr. So-and-So. I think he lives at such and such."

But this night, I called up the operator, and I said, "Operator, I'm looking for a good time."

"I'm sorry, sir. There is no such listing."

"Thanks, Operator. But I'm looking for a really, really good time."

"Oh," the operator said. His voice changed. "Let me connect you."

The phone rang, and there was a click of a good connection.

"Hello," said the man on the phone. "My name is Yon Yonson. I work in Wisconsin. I work at the lumber mill there."

He sounded like a lumberjack. His voice was a pleasant, deep growl. I knew a man who sounded like that once. He was making love in an old-style elevator, and the foreskin of his wedding tackle got caught on the wrought-iron grate, and the elevator went down and he went up and he was crushed to death.

So it goes.

"Hello," I said, and I told him my name, which is the only polite thing to do. You can't let a main character run around without a name for an entire short story, let alone an entire book. That would be fucking annoying, KURT. Then I told him what I was looking for. "I'm looking for butt stuff," I said.

I was looking...for butt stuff.

"Come over," he told me.

"But you work in Wisconsin, Yon Yonson. And I live in...Schenectady, I think? Maybe Cape Cod? It's not really clear from the narration."

"I'll send a friend," said Yon Yonson, and he hung up manfully, like a sack full of muscular sausages.

I stepped outside, and with a hoot like an owl, a flying saucer appeared above me. It seemed like it was coming everywhere at once. Basically a transdimensional bukkake effect. You'd recognize it.

The saucer was a hundred feet in diameter, with throbbing purple portholes around the rim. A puckered hole opened at the bottom and a thick, veiny shaft of purple light extended to the ground and then began sucking me in. It drew me upward with quick, flicking motions, and then let me drift down a little before pulling me back up.

I understood what was happening. Some animals like to toy with their prey. I once saw a bear go to town on an otter for like two hours before he finally finished the job. So it goes.

All at once, I was inside the spaceship, inside its airlock. The door whooshed open and an alien entered. The alien looked like a plumber's friend...with benefits. So basically like a plunger you could fuck.

"Are you ready to party?" I asked the alien.

"That is a very earthling question to ask, Mr. Narrator," the alien told me. "This moment simply is."

Then it began giving me a sad hand job with the cup part of the plunger, focusing mainly (and unsatisfyingly) on the balls. Some aliens out there are probably eight-foot tall blue catpeople with perfect bodies just waiting to give it to me up the rear. I got a handie from a toilet-related home appliance.

So it goes.

The flying saucer navigated through time as well as space, and so it took no time at all to travel to Wisconsin. The sad plunger hand job had barely succeeded in making me erect, but before I left the flying saucer I pretended to have an orgasm anyway. I thought it was the only polite thing to do, and besides, since it was an alien, it would be easy to fool. So I flailed my arms around and screamed, "I'm coming! I'm coming!"

The alien's plunger-like countenance remained inscrutable.

Outside the flying saucer was a lumberyard. Inside the lumberyard was an orgy. Lumberjacks dashed back and forth, wearing only flannel thongs and occasionally pasties. A man named Wild Bob, whom I had known in the war, operated a machine made from a Sherman tank and about fifty German bayonets. What you do is, you take the bayonets and you dip them in condom molds filled with Lucite, and then you have a transparent dildo with a knife in it. Some men remember the war differently than others.

Wild Bob had attached about fifty of these dildos to the front of the Sherman tank and he was maneuvering the tank back and forth very carefully, fucking fifty brawny lumberjacks at once. I was sure this was all going to end in tears, but Wild Bob was topless and having the time of his life.

I knew a man who got topless and enjoyed himself once. The Nazis got him. Got him good.

So it goes.

And that was just one of the many things I saw people doing to butts, doing with every piece of equipment anyone had ever used on a butt: penises, dildos, cucumbers, gourds, sausages, bananas, empty wine bottles, wine bottles filled with wine, unusually large cigars, human fists, rubber models of human fists, an empty bottle of lube, a bird in a state of hypnosis, a gerbil in a ball, two gerbils in a ball together—the gerbils themselves in a post-coital state of repose—a swimming trophy, an Oscar, a toothbrush case, a mortar round, the hilt of a ceremonial saber, a plunger, a butter churn, and so on.

I saw Yon Yonson presiding over the crowd from atop a throne of manflesh like some sort of ancient Caesar, so I walked on over to him.

He saw me and gave me a hug. It was like being hugged by a really butch walrus, all muscle and bristly mustache.

"I'm glad you came," he said. "How can I help you?"

"I'm here for butt stuff," I said.

I was there...for butt stuff.

And oh boy, did butt stuff happen to me. Yon Yonson tossed my salad as only a Yonson can, licking from the wet ring around my balls left over from the sad alien hand job all the way up to my coccyx, which is a bone that has nothing to do with your cock. He penetrated my ass slowly at first, and then faster, like a prison train accelerating as it loses coaches on the way to its destination, until he began pounding my prostate the way American firebombs had pounded the city of Dresden.

"Uhn uhn uhn" I went, until I orgasmed. The French call orgasm *le petit mort*, which means "the little death." Everything is about death, even sex.

So then it was after the orgy. And there is nothing intelligent to say about an orgy, because everyone is supposed to be passed out from having come all over the place. Everything is supposed to be very quiet after an orgy, and it always is, except for the cocks.

And so it was, and I lay there, and my cock went "Poo-tee-weet?"

# THE HITCHHIKER'S GUIDE
# TO THE GALAXY

Few books capture the "look how clever I am" sweet spot of adolescence quite like The Guide. Grab a copy, take a whiff of the pages, and tell me it doesn't smell like nascent facial hair and Monty Python quotes in a used Honda Civic. We loved so many of the pieces in this episode of the show, but most were so true to the material that they came off like an inside joke for thirteen-year-old me. Alan went another way, though, and in his big tent approach to popular science fiction he called bingo on the genre while staying true to Adams's spry wit. —Casey

## "Trillian" by Alan Leggitt

After their daring escape from Magrathea, Ford took the *Heart of Gold*'s crew aside and asked them all to be extra nice to Arthur. "He's been through a lot these past few days. Now that the dust has settled, the grief of losing his home and family will finally hit him."

Apparently, everyone had forgotten that Trillian was also from Earth. Even her deranged lab mice had wanted to scoop out Arthur's brain, without even considering how valuable her brain was.

It was a sobering reminder of why she left Earth in the first place. As a female scientist, she had grown used to being passed over by her male counterparts, while being made to swallow a bunch of bullshit about the changing demographics of her field.

She needed a break from the inconsiderate crew. Luckily, they were still outlaws and took turns navigating the improbability drive to obscure destinations.

"Bring me to some shithole where I can get a stiff drink," she ordered the ship's computer on her first night shift.

"Coming right up," replied the computer in its annoyingly helpful tone.

After a burst of light, Trillian tasted purple and played hopscotch with Aaron Burr as the improbability drive did its thing, until they whirred to a halt in orbit around a meek desert planet.

"Mos Eisley spaceport," reported the computer. "You will never find a more wretched hive of scum and villainy."

"I thought that place existed a long time ago," replied Trillian "in a galaxy far, far away."

"Well you see—" began the computer.

"You know what? I don't care," she interrupted. "Just beam me down."

"This ship is not equipped with an onboard—"

"You're an improbability drive. Just figure it out!" she interjected.

Moments later, Trillian sat on a bar stool, drinking a pan galactic gargle blaster and watching some creepy animatronic band. The bar had the gritty clientele she'd been hoping for: Wookies, space orcs, Klingons, Dark Eldar. She was feeling quite pleased, until a man started eyeing her from across the room.

He was devilishly handsome, sporting a smedium yellow shirt with a Starfleet emblem above his left nipple. After making eyes at her, he swaggered over.

"Hey, baby," came his buttery voice. "Buy me a drink, and I'll boldly take you where no woman has gone before."

"Ugh! Get lost," replied Trillian. She was in no mood for even a gorgeous creep.

"Come on, doll," he persisted. "I'm captain of the *Starship Enterprise*! Every creature in the galaxy wants my cock in one of their holes."

Trillian splashed her drink into the captain's face and shouted, "I said get lost!"

A few heads turned and chuckled. The captain wiped his eyes and grabbed Trillian by the wrist. "That was a mistake!" he growled.

"GET AWAY FROM HER, YOU BITCH!!!" cried a voice from across the bar. The music stopped. Trillian turned to see a handsome woman clad in sweaty overalls, pointing a flamethrower at the captain.

The pretty young man released Trillian and turned to the sweaty woman. "You even know how to use that thing, toots?"

There was a hiss and a whoosh as a burst of flame engulfed the space captain.

Despite being startled by the sudden barrage, Trillian could not look away from the smoldering amazon, whose skin glistened in the fire's glow.

The smell of cooked flesh filled the bar. When the lady ceased her inferno, a blackened corpse fell to the ground, and the band resumed playing.

"Two more of what she's having!" the woman called to the bartender as she stepped over the charred body.

Trillian smiled awkwardly. She was kind of turned on. "Thanks, that guy was a jerk," she stammered. "My name's Trillian."

"Ellen Ripley," came a curt reply. "You should be carrying one of these if you're gonna be alone in a place like this," Ripley said, stroking her flamethrower. Trillian admired Ripley's rough fingers, which were caked in grease and ash.

The drinks came and Ripley slid one over to Trillian. "To the *Starship Enterprise*!" Ripley said, lifting her glass. "Let's hope the next captain isn't such a douche bag."

Trillian giggled and sipped her drink and watched Ripley down hers in one gulp. Ripley slammed the glass down and gestured for another. "What brings you to this shithole?" she asked.

Trillian frowned. "My home planet's been destroyed and my crew is a bunch of sexists," she said grimly, then added in a polite tone, "What about you?"

Ripley took a swig of her second drink and looked Trillian up and down in a way that made her feel dirty. "Every time I wake up, I find out I've either been cloned or frozen for a hundred years."

Trillian hardly heard a word she said, she was so preoccupied by Ripley's fierce stare and deep brown eyes. She almost looked away in fear, yet she felt a strange determination to meet Ripley's gaze.

Without looking away, Ripley finished her second drink and said, "I got a room upstairs. Wanna get out of here?"

Trillian felt excitement in her loins and nodded. She left her drink half finished and followed Ripley out the door.

They stepped into the glass tube of the Televator and Trillian instinctively moved her hand to the control panel. She was about to ask, "What floor?" when Ripley's hand reached for the panel as well. Their hands touched, and both women paused. Trillian looked into Ripley's eyes, unsure whether to smile or stare or maybe just kiss. Ripley smiled, leaned forward, and pressed a button. A flash of blue light engulfed them and transported them to Ripley's motel room.

Every surface, including the bed, was covered in guns, grenades, and ammo. Ripley pushed it all to the floor and pulled Trillian onto the mattress. The two women rolled around the bed, stripping off each other's clothes in a frenzy of kissing and sucking and biting, until they were both naked.

"I should warn you," Ripley said. "I'm one of Ellen Ripley's clones, and I'm part alien."

"Which part?!" asked Trillian, with equal parts thrill and terror in her voice.

Ripley opened her mouth wide and stuck out her tongue. It was ten inches long and a small alien head protruded from the tip, with a mouth and teeth of its own.

Trillian took one look at the mighty alien tongue, then grabbed Ripley by the hair and pulled her head down to her soaking wet cunt. Ripley's saliva had a sort of chemical heat to it, like Icy Hot. The tongue crept up Trillian's pussy until it was scraping against her uterus, bathing every inch of her lady parts in the acidic alien fluid.

Ripley folded her tongue so that the base of it was rubbing against Trillian's clit and the end of it was gnawing at her G-spot. Nobody, not even Zaphod Beeblebrox with his two heads, had ever eaten her out like this before.

Within minutes, Trillian felt herself coming. Ripley withdrew her head slightly, so that when Trillian reached climax, she squirted all over Ripley's face.

Several days later, a Xenomorph burst out of Trillian's chest and it lived happily ever after.

# FRANKENSTEIN

## "Skull Emoji, Lightning Emoji, Eggplant Emoji" by Joe Wadlington

Victor Frankenstein and Henry Clerval played Magic: The Gathering in an empty pub with no setting details. Victor kept using zombie cards.

"Victor! You are a force with necromancing cards!" Henry laughed.

"I did this a lot in college," Victor mumbled.

"Victor, I would love to hear more about your time in seclusion. You didn't send word to the family for years—then showed up with sagging skin, black lipstick, and smelling of embalming fluid," Henry said. Victor rolled his eyes. "Adjust your countenance, Victor! You've been a fountain of misery for all of our trip from Europe to a different part of Europe. I hoped we'd get blacked out, then go to brothels and pay to cuddle—but you're acting like someone deleted your Tumblr!"

"UGH FIIIIIIINE!" Victor tossed his head, shifting dyed black bangs from one eye to the other. "I spent my time in seclusion working on my art. It's ummm...found-object sculpture. I'm playing with the idea of creating life," Victor said.

Henry's eyes narrowed. "Like, in an abstract way?" he asked.

"NOPE!" Victor said, laying down another zombie card.

A village person with no physical description burst into the pub.

"THE DEMON RETURNED! He killed nine people!" the man yelled.

"Well, I hope no one was hurt!" Victor said with fake concern.

Henry ran to the man. "Sir! What is this demon you speak o—"

"SCIENCE!" Victor screamed, breaking a bottle over the peasant's head. Victor cradled the man's body and looked innocently at Henry. "It's okay! We can put lightning on it!" he said, then broke the man's neck with his hands. "Whoopsie." He flashed a cute little smile.

"Lord spare us! Victor, you devil! What have you done?!" Henry yelled.

"I need more parts for my second monste—I mean my art project," Victor said.

"Are you dismembering people again?!" Henry said.

"NO ONE WE KNOW!" Victor dropped the man in defeat and pouted on his way back to the table.

"All this time we hoped you were just jerking off and threatening people on the internet," Henry said.

"Only on my breaks," Victor mumbled, brushing his bangs over his eyes.

"As a kid, you tortured small animals and showed no capacity for empathy, but we thought giving you half a science degree, two years of funding, and no follow-up questions would help," Henry said.

"Yeah, that was a bad idea—I chased nature into her hiding places, dabbled through unhallowed graves, and tortured the living animal to build my lifeless clay—but we all make mistakes, right?" Victor said, playing another zombie card.

"Stop that! You aren't even tapping mana. And I can't believe a maniac like you was granted a lab!"

"Do you know how easy it is to get a lab in this country? Only slightly harder than getting a semiautomatic rifle. And demented science is a natural urge for me: like dancing in the rain or falling in love with my sister. It just happens," Victor said.

There was a pound on the door. Victor shrieked and ran to bar it.

"That has to be the monster! All the other characters are dead by now! Henry, he's horrifying: violent, angry, and, worst of all, not conventionally attractive." Another pound. "Please don't let it get me!" Victor pleaded. "I'm just a misunderstood white kid. I didn't know what I was getting into—well, I did know, but I hoped none of the obvious consequences would happen to me. Please! I'm done with my wicked occupation. Now my happiness lies in one day marrying Elizabeth and blindsiding her with my horrifying past."

"How can I kill it?" Henry asked.

"IDK just shoot it! This isn't Beowulf!" Victor said.

"Victor, my dear playmate. I will stay and fight this beast with you. For your father took me in, clothed me—I am only medium-rich, so it was charity. I owe you my loyalty!" While Henry was monologuing, Victor had slipped out a back window. Something pounded on the door again.

"Ah, shit." Henry kicked the door open and stood at the ready.

The night was completely black, to build suspense. Henry could see nothing but heard a sound like bean bags being tossed and snakes slithering. As the monster filled the doorway, Henry realized Victor had been wrong: This wasn't the demon; it was the demon's half-finished wife.

Victor had run many experiments aside from his monster. They had organized and escaped their prisons. Hundreds of zombie body parts flooded the doorway—and mostly the sexy ones. Vaginas of every shade and dilation were jumping across the ground like suction cups being plucked, then relocated, plucked, then relocated. Strong arms wobbled in like uncertain toddlers and the dicks slithered on the ground like dicks always fucking do—but the breasts...oh the bushels of breasts! They leaped through the world like a water balloon toss, with invisible players. One of the vaginas appeared to be the leader and spoke boldly.

Hundreds of zombie body parts flooded the doorway—and mostly the sexy ones. Vaginas of every shade and dilation were jumping across the ground like suction cups being plucked, then relocated, plucked, then relocated. Strong arms wobbled in like uncertain toddlers and the dicks slithered on the ground like dicks always fucking do—but the breasts...oh the bushels of breasts! They leaped through the world like a water balloon toss, with invisible players.

"YOU DOWN TO…EXPERIMENT???" she cackled, speaking exactly how you would envision a vagina to speak. The breasts began organizing into a colony that spiraled higher and higher—using a few penises, but only auxiliary for structure, NOT because they needed them.

"Nooo-ooo," Henry stammered. "That's disgusting!" He was so turned on. "I don't want this to happen to meeeeee." He wanted this exact thing to happen to him very badly and for a long time.

The breast coven was taller now. Four legs slipped under it, then stood, bringing the tit teepee to eye level. It looked like the back of every twelve-year-old boy's notebook. The Wankenstein moved forward slowly, with considerable tit bouncing. All Henry could think was, *Boobs, boobs, boobs, boobs, boobs, boobs, boobs, boobs, boobs, boobs, boobs, and some dicks.*

An army of hands walked through the door, carrying a woman's head. She was passed from the floor to the top of Chesticle Mountain and leered down at Henry. The hands began running up Henry's body—massaging him, relaxing him. This was all the foreplay Henry needed. His oven was preheated and about to burn the house down.

"I see you don't need rigor mortis to get hard," the head said with a poisonous laugh. She stared at Henry's bulging monster and licked her lips with a tongue that was clearly four tongues sewn together. One of the hands undid his pants.

"I…I just want to be held," Henry said. The head nodded knowingly. Mammary Mountain parted in the middle like a bathrobe, and Henry stepped inside. He was surrounded by a patchwork of skin tones, like a quilt, if a quilt could fuck you. One penis slipped into Henry's butt comfortably and on the first try—because that's how anal works in fiction. The walls burritoed him—he felt safe but in a sexy way.

Henry heard the glasses behind the bar trembling, then the floor. The shaking moved through his body too. Henry realized the boob quilt was revving up to motorboat him. The shaking increased, and the bosom bushel waved like it was being wrung out. It felt like being in a cement mixer filled with water balloons. More dicks and hands joined the mix, making it a penetration tornado. The head began yodeling wildly in time with the tit pummeling. Henry pulled his arms above his head and started leaping up, into the corpse cavern. The shaking increased and the yodeling got louder, until a final pleasure seizure began vibrating the tower to pieces. Before the head fell, she yelled, "It's alive! IT'S ALIVE!"

The pieces disassembled quickly and exited. Henry lay on the floor sweaty and covered in bruises.

"I love you!" he yelled.

"Let's keep it casual," the head said, rolling out.

Henry lit a cigarette and took a long drag. "Fuckin' science, man!" he said, shaking his head.

# "Safie's Choice" by Kitty Stryker

It was a dark and stormy night.

Well, it was dark, anyway, something the Creature was thankful for as he settled in for another long night of peering through a stranger's window. He told himself it was for "educational purposes"; the fact that his hand very often ended up in his pants was merely coincidence. Correlation is not causation, after all.

That's a science reference, because this is a science-fiction story.

The Creature had been peering through this particular window for many nights. It was a lot more interesting than reading *Paradise Lost*, which isn't terribly surprising if we're being honest. The goings-on inside the cottage, meanwhile, were a lesson in open-mindedness. Not in an intersectional awareness sort of way, but more in a "wow I had no idea all those things could fit inside a butthole" sort of way. The Creature was pretty into it.

The window belonged to a cottage housing three peasant youths, who, despite being peasants, were all strikingly attractive and miraculously free of smallpox. There was Felix, the dashing young man with firm, tanned muscles who seemed sad and therefore probably would have loved *Paradise Lost*. There was his sister Agatha, a blond-haired and freckled young woman with a mischievous twinkle in her eye. And there was Safie, a bright-eyed and dark-haired beauty who enjoyed accommodating the siblings' many pleasures.

Look, it was winter in Germany; there wasn't a lot else to do. And sex is cheaper than coal. YOLO (well, unless you're a reanimated corpse, but I digress).

Safie, who was not from around here, was being coached on how to speak French by Felix, even though they were in Germany. This ended up being a euphemism for "having a lot of kinky threesomes with his sister when Dad's not home." It was a hands-on education in the various ways one could pleasure themselves with their hands, someone else's mouth, or a convenient gourd if the mood was right. The Creature, who had never seen such things and had only read about them in whatever the eighteenth-century version of Cosmo was, studied their behavior obsessively, learning words like *shaft* and *cunt* and important phrases like *Use more lube* and *If you move from that spot on my clit before I come, I'm going to punch you*. Occasionally the Creature would see an older man in the cottage, father to Felix and Agatha and blind, but he seemed more inclined to wander around the woods than stay there, probably in part because it reeked of sex and he really didn't need that kind of intimate knowledge of his children's sex lives.

The first time he observed the three fucking, he experienced a strange engorgement of the flesh and a wetness in his trousers. Reading Milton had not really prepared the Creature for the mysteries of his body, and he didn't really speak to his Maker about the birds and the bees. Watching Felix orgasm onto Agatha's face while Safie stroked his cock gave the Creature some context for what jizz was, and he began to put his hands down his pants in order to catch the curious fluid from its source. He told himself it was to save his clothes from staining, but secretly he just liked to lick it off his palm.

On this particular evening, the Creature peered through the window to see they were left to their own devices yet again, in part as their dad was blind, not deaf. Today's devices appeared to be a broom handle, a zucchini, and a vibrating contraption that probably shouldn't have been invented yet but we'll pretend was in order to aid the story.

Agatha had blindfolded Safie for some sort of game—she held the anachronistic vibrator in one hand and the broom handle in the other and was teasing Safie to reach out and pat the arm that would be her pleasure object for the evening. Felix had pulled down his lederhosen and busied himself with the zucchini, putting on quite a show as he thrust the vegetable in and out of his eager asshole for the amusement of his sister. Safie, nipples hardening as she heard the moans coming from one side of the cottage, eagerly reached out and patted the arm with the broomstick, causing Agatha to giggle with devious delight. Because I cannot possibly write about the sexual use of a broom handle without shuddering thinking about splinters, I think we'll adjourn back to the scene outside.

The Creature stared through the window, transfixed by the whimpers and gasps coming from within the cottage, his jaundiced hand stroking his dick, which was quickly resurrecting.

He felt a hand on his arm. It was the father, De Lacey, home at last from the village.

"Ah," said De Lacey, "have you been spying?"

The Creature just sort of made an affirmative groan in response, partially because he had been really close to orgasm and this was really inconvenient timing. De Lacey, totally nonplussed by the nonverbal response, began to feel his way up the Creature's broad chest, past his scars, up to his face.

"You're a strapping young lad," said the old man with a furrowed brow. "Why wouldn't you knock on the door and say hello? As you can see, they're pretty experimental, though I wish they did chores with the same enthusiasm."

The Creature shook his head frantically. "I...I couldn't possibly. They are so beautiful, and I am so hideous."

De Lacey snorted in response. "Humph! Well, looks aren't everything, my boy, take it from me. An eagerness to please wins out over a handsome face any day of the week." He grinned, a smile that, sure, was missing a few teeth but made up for that in warmth. "Perhaps I could show you a bit of the old 'brotherly love,' if you think you'd give an old fellow like me the chance?" And with that he reached down to cup the Creature's stiff prick in his hand. "It seems like you might."

The Creature had never been touched like this before, and the warmth of the old man's hand against the cool but throbbing meat of his cock was a new, welcome sensation. Then De Lacey kissed him, hard but tenderly, his beard sloughing off the top layer of the Creature's skin—it was okay, because De Lacey was blind and the Creature couldn't feel it. Soon De Lacey had spit in his hand and began stroking the hard flesh of his companion, beginning with a slow, gentle jerking off, then getting faster and firmer. "Yessss," De Lacey murmured. "Just like we used to do in the army…"

"Um," said the Creature, feeling a bit embarrassed but also very aroused, "I'm not entirely sure that's the best idea…"

The next tug left De Lacey with the Creature's cock in his hand, feeling like a bratwurst that had been left on the counter overnight.

"Oh," said De Lacey. "Awkward." He lit a cigarette and offered it to the Creature.

The Creature shrieked and flung the cigarette at the cottage in horror, which immediately caught on fire.

## "Love is Deafblind" by Molly Sanchez

"I can't believe you're leaving me for this asshole," Helen Keller signed angrily into the palm of Anne Sullivan. It was a lovely Alabama spring day and the pair of them, along with Anne's fiancé, John Albert Macy, were strolling around the local carnival. "I mean, does the phrase *bros before hoes* mean nothing to you, Anne? Like, what the actual fuck?"

"What is Helen saying, dearest?" John asked as he guided them past the many sights and sounds of the fair (all of which were lost splendidly on Helen). Anne rolled her eyes and cleared her throat. "Oh nothing, pumpkin. She just said she's frightfully excited about our wedding."

"Listen, bitch, John is not a dingbag and he is not a ho. He's an English teacher, for Christ's sake," she signed furiously into Helen's hand, all the while smiling as John nodded toward the cotton candy vendor. "P.S. I know you can't see it but he is really freaking hot. Like super hot. He has an ass like a layer cake and last week I definitely got some over-the-pants action while you were in the room."

Helen shook her head. "Yeah, asshole, I'm blind and deaf but not stupid. I can feel your BJ vibrations from across the room. Also I have touched the dude's face, okay. He's a six at best. I just don't know why you're abandoning me for a six!"

"Are you and Helen all right, sweetness?" John asked.

Anne smiled and nudged Helen with her shoulder. "Of course we are, my darling. Helen was just saying that she couldn't be happier that I'm settling down with a man like you and that she's really jealous."

Helen smiled sweetly at John and gave a little wave. "I will fucking murder you," she signed to Anne.

Helen was lonely. Annie, her best and only friend, the only person who she could really be herself with, was ditching her for a nerd. At nights when Helen fondled herself in the dark, she longed for a partner more substantial than her usual handle of a hairbrush. Someone who would hold her and talk to her and see her as more than just the waaater girl. As she lay there, panting, her hairbrush sullied, she wished someone loved her, or at least wanted to fuck her like they did.

Suddenly Helen smelled something interesting. A cold smell, a musty comforting smell that reminded her of soil after rain. And as she inhaled deeper, she sniffed something familiar, keen loneliness. She nudged Anne. "What's going on?"

Anne signed, "They just wheeled out this dude they found frozen in the ice caps years ago. He's still frozen."

Helen sniffed again and signed, "Is he cute?"

She knew if she put her hand to Anne's face, she'd feel an eye roll but she felt her friend pause for a second before answering, "Hard to tell, but very tall...Oh fuck."

What Helen couldn't see was that the scorching Alabama sun had been melting the ice block all afternoon and suddenly the Monster broke free of his cold prison and started stretching his limbs. The crowd started screaming and running and Anne furiously tried to explain the situation to Helen.

"But you say he's tall?" she asked.

"Jesus, Helen, that's not the point. He's a hideous mansicle!"

"Okay, but tall?"

"Fuck it, yes!"

"He smells good. Let's take him home!"

And so they did. Anne, being used to dealing with frustrating people, offered the Monster her coat and coaxed him to join them on their way home (in the most awkward carriage ride in recorded history). Eventually he became a staple in the Keller household.

It took some time for him to adjust to living somewhere that wasn't a literal hovel. He was an eloquent conversationalist (though with obvious daddy issues) and soon he was able to join the Kellers and Anne at the dinner table.

He was fascinated with Helen but kept his distance, learning her movements as he had learned those of Felix, Agatha, and Safie years ago. In her he recognized an all too familiar sadness.

He was entranced and sometimes in his room at night his member became stiff and uncomfortable at the thought of her body so much so that he had to abuse himself between the box springs for relief.

He was charmed to see the candor with which she and Anne conversed, a candor only the keen observer could catch. He first noticed this when Anne told John Macy aloud that she had been "simply contemplating what a joy it would be to be your wife, dear heart" when in reality he had seen her sign, "He has a dick so pretty I want to make an oil painting of it!" as Helen laughed, her small breasts heaving with wanton abandon.

Yet he could not bring himself to approach lovely Helen. How could he cope if yet again he had found the perfect mate only to be so grossly rejected?

But he could not contain his passion long. One fateful night when the family had gone to the theater and left Helen to rest, he crept into her room and sat down on her bed beside her. He took her hand.

"May I lay with you?" he asked meekly into her palm.

A smile quirked Helen's lips "About fucking time!" she signed, and laughed slightly.

They lay down to face each other.

"You learned to sign?" she signed into his rough palm.

"Obviously," the Monster signed playfully.

Helen laughed a husky laugh before putting her hands over her mouth. She cleared her throat and said shakily, "I'm ashamed of my voice. I think it makes me sound stupid."

"You're not stupid," the Monster said, holding her hand to his lips.

Helen blushed and said more confidently, "Such a way with words."

She ran her hands over the Monster's face, feeling the lines of grafted skin. She traced her hands down his neck and under his shirt to rest over his heart, which was racing.

"Do you think I'm a monster?" he asked into her free hand.

She looked up at him and with her high voice she replied, "Do you think I am?"

The Monster kissed her then, the way he'd seen other couples kiss. He kissed her softly like Agatha had kissed her father's cheek, then tenderly and openmouthed the way Felix had kissed Safie on their reunion; then he drew her to him by her waist and kissed her hard like Victor had kissed Elizabeth on their fateful wedding night.

Helen groaned and pulled her nightgown over her head. The Monster had never seen the female body before and he wept at the sight of it.

Helen chuckled. "Come on, crybaby," she signed. "Fuck me already."

And so they made monstrous love until the power of their thrusting broke the antique bed frame and they went crashing to the floor.

Sweaty and sated, Helen rolled to lay her head on the Monster's chest. "If we're going to do this, you should know that sometimes I swear and I am definitely planning to be a socialist."

The Monster heaved a sigh and placed her hand to his lips before saying, "If we're planning to do this, you should know I accidentally killed a kid once."

Helen cocked her head and looked at him with sightless eyes.

"Accidentally?"

"Yes, it's a long story."

Helen shrugged and kissed him deeply before snuggling back onto his chest. "Well, might as well start. We have allll night."


## "Juicing the Saddle" by Evan Burton


Elizabeth Lavenza sat at an open cottage window awaiting the return of her husband, the pompous taint worm, Victor Frankenstein. The purple-black night made it impossible to tell the road from the trees that bordered it, so she closed her eyes and simply listened. It was, after all, the surest way to tell if her husband approached on horseback. Among his many quirks was that Victor Frankenstein rode with his saddle backward, the hard shaft of the horn in the rear instead of in the typical front position. As he rode, constantly prodded by the horn behind him, Victor grunted quite audibly above the clip-clop of the horse's hooves. Elizabeth once asked why he chose to be continually poked by the wood-hard horn—didn't it distress him? Frankenstein responded tersely that he preferred it that way. It braced him.

And nothing more was said about it, which was representative of their relationship. As the self-absorbed perineum parasite, Victor Frankenstein peered boldly into the soul of creation and slid all up in the DMs of nature, battering its inbox with requests. He permitted nothing to be asked of himself. This one-man circle jerk of vanity, ignorance, and daring is what led Victor to birth a monster he could not control.

Elizabeth sat waiting and waiting and listening to the nothingness. It was their wedding night, and her husband had promised to return after securing a pack of cigarettes and a bottle of Tropicana orange juice from the local merchant. This, of course, was a ruse. In fact, he had set out on horseback for the pleasure it gave him, and because he meant to find and destroy the monster before the monster destroyed him.

Elizabeth embraced her solitary woes. How lonely to be totally possessed by another. And yet how necessary. Just then she heard footsteps in the hallway and thought perhaps she'd fallen asleep despite herself, missing her husband's approach. As she turned to face her bedroom door, a giant figure emerged, filling her with a fear so immediate and absolute that it passed as easily as it had entered. She felt suddenly like an observer in her own body, free to act and yet unafraid of consequence. Elizabeth regarded the monster coolly, which was awkward because he had been counting on her to at least shriek or something, so that he could deliver his death sentence with dramatic flair. After a lame interlude of standing in the doorway menacingly, grunting and flailing his arms to no effect on Elizabeth, he went ahead and delivered his line.

"I have come to take what was taken from me. Since I cannot feel love, I will destroy it."

Elizabeth laughed from her gut, and the monster plodded toward the table where she sat.

"Do you not fear me?" The monster placed his icy hands on Elizabeth's shoulders and neck.

In a fluid motion, Elizabeth slid out of her chair and spun behind the monster, lifted herself to the tips of her toes, and leaned into the monster's ghastly ear.

"One cannot fear what one claims. You are mine now."

"Thank you, yes," said the monster, weeping openly. "I have been so lonely."

Elizabeth extinguished one of the lamps on her table, dipped her fingers in the oil pit, and dropped the monster's pants. She then copiously slathered his infernal asshole with oil, which the monster found hella pleasurable. His rigorous erection served as a confirmation to her powerful technique. The two slid into an unhallowed trance unified in the depths of their respective loneliness. Elizabeth, absorbed in her work, didn't hear the grunting approach of her husband.

When Victor Frankenstein entered his home—with his saddle in one hand and an orange juice in the other—to find Elizabeth five fingers deep inside the monster, fisting him with all the gusto of a banana cream daisy bursting forth, after a long winter, into spring, he stood for a moment speechless. Victor dropped his bottle of Tropicana orange juice, disturbing the two from their dark reverie. Victor met the monster's perpetually watery eyes, which were now extra watery.

"You fiend!" said Victor. "What are you doing to my dear sweet Elizabeth?!"

"Shut the fuck up, Victor," said Elizabeth without breaking the motion of her arm, pumping the monster's purple flower like a piston on a gas locomotive, "and come here!"

Victor obeyed, dropping the saddle as he approached.

"No," said Elizabeth, "bring it to me."

Victor picked up the saddle again, shaking and mesmerized by the unprecedented power he was witnessing in his wife. The scrotum muncher Victor Frankenstein had forced Elizabeth to wait for his attention and his affection at every turn as he projected his own monstrous image onto the screen of the universe. Now there was no more waiting.

Through the magic of ecstasy, Elizabeth intuited that the monster's dick was detachable, so she gently reached around and removed it. She gave him a rest from the fisting and the monster exhaled like the bag of flesh he was. As Victor came closer to the pair, Elizabeth held the monster's dick above her head and motioned with it to Victor.

"Do you want this daemonic dick, Victor?"

"I don't deserve it."

"Do you want this monstrous devil's eggplant, Victor?"

"I am a wretch."

"Do. You. Want. It. Victor?!"

"Yes! Yes! YES! Rejoin me with my own repulsive creation."

With that, Elizabeth took the saddle and slung it on the monster's back, who continued to weep joyously, facedown on the table. Wasting no time, she picked up the open oil lamp and poured it down Victor's ass crack. Victor shivered in response, murmuring, "I am a wretch."

Elizabeth guided his chest to the table next to the monster and mounted the saddle on the monster's back. She leaned over and began fucking Victor vigorously with the monster's dick.

"Ah," said Victor, "sweet nature!"

The harder Elizabeth fucked Victor with the monster's detached dick, the more the monster bucked, and Elizabeth found deep pleasure against the horn of the saddle. Now she understood why Victor liked to ride, and she resolved to do more of it herself.

"Yes, yes," said the monster, feeling Elizabeth's masterful operation of his dick inside Victor. "I am finally loved!"

With that, the monster came explosively and Elizabeth withdrew his dick from Victor, letting it spurt all over the curtains, and the floor, and the forgotten bottle of Tropicana orange juice, and finally out of the window. Reaching the pinnacle of her own pleasure, Elizabeth, too, came out of the window, followed by Victor Frankenstein, the ultimate fuckboi and deadbeat dad.

The moment their cum trifecta hit the ground, a dark forest teeming with vines and all manner of green life sprung up around the cottage.

Wrecked, Victor Frankenstein said in a soft voice, "If only I had known to look to the divine feminine as the source of life, I might have saved myself much tribulation."

"Shut the fuck up, Victor," said Elizabeth, still riding the wave of her orgasm.

Elizabeth patted the monster on the ass, and he helped her down from the saddle, which she then carried into another room to place among the rest of her belongings.

# JURASSIC PARK

Jurassic Park is one of those crazy things that seems to have existed long before the instant it existed. Part cultural landmark, part theme-park ride, and above all it's a perfect storm of dudes saying #actually to anyone who'll listen. With the possible exception of The Name of the Rose, you'd be hard pressed to find a greater testament to the dramatic power of mansplaining. Yet high above it all stands Dr. Ian Malcolm, cool and disinterested in the inevitable doom his mathemagical formulae predict. So, too, this story from our JP show rises above the action to coolly comment upon it all. —Casey

## "Ian Malcolm" by John William

It was the very early nineties, and renowned chaos theorist Ian Malcolm was putting his favorite Deee-Lite CD into his Discman as he slowly bled to death in a medical evacuation helicopter. Groove was in his heart, but also a ton of morphine, which the paramedics had given him on account of his getting mauled by a dinosaur. Being cool, he'd

167

let the two helicopter pilots crush his fentanyl lollypops and snort them off his dick just before takeoff, and now they were all tripping balls. Let me tell you it was some good shit. The sky was singing, the air was laughing, and they were all beginning to smell the texture of the walls.

"Would anyone like another opiate-fueled lecture on fractals?" Ian Malcolm offered. His words danced through the air, leaving pulsing trails of light and color.

Instead of answering, one of the pilots, a busty brunette whose pupils had dilated to the size of coffee mugs, flashed Dr. Malcolm a seductive grin and slid the zipper of her jumpsuit down to her waist. She wore nothing underneath. The other pilot, a well-muscled daddy with a jaw like a granite countertop, did the same thing. Because renowned chaos theorist Ian Malcolm was also a renowned bisexual.

"I'll tell you about chaos," Ian Malcolm said. "Chaos is math, but not regular math. Cool math. Math that punches you in the face and steals your little brother's Ritalin. You see, everything in the universe is connected, but in this fucked-up, passive-aggressive way. Like a butterfly goes to a fisting party in Botswana, and the next morning Kate Bush wakes up on a Montreal city bus with a condom in her ear. Chaos did that. Or, a character fucking dies at the end of a novel and then is somehow the protagonist in the sequel."

The pilots had stopped listening some time ago. They were half naked and exploring each other's bodies with their mouths. The male pilot cupped one of the female pilot's breasts, teasing her large brown nipple with his tongue. Dr. Malcolm wasn't sure if it was the copulation or the recent talk of math, but blood was suddenly rushing to his dick. He grew light-headed as his cock sprang to life, and the atmosphere in the helicopter seemed to shiver and gleam. Strange shapes passed before his eyes, and when his vision cleared the world had changed.

"This is probably the drugs talking," Ian Malcolm said, "but did you just turn into Counselor Troi from *Star Trek: The Next Generation*?"

"Oh my God," said the male pilot. "She did!"

"I sensed that I was turning into someone," said the female pilot, who suddenly was season two Counselor Troi, in her low-cut burlap catsuit and sexy, eggplant-shaped up-do.

"What about me?" the male pilot asked. "Am I turning into anyone?"

"You are!" exclaimed Counselor Troi. "You're turning into teen heartthrob Joey Lawrence from the current hit TV show *Blossom!*"

"Whoa!" said Joey Lawrence. No one was flying the helicopter.

Ian Malcolm gazed lustfully at Joey Lawrence, his eyes dancing over the young man's supple bronze skin and feathered pseudo-mullet. He was like a Greek statue of a lesbian tennis player. But was he also a little too young?

As if he could read Ian Malcolm's mind, Joey Lawrence spoke the sweetest sentence known to humankind: "I'm exactly the age of consent in the Central American dictatorship we're currently flying over." Then he knelt and swallowed Ian Malcolm's leaky meat pole all the way to the hilt.

"I'm sensing my gash is totally wet," said Counselor Troi. She stepped out of her uniform, mounted the gurney, and mashed her sopping pussy against Ian Malcolm's mouth. If you've never encountered a Betazoid vagina, it's a thing of wonder and beauty. It is a deep, cleansing well of silken mystery, an unfurling lotus made of sunlight and birdsong and children's prayers. Ian Malcolm lapped at it like a greedy kitten, savoring the tangy alien jizz that coated his lips and mouth. As he sucked away at her goo pot, he felt her moist minge sucking back, grabbing teasingly at his tongue. Counselor Troi had been doing her space Kegels.

Meanwhile, at the other end of the gurney, Joey Lawrence tongued his way from Ian Malcolm's balls to the tiny pink furrow of his tender man passage, by which I mean his butthole. He fingered a gob of spit into it.

"Fuck me, Joey Lawrence," said Dr. Malcolm.

Joey Lawrence's cock was thick and manly and impressively veined, but it also curved sharply to the left an inch below the tip, because life is chaos. He thrust his turgid spoo hose into Dr. Malcolm's quivering

under-mouth. All around them, medical equipment squawked and hol-
lered, as Dr. Malcolm's vital signs fluctuated dangerously, but nobody
heard.

"I'm sensing you've never been sounded before," Counselor Troi
said.

"I don't know what that is," said Dr. Malcolm. "But I don't think
you're actually psychic..."

"Shhhh," said Counselor Troi. "No words. Only feelings." From
somewhere beneath the gurney, she produced an eight-inch steel wand
and a tube of surgical lubricant. She greased the wand and pressed its
rounded tip against Dr. Malcolm's pee hole.

"You're going to like this," she said.

Ian Malcolm felt his piss slit pull apart as she nudged the wand gently into the head of his cock. He shuddered, and his velvety fuck cavern
clamped down around Joey Lawrence's cock. Counselor Troi inched
the sound deeper, deeper into Dr. Malcolm's urethra. The feeling of his
dick expanding from the inside out was like nothing he'd ever experienced before, and also it burned a little. Joey Lawrence gave a sudden,
wild buck of his hips, his baby cannon punching to the farthest recesses
of Dr. Malcolm's sweet, sweet love gutter. The wand slid deeper.

The pleasure was mounting, mounting, until it was almost unbearable. But the feeling of ecstasy overtaking Ian Malcolm wasn't coming
from his dick or his ass; it was coming from all around him. The world
was collapsing into a field of light, and he felt the invisible filaments
that tethered him to his body strain and break.

Suddenly he could see himself, sweaty and impaled on Joey Lawrence's frantically thrusting cum hammer, as if from above. He was
leaving, letting go of everything that had once meant so much to him,
like math and Jheri Curl and black leather jackets. He was walking,
no soaring into a brilliant light, while somewhere far behind him Joey
Lawrence and Counselor Troi shrieked in ecstasy. He wondered at
what point the pilots would stop fucking his body, and he hoped they
would at least get off, because they would probably be court-martialed,
and they deserved a moment of happiness first.

Even as they came to him, these thoughts were hard to hold on to. His consciousness was expanding like a cloud, diffusing, and the connections between ideas were getting harder and harder to make, as he slowly became light, became warmth, became peace.

But don't worry; he totally comes back for the sequel.

# CARRIE

## "Principal Grayle" by Spencer Bainbridge

"We escaped England to get away from the cold," John Smith grumbled as he put another log on the fire and dusted his meaty hands. "'Tis as cold here in Jamestown as any winter in Sussex, says I."

"John Smith, temper your moaning." His goodly wife, Mary, frowned over her knitting. "You know as well as I we came here to practice our religion freely. So don't utter such blasphemy of this beautiful land we call Virginia." Even when she was cross with him, John Smith could see the sparkle in her brown eyes, and he couldn't help but notice the heave of her ample bosom as her fingers worked the thread.

"You are right, Mary," he said. "'Tis such a blessed place, we named it for our savior's virgin mother. But that needn't mean there be any virgins in this house."

She smiled coyly, turning away slightly. "Why, John, there is much work to do on this wintry night if we're to survive."

He put his hand on her left breast and felt the erectness of her nipple. "Then let us be warm."

She rose, letting her garment fall to the wooden floor. "Ravage me, John," she whispered. "I want you to attack my feminine mound like a tribe of warring Iroquois."

"I shall," he said. "I'll get on my knees and eat a mighty feast. Then you'll take my stiffened manhood in your sweet mouth, as that is the spirit of Thanksgiving."

"Ah, John. I would receive your...your..."

Damn it! Stuck again. Henry Grayle had been on such a roll. Who knew writing an erotic novel about colonial Jamestown would be so difficult?

It was a Friday afternoon, always a quiet time at Thomas Ewen Consolidated High School. This was Henry's favorite part of the week. He deemed it more wonderful than Spaghetti Wednesdays, the highest praise he could bestow. As quiet finally fell over campus, he'd reach into his top desk drawer, pour himself a paper cup of VO, and settle in to work on his long-gestating masterpiece.

Being a high school principal was hard enough. But finding the time to write historically accurate colonial eroto-fiction was damn near impossible. Research wasn't necessary; he had been a history teacher for seventeen years and he knew the ins and outs of early American copulation. It was the sheer hours it took to find precisely the right words to express his most vivid fantasies of pre-Revolutionary rumpy-pumpy that delayed his progress.

His latest roadblock was finding new synonyms for *erection*. He stared out the window, his hands hovering over his Adler Eagle typewriter. "Boner...," he muttered aloud, not for the first time. He said the word again, carefully considering every letter. "Boooonnnnneeeerrrr."

The intercom buzzed. "Principal Grayle?"

"Uh, yes, Catherine. What is it?"

The last thing Henry wanted to hear was his secretary's nasal whine crackling over the intercom, not while he was struggling with penile synonyms.

"I just wanted to remind you you're meeting with Chris Hargensen's father first thing Monday."

Boner. It just doesn't sound very seventeenth century, he thought.

"Principal Grayle?"

"Uh, yes, thank you, Catherine. You can go home now."

The intercom clicked off. Sinking back in his chair, Henry could hear Catherine gathering her things in the outer office. Funny, he thought. She sits just feet away, behind a flimsy wall, and even she has no idea he was cooking up such steamy yarns.

Suddenly, Catherine entered, startling Henry. "Oh, didn't mean to surprise you," she said. "I left my coat in here this morning."

"Actually, Catherine, can I ask you something?" he ventured.

She looked at him quizzically and sat. "Sure."

"I know you're involved in the community theater."

"Oh, yes. Well, a bit. I assist with the costumes when my aquasize schedule allows."

"So you're a creative type. I feel we can discuss this as colleagues. I'm working on a project. I can't tell you too much. But I'm afraid I'm a bit stuck."

"I see. Is this about your book?"

Henry froze in terror. "Uh, I'm sorry?" He could already feel beads of sweat forming all over his lumpy frame.

"Your book. The sexy one about the pilgrims. Are you having trouble?"

"Catherine, how did you know about my book? That's private!"

"It's not that private, Principal Grayle. You just leave it sitting in your desk drawer with the whiskey. I've read it many times. I think you're coming along nicely."

"Well...thank you, but that's not the point! Drinking my whiskey during school hours, that's all well and good, even expected. But how dare you read my private fiction?"

Catherine arched an eyebrow, giving a sly expression Henry had never seen. "Oh, come on. I think you wanted someone to read it."

Henry, apoplectic, could barely summon coherent speech and sputtered an embarrassed string of discordant syllables.

Catherine reached for the paper cup and took a swig, then offered it to Henry. Obediently, he sipped. The two sat in silence for a moment.

"So," Catherine said at last. "Where did you get stuck in the story? Has John Smith's comely sister-in-law already discovered how to flick her bean?"

"Catherine, when did you decide you could speak so freely to me?"

"Can it, boss. You know you want to ask me something." She licked her lips slowly in a clockwise motion. "So ask me."

Henry reached deep inside himself and summoned the courage he needed for such situations. It reminded him of when he told his father he wasn't going into the napkin-folding business or the difficult day he had to choose between gray kitchen marble or light green. Finally, he had the nerve to speak.

"Well, Catherine, I'd like to ask you. Do you have any, uh, ahem, suggestions for further synonyms for...for...for an erect male member?"

"Oh, Principal Grayle!" She threw back her head and let out a powerful, single-burst laugh. "I thought you'd never ask."

She produced a small notebook from her skirt pocket and flipped back several pages. Clearing her throat, she began.

"Hard-on. Stiffy. Rod. Sex stick. Big hard cock. Blackbeard's flagpole. Love bulge. Flesh axe. Mighty pants oak. Sword. Cum musket. Wooly willy. Engorged member. Third leg. Furry hot dog. Cucumber down under. Dong. Thor's hammer. Pussy drill. Pleasure zucchini. Captain's baton. Splooge hose. Travolta. Rolling pin of delight. Swinging John Thomas. Tallywacker, I barely know her. Diiiiiiiick. Broken flashlight. Give her hell, hairy. The long arm of the balls. Bearded gourd. Trouser fugitive. Hymenus interruptus. Brian de-palm-ya. Skin sledge. And, of course, boner."

Henry was absolutely stunned. "My God," he said. "Catherine, that was remarkable!"

Catherine nodded with satisfaction and put the notebook back in her pocket. "My pleasure, Principal Grayle."

"I appreciate your help, but we must keep this strictly between the two of us. I don't think people at Ewen High would be very understanding about this project of mine."

"Of course," she said. "You're right, they wouldn't be able to handle it. Nothing exciting ever happens at this school."

## "Teenage Dream: A Friend-Fiction Period Piece" by Lilly Miller

Tommy had been going steady with Sue about half a year. He was into her slammin' bod and sweet demeanor and had already asked her to prom. But ever since the newest student transferred to Ewen High's senior class, Tommy wanted nothing more than to make love to her and moan her name: Tina Belcher. The eighteen-year-old New Jersey transplant captured Tommy's eye as she slumped and schlepped past his locker every day.

Tina and Tommy only shared one class—health—where the teacher's monotonous droning had put nearly everyone to sleep. While Tommy's attraction to Tina was intense, not even the sound of her sexy, uninterested sigh could deter his sleepiness.

"There is more to the female anatomy than the vagina; the vagina is merely part of the vessel of life," the teacher said, barely eliciting a response from the class. "The uterus, ovaries, fallopian tubes, and cervix all play an integral part of human reproduction." Tommy's eyes glazed over as he glanced at the female anatomy poster, aroused only by the thought of Tina's drooping knee socks. "The menstrual cycle is a result of monthly ovulation..." Tommy tuned out; he was done. He closed his eyes and gave in to sleep, still thinking about Tina.

Suddenly, he could see her clearly. He dreamt of Tina naked in the girls' locker room shower. Water dripped from her short black bob down her mosquito-bite-sized breasts; steam filled her thick, square-rimmed glasses.

"Oh, the humidity!" Tina said, smiling over at Tommy. Her feet squished into the mildewed tile floor as she walked over to him. "Isn't it just too much? You should drop your towel."

Tommy glanced down—he only had a towel neatly wrapped around his hips. Blood was starting to rush to his groin.

"Uhh...I'm not wearing anything else," he said, blushing, as he clutched the towel and readjusted.

"It's okay, that's just how I want you," Tina said, pushing him up against the wall. Tommy could feel her majestic bush rubbing against his terry-cloth-cloaked erection as she leaned in for a kiss. Just as Tommy puckered his lips, the bell rang.

"Quick! We have to hurry!" Tina grabbed his hand.

"Where are we going?" Tommy asked.

"I'm taking you to class—to a special class," Tina said, leading him to the pool. "Don't worry, it doesn't require any clothes."

Tina yanked Tommy's towel away from him and dove in. Carrie and Sue, also totally naked, were on the other side. Carrie floated around while Sue kneeled at the edge of the pool.

"Today's lesson is about how to eat pussy," Sue said. "Tina, get over here. This is really important."

"Sorry, I was distracted by Tommy's butt." Tina's glasses reflected his tan, perfectly sculpted cheeks as she continued to stare, mouth agape.

"Tina! We don't have all day!" Sue yelled. Tina made her way over to the girls, where Carrie was absentmindedly stroking her engorged clit. Tommy leaned against the bleachers, not sure what was happening.

"Okay! So." Sue cleared her throat as she spread apart her knees. "To review from last week, you can stick your fingers up inside the vagina to find your G-spot. This is what most boys think is what makes us come, but REALLY what we want is more clit action. By the way, good job with your clit action, Carrie!"

Carrie smiled and continued to euphorically flick her bean. Sue glanced over at Tina, who had stuck her fingers into her pussy and let out a llama-esque moan. Tommy had never been so turned on before.

"Excellent work, Tina," Sue said. "But there's so much more to female pleasure than penetration! Carrie, are you ready for a demonstration?"

Carrie blissfully nodded and stood up in the pool as Sue slid in. She joined her mouth to Carrie's tight pink cave; the lights flickered as Carrie gasped and sighed. Sue popped back up. "See? You can lick too. We call it 'eating out.' You know, like takeout, but with pussy instead of burgers."

"That's incredible," Tina murmured in amazement as she continued to pleasure herself. "Can I get a piece of that double-trouble action?"

Sue and Carrie pulled Tina closer, and the three girls started making out as they furiously fingered each other.

Tommy just stared as he watched the girls go at it. They splashed and licked and kissed and moaned. Sue hopped out and kneeled at the edge of the pool. "Eat the food, Tina," Sue groaned. "Eat it."

Tommy let out an audible choke as he watched Tina lick Sue's pussy from crack to front.

The girls turned around and gave Tommy a come-hither look. "Come on, Tommy, join us," Tina said, beckoning him into the pool. "Don't be such a heinous anus."

Tommy stammered nonsense as he tumbled his way into the pool, paddling toward the girls. Carrie and Sue started nibbling along the sides of his neck as Tina straddled him. Tommy's member hardened, rubbing ever so slightly against Tina's clit. He slid into Tina easily while inserting his fingers into Sue and Carrie. All the girls moaned in unison, the water splashing rhythmically against them, and Tommy leaned his head back in ecstasy. He sat up after a minute and opened his eyes to take in everything, only to yelp and jump out of the pool— Sue had started menstruating.

"Gaaahhhhhh! Go clean up," Tommy said nervously, trying to avert his eyes. He rubbed his fingers hastily and stood with the girls at the edge of the pool. "I'm sorry. That's just a lot of blood."

"You think you've seen blood? I'll show you blood," Carrie barked. She closed her eyes and pressed her hands firmly against her hips, and all three girls started simultaneously menstruating.

"AAAAAAAAAHHHHHHHHH!"          Tommy screamed. He tried to back away but slipped and nearly lost his balance at the edge of the pool. "What the hell?!" His body tensed up as the blood started to gather at his feet, slowly dripping down the tile cracks. Carrie smiled, and the chlorinated water turned dark red.

Tina took a step back, glancing briefly at the girls. "THIS...IS...

MENSTRUATIONNNNNNN NATIONNNNNNNNNNNNNN!"
she screamed at the top of her lungs as she kicked Tommy into the pool.
As he came up for air, he felt something hitting his head, like cottony
hail. Carrie stared at the rafters and wiggled her fingers, creating a
hailstorm of used tampons. Shrieking, he paddled away from the girls,
only to slam his head on the pool ladder and suddenly wake up.

"Tommy, are you all right?" Tina squinted at him. Tommy had
tumbled out of his desk and hit his head. He pulled himself up, tasting
blood—he split his lip in the fall.

"Yeah, I...I...I'm fine," he stammered, wiping his mouth.

"I hope so," Tina said as she walked toward the door. Tommy
watched her move, still entranced by her uneven bangs, only to notice
a line of blood dripping down her left leg. He shuddered in disgust but
felt his member stiffen in delight. Tina stopped briefly to glance back at
him. "Class dismissed," she said with a wink as she walked away.

# "Carrie" by Virgie Tovar

Thanks to the technology, Carrie was able to be revived from death
and begin her lifelong dream of becoming a therapist.

She moved to Pacifica and commuted to the Masters of Social Work
program at SF State. She married a dude she met on craigslist Casual
Encounters named Raven. Raven was a white man with dreads. They
had butt sex twice a week, which Raven found thrillingly perverse. Carrie observed in her private notebook of therapist thoughts that Raven—
whose real name was Bruce—rebelled against his upper-middle-class
roots by doing things like making marijuana puns at dinner parties
and his obsession with "da butt." He had a strict mother, who gave him
an enema every night before bed until he was seventeen. This led to an
anal fixation. Carrie knew all about the ways that mothers weave their
way into our fantasies.

Carrie began her intern hours. Her primary interest was in patients with unusual sexual proclivities—fetishists, in particular.

The first month of her internship was spent talking with primarily men about things like an unbeatable desire to drink young women's urine. Her most interesting patient was a man who enjoyed pretending he was an amputee and having women poop on sponges and pretend to trick him into believing the poop was soap.

Carrie had read that fetishists were primarily men. Freud only wrote about male fetishists, but what would Freud say about Carrie's sexual proclivities, then?

Two months later she got a new patient, a woman. There was something about her that felt vaguely familiar.

Unlike her other patients, Claire spoke very little. This made Carrie flustered and she began to talk aimlessly. Each session she promised herself that THIS time would be different, and each time she talked even more than the last. In their eighth session, Carrie asked, "What excites you sexually?"

"What excites you, Carrie?" Claire responded. The question gave Carrie a massive lady boner.

Afterward, Carrie went home and lay in bed, thinking about Claire. She was uppity and controlling, the kind of woman who'd bring a crucifix or straight razor to bed...or better yet, a bucket of...No. No. Carrie couldn't. She'd come this far and she wasn't going to relive those old days. Carrie turned on her Hitachi Magic Wand. She didn't need to plug it into the wall. It was powered by her telekinesis. Score.

In the next session, despite all her will, she found herself confessing things to Claire. She wasn't sure who was the patient and...who was the therapist. One afternoon Claire came in wearing a corsage. When Carrie saw it, her eyes began to focus in and then out and then in and then out, while violin-heavy stabby horror music played. She began to sweat.

"A corsage? What an odd fashion choice."

"I never went to my prom, but I've always fantasized about what it could be like. Did you go to your prom, Carrie?"

*Carrie turned on her Hitachi Magic Wand. She didn't need to plug it into the wall. It was powered by her telekinesis. Score.*

"Yes, I did." Despite herself, Carrie began to get moist in her lady parts. She couldn't control it. She had studied this in her Sexual Deviations class: in some rare patients traumatic events became part of sexual desire, sometimes causing sexual fixation.

There was something about the corsage that loosened something within Carrie, and she couldn't stop herself from telling Claire all that had happened, and the fetish that was the product of it all.

She told Claire about her mother's religious fanaticism, the prom… the pig's blood… the fires. How what she wanted more than anything was a sick and twisted mommy who would throw her into a prayer closet and pour a bucket of blood on her. She wanted to feel that sort of humiliation—and PAIN—again.

There, she said it. Out loud. It was no longer rattling around inside her mind, haunting her. She knew she had broken the code of ethics, but she felt so relieved. After the wave of blissful relief came the embarrassment of having told this to a patient.

She began to stammer: "Well, I'll see you out and the secretary can offer you some suggestions for a new therapist who is—"

Claire interrupted Carrie: "I want to humiliate you, Carrie."

Carrie stood wide-eyed, practically drooling lady jizz from her v-hole.

They set up a time and place to meet—there was a motel near the beach. Carrie got there early, waiting.

Claire knocked on the hotel room door.

"Put this on." She threw a bag at her and there was a tight slinky prom dress inside. "No bra. No panties," she hissed at Carrie.

Carrie put it on. The woman jumped on top of her, kissing her, pushing her body into her.

"You can't go to the prom, Carrie! You look like a harlot! Look at your DIRTY PILLOWS!"

Carrie's nipples stood on end.

"No, Mama. I'm not a harlot. I love Jesus."

"Jesus McPenis Pumper is the Jesus you serve!"

"No, I don't even like penis, Mama."

Claire slid her hand between Carrie's legs.

"The Baby Jesus Butt Plug is your God!"

"No, Mama, please let me go to the prom."

Then from out of nowhere Claire pulled out a giant Costco-sized ketchup bottle. She opened the top, teasingly squirting a little between Carrie's boobies. She made Carrie get on her knees while she stood up on the edge of the bed.

"Announcing...your prom queen...the Queen of Whore Island...Carrie White."

And with that she squeezed nearly the whole bottle of ketchup onto Carrie's head. Carrie never knew she was a squirter, but OMG she totally was. And then Claire began to chant:

"Pig's blood for a pig. Pig's blood for a pig! PIG'S BLOOD FOR A PIG!"

Arousal turned into the deepest kind of humiliation and then at the edge of her consciousness...a SHOCKING REALIZATION.

"I never told you that the kids at the prom had chanted 'Pig's blood for a pig!' How...did...you...know...that?"

She looked at Carrie and CACKLED. She jumped off the bed and grabbed Carrie by the neck; ketchup and squirt was EVERYwhere.

"You silly bitch! I AM CHRIS HARGENSEN...the one who got kicked out of prom for throwing tampons at you! After the prom disaster I didn't die. I moved into a lesbian separatist community and learned that my cruelty toward you was a product of my deeply repressed sexual desire for you. I didn't want to ruin your life. I wanted to FUCK YOU. I had a feeling you'd moved to Pacifica. So I got facial reassignment surgery much like that which was done in the 1997 film *Face/Off* starring John Travolta. Carrie, that's not all—I'm...I'm YOUR REAL MOTHER! I had to let you go at birth because...I'm a vampire. Carrie, GODDAMNIT you're half vampire!"

"OMG. That would explain my telekinesis and also how you looked so young when we were in high school, but I thought vampires couldn't have children."

"No, that's a myth of the patriarchy…and…so…is…the TABOO OF INCEST."

And with that they proceeded to have the sweetest Mommy Play there ever was—the real vagina-bumping your actual mom kind.

# JAWS

Every once in a while a writer just perfectly nails our FEELINGS about a book, and straight out of the gate, this story by Joe Wadlington delivers. In a sea (sorry) of shark jokes, Joe latched on to all the false male bravado and suburban housewife ennui so typical of the denizens of Long Island, which is a thing I am allowed to say because I am from there, and now you know my terrible secret. —AMY

## "10,000 Leagues Under the D" by Joe Wadlington

The Amity courthouse walls were sweating—a combination of summer heat and small towners turned on by controversy.

"We can't close the beach!" the crowd yelled. Police Chief Brody held up a cautionary hand.

"That shark killed a white man yesterday—we can't ignore it anymore," he said.

"Please, Brody! Can't we just wait until another kid dies?! Amity is a summer town. We need summer money!" one man said.

"Are you asking me to turn a blind eye to a horrific massacre so that your businesses can thrive?" Brody said.

"It's July Fourth—what could be more patriotic than that?" the mayor said.

The crowd erupted into homogenous agreement, until a bottle of white wine was shattered on the chalkboard. Silence.

Ellen sloshed her glass of Chardonnay.

"It's not just any shark—it's a great white," she said.

"At least it's white," the innkeeper murmured.

The mayor stepped forward. "How do you know?" he asked.

"I read my kids' Zoo Books when they're at school," Ellen said. "The bite marks from the chunks of the victim match, and great whites migrate here in the summer."

"They spend winter in Florida?" someone asked.

"Farther south," Ellen clarified. The crowd's faces got scrunched and puffy as they tried to think of Geography outside the United States.

"Mexico. It's from Mexico!" one brave voice said.

"That shark wants our jobs!" the mayor erupted.

"What? No," Ellen said. "It just follows the fish. Why do you feel so threatened?"

The mayor stood to his full height and glared.

"I'm a man! I always feel threatened!" he bellowed.

Ellen covered her face. She hated life in Amity. It was too small. She was jealous of the summer visitors—people who had P.F. Chang's in their towns and cute coffee shops with that classy shit in the tiny cups. Ellen had once been on her way to a fulfilling career—now she just did Kegels in the grocery line and waited for her husband to tell her dinner was good. She only came to the meeting because she thought they were getting a Whole Foods.

"Ellen, you're the most bitter character on the island. You have to kill this shark for us," the mayor said.

"Then what?" Ellen asked.

"Well, hopefully it's the only shark in the ocean and then we're done," the mayor said.

"Unless that shark has the last fifteen years of my life in its belly, I don't give a fuck," she said.

"Ellen, if you kill the shark, we'll build a Super Target."

Ellen was taken aback. They'd denied the permit for years. She choked back tears with a swig of Chardonnay.

"Add an in-store Jamba Juice and I'm out of here."

"Deal!" the mayor said.

Ellen threw her wineglass at the shark drawing and put her face exactly where the little sharky ears would be. She whispered, "You think you're dead on the inside? I'm from Long Island."

The boat swayed gently with the waves. Ellen's character didn't have an identity outside of wife or motherhood, so Chief Brody came along to give her context. They sat in the cabin taking shots of white Zinfandel, making out, and comparing scars.

Brody ripped open his shirt. A scar slashed across his hairy barrel chest. It was from their first date, when Ellen blacked out and thought Brody was a ghost from the Civil War. Ellen stroked the scar. They hadn't touched in a long time. It was nice to be away from the kids—whatever their names were.

"Now, I want to see your biggest scar," Brody said.

"If I could rip out my heart, I'd show ya—but my character doesn't express feelings besides weeping. I was an eighties lady, Brody. Shoulder pads, thick belt, hair to Jesus. The testicles of my entire company were below my stiletto and my company LIKED it. Then I met you, put on Jordache jeans so high-waisted that I stopped breathing—woke up fifteen years later with two kids yelling at me for being 'bad at texting.' One day you're ignoring a French triathlete because he's only a primary care physician, and the next you're at T.J. Maxx, doing Kegels and looking for discount Spanx that can convincingly fit under a one-piece," Ellen said.

"Can you even get Spanx wet?" Brody asked.

"No, Brody, there's no love in this world," Ellen said.

Brody hadn't realized how distracted he'd been the last few years. Ellen had streaks of silver in her hair now and new wrinkles in her face from all the shit he did to her. She was just as beautiful as she'd been on their wedding day. He started kissing her hard and unsnapped her mom jeans. The boat slammed to the side and they went tumbling. Another slam and the ship's hull started leaking. Another slam—the boat was sinking—and fast. Ellen and Brody crawled to the deck. The massive shark was circling the boat, fucking with them.

Ellen grabbed the harpoon gun and Brody pulled out his pistol. Brody sunk a few bullets in the shark before it slammed into the boat again, sending them flying. The mechanism on the harpoon gun broke completely and Brody's pistol went overboard.

The back of the boat had broken off. The shark was weighing it down. It snapped and snapped at them, swallowing the inner tubes, oxygen tanks, and white wine bottles that rolled toward it. It flashed a smile that was ten feet across, then retreated to deliver a final blow.

Brody started making out with Ellen immediately.

"What, are you doing?!" she exclaimed.

"You have to shoot it with the harpoons!" Brody said between kisses.

"It's broken," Ellen said.

"No, we need more force than that," Brody said, handing her a harpoon. "Use your Kegels."

Ellen's eyes grew wide as her husband dropped to his knees, immediately swabbing her deck.

"Don't stop!" she said.

Brody's tongue moved in double time with the waves. Ellen was fully sitting on him now and opening compartments of herself that had been closed for years. Brody was so hard his pants looked like they had a dorsal fin. He lay Ellen down and handed her the blunt end of the harpoon. She moved the smooth pipe in gently and let her body engulf it.

When Ellen saw her new harpoon dick, she felt comforted—as if she'd always had a horrifying penis but now others could finally see it too. And, thankfully, the shark was taking a really fucking long time to come back.

Brody knelt around Ellen, kissing her and moving the harpoon

*When Ellen saw her new harpoon dick, she felt comforted—as if she'd always had a horrifying penis but now others could finally see it too. And, thankfully, the shark was taking a really fucking long time to come back.*

gently. She got so wet it made the boat sink faster. The shark started rocketing toward them. Ellen's body was bent in pleasure as they moved the harpoon faster and faster. Her howls rose like sonar until both she and the shark couldn't be any closer.

"THIS IS WHAT A FEMINIST LOOKS LIKE!!!" Ellen roared. Her orgasm tidal waved and her Kegels threw the harpoon like an Olympic javelin. It went straight into the shark's open mouth, cutting the oxygen tank in half and blowing the bastard to pieces.

The two lovers didn't skip a beat. As bloody shark confetti covered them, Brody entered Ellen and they bucked and bucked with the new waves. Ellen looked at the sinking boat, the pool of blood, and her handsome husband. *I can have it all,* she thought peacefully.

# THE MALTESE FALCON

## "Private Eye, Private Time" by David Cairns

The dawn of a new day burned the remaining blackness of the night to a simpering gray, the color of diluted squid ink. At his side, Brigid O'Shaughnessy's soft snoring gave the appearance of a deep slumber. Spade was quiet leaving the bedroom and shutting the bedroom door. He examined the sleeping girl's clothes, took a flat brass key, and went out.

He went to the Coronet, letting himself into the girl's apartment. Inside, he switched on all the lights. He searched the place from wall to wall, checking every drawer, cupboard, cubbyhole, box, bag, trunk— locked and unlocked both. He passed his tough hands along the wall-paper and felt for wires, hidden microphones, peepholes. Having found none, he checked his pocket watch. It read a quarter till seven.

"Finally, a little peace and quiet," he remarked to the empty room, and slipped the watch back into his pocket, where it nestled against his already growing cock.

Spade strode carefully from room to room, making as little sound as might be. He parted the Venetian blinds with his left index finger and worked open his trouser buttons with his right. His yellow eyes rolled across the scenery of San Francisco and settled on a middle-aged woman hanging laundry in an alley off Sutter Street.

191

"Not the bird I'm looking for, but she'll do," he muttered.

Spade twisted the Venetians open, his fingers mildewed with sweat. He brought his hands together in front of his mouth and spread his thin lips, blowing hotly and rubbing his palms together. The rasping of his calloused hands filled the room and his palms warmed like a pair of Chinatown biscuits. He slipped the fingers of his right hand into his trousers in search of his Butcher's Prize.

He coaxed the tender muscle from its tweed birdcage and rested his thumb across the thatched bridge of his Naughty Little Man. His fingers relaxed around the lower third. The woman hanging the wash in the alley bent to retrieve another handful of rags from her basket, revealing her copious baby-feeders. The tendons in Spade's fingers contracted and his cock became turgid and red with blood pumped in from his feet and ears.

Spade cleared his throat. His cock was ugly, he knew, but it could handle itself in a fight. It had a long protruding vein running the length of it on the right side, and the skin was mottled, pink and brown. On the underside was a small reddish mark, which Spade had obtained from masturbating too much during a family trip to Oswego Lake when he was fourteen. It was his only souvenir.

Spade rubbed and a bead of milky precum started to collect at the tip of his cock. The woman in the alley hung the last of her whites and went inside.

"Damn!" said Spade. "Just as I was getting a usable erection!"

He turned his head and surveyed the rest of the hotel room. His eyes presently struck a look of curiosity, and then one of devilish cunning, like a man who had just found a place to masturbate.

Spade rolled a cigarette and placed it between his lips. He lit it and checked his watch again. Seven-oh-four. He crossed the threshold into the bathroom. His cock was softer; it was at three-quarters mast. If it were a flagpole, people would assume an important dignitary had been killed.

Spade kicked off his shoes and socks and jostled his cock like he was interrogating it. His eyes were placid, but the set of his jaw indicated frustration. He shoved off his jacket and suspenders and trousers and then his long underpants, his sock garters and underdrawers and his shirt and undershirt. His hat he left on. He turned and gave the pile of clothes a savage kick and they scooted back into the adjacent room like the Invisible Man falling down the stairs.

Spade pulled at his rubbery wad and spat on it—a viscous spit, stained tan from his unfiltered cigarettes. He rubbed the tan goo into his cock and sat on the edge of the claw-foot bathtub. Spade shivered from the coolness of the marble and shut his eyes tight, forming a V in his rapidly balding brow.

"Come on, Mack!" Spade searched his mind for a fantasy, a vision, a glimpse of leg or a bit of lipstick on a glass—y'know, erotic imagery—but found only his recently shot partner, Archer.

Archer approached him, shirtless. "So I heard you been screwin' around with my wife, Spade," Archer said. "How'd you like a little screwin' of your own!"

Spade grunted unhappily and waited for another fantasy to take the place of this one, but when none did, he allowed it to continue.

Archer removed his trousers and revealed his thick manhood, which bent like a napping swan. It was beautiful, unlike Spade's. The skin was smooth and tanned like a new wallet, and his hair was flaxen like an angel's pubes. "I'm going to put this in you, Spade," Archer said.

Spade's eyebrows lifted, as if awaiting one or more women to appear in his mind, but his yellow eyes remained closed. The imaginary Archer gripped Spade's haunches and eased his whole canary into Spade's deep, dark coal mine.

Spade shuddered and bent himself over the bathtub, stroking his beige shillelagh in long, bold arcs. He coated the thick fingers of his left hand with another dose of tobacco-laden mucus and moved them with fumbling haste to his puckering rectum. He rubbed in the greasy funk with slow, manly circles.

The chubby middle finger groped farther in, as the second digit became obscured, and then the third. Spade began to work his ring finger in, too, and at that moment, he was happy he'd never married.

"How do you like that, Spade! I've got my whole cock in your ass-hole!" Archer taunted plainly. Spade made it work—he needed this—and continued to whale on his own Moby Dick and, losing his balance, slid forward into the tub until just his legs stuck out. His scalp pressed hard into the icy marble. "Spade, I'm going to come! I'm going to baste your little turkey!" Archer said.

Spade opened his feverish yellow eyes and looked up to find the salmon eyehole of his phallus. It looked back at him like a blind oracle and released. Spade's chest and neck were buttered, as were his eyes. His mouth was treated to a steaming spoonful of salty dick grits.

He showered and when he had finished dressing, he made and drank a cup of coffee. Then he unlocked the kitchen window, scarred the edge of its lock a little with his pocketknife, opened the window—over a fire escape—got his hat and overcoat from the settee in the living room, and left the apartment through the front door, as he had come.

## "Wilmer Cook" by Leena Rider

After that whole mess with Sam Spade, that dame, and that cop Pol-haus, Wilmer Cook made a deal with the feds that would keep him out of prison in exchange for testifying against Kasper Gutman's boss. He was a little confused why they hadn't moved him out of San Francisco and why he still had his own name if he was in witness protection but he was sure they had their reasons.

And he'd landed this sweet job working security at Club Rule 34 in the old Belvedere Hotel.

And he never had been that bright.

Wilmer had traded his two comically large pistols for a full-color, sound-optional, closed-circuit monitoring system and a personal pref-erence for self-denial. He squinted his hazel eyes at the monitor bank in front of him and adjusted his member, enclosed in a CB-10,000 male chastity device. He'd been at work for a few hours already; it was both difficult to concentrate and impossible not to concentrate on his job: watching all these fucking freaks.

Or watching all these freaks fucking. Whichever.

The Keystone Kops were in room 5, haphazardly daisy-chaining their way through the evening. Their uniforms were in various stages of disarray and each pelvic thrust set off a Newton's cradle of anal drilling around the circle that looked like it should result in pratfalls but somehow rarely did.

In room 2, a brunet, hirsute man was strapped facedown to a table, legs spread. Four others wearing gray latex suits with large heads and big black eyes milled around him. The gangliest one worked the brunet man's scrotum and cock with his incredibly long fingers while one of the smaller two manipulated the man's nipples and played with his hair. The broadest one expertly traced the man's body with a violet wand while the smallest—was that one wearing glasses?—worked a vaguely falcon-shaped toy into his rectum. They all worked in concert until the hirsute man tensed and shouted, "I WANT TO BELIEVE!!" and came all over the gangly one's hands.

After he ejaculated, the four creatures pulled their masks off dramatically, revealing an unkempt, brunet man; a redheaded woman with a stylish scarf; a blond man wearing a neckerchief; and a brunette, bespectacled woman.

"Jinkies, it's hot in these suits!" the brunette, bespectacled woman said.

"I, like, heard that," the unkempt gangly man said.

"Thanks, guys. I never would've gotten off if it weren't for you probing aliens," said the man strapped to the table.

"Anytime," said the redhead, fingering her scarf and batting her eyelashes furiously at him.

The blond man straightened his neckerchief, looked at his alien mask, and said, "Quite a turnabout, isn't it, guys? Us in the masks?"

"Oh, Fred," said Velma, Daphne, Shaggy, and Mulder in unison.

In room 15, two regulars—Shaft and Miss Marple—were going

at it. At the moment, Shaft was thrusting his massive cock between the soft, papery folds of Marple's aged titties, which wrapped entirely around it in almost a double helix. Even without the sound on, Shaft's contented, "Ya daaaaaamn right," reverberated up to the control booth.

In room 10, Kinsey Millhone, V. I. Warshawski, Kay Scarpetta, Cassie Maddox, Temperance Brennan, Thursday Next, and all four members of the Women's Murder Club were stacked like Lincoln Logs in a slurping, moaning circle of oral pleasure.

Wilmer's cock twitched again in the unforgiving sheath. He balled his tiny fists and turned his attention next door for relief. In room 9, the saddest circle jerk ever was in progress.

Room 9 featured the who's who of dark and tortured souls. They were all white middle-aged men, grizzled, unpleasant, not attractive but sort of attractive. Standing in a wide, ragged circle were Harry Bosch, Lord Darcy, Hercule Poirot, Aloysius Pendergast, Jack Reacher, Thomas Magnum, Lucas Corso, Harry Dresden, Albert Campion, Nero Wolfe, Auguste Dupin, Jacques Clouseau, Dale Cooper, Will Graham, Philip Marlowe, and Clancy Wiggum. They worked their respective cocks fervently until each shot their hot man juice onto a short, squat black falcon secured in the center of their masturbatory circus on its suction-cupped base.

Wilmer felt calmer.

In room 18, former child prodigy Nancy Drew and Sherlock Holmes sat on the floor fully clothed and snorting platonic lines off of a mirrored table with falcon-shaped legs.

Wilmer unzipped his fly and checked on his plastic-encased man-meat. A fine misting of dick and ball sweat fogged the inside of the cage but the WilmHammer was otherwise passive.

In room 14, Kojak held his lollipop aloft with one hand and firmly ensconced his just-as-bald little head in the other while he motorboated Jessica Fletcher, who was gyrating atop Easy Rawlins, reverse cowgirl style.

In room 6, Jessica Rabbit rode Lincoln Rhyme while he circled the room in his candy-apple-red Storm Arrow power chair. He alternated between taking her entire tiny foot into his mouth and enthusiastically tonguing between and around each dainty toe. Amelia Sachs, in a full Tyvek body suit, documented the scene extensively with her camera.

Turning his attention to room 1, Wilmer saw all three doors burst open. A redhead, a blonde, and a brunette—all wearing sensible shoes and conservative black suits—burst in and announced themselves at each other, waving their badges and shouting:

"Dana Scully, FBI!"

"Olivia Dunham, FBI!"

"Clarice Starling, FBI!"

Wilmer could feel the WilmHammer straining against the plastic casing like a kid up against a candy store window.

"What's that?" Dunham asked, gesturing at a mass of fluff in the brunette's arms.

Clarice shifted it from one arm to the other. "Well, you see, I used to live on a farm that slaughtered lamb and sheep and..."

Scully sighed. "Just put it on, why don't you... Or is one of us supposed to wear it?"

Clarice donned the sheep costume and climbed onto the circular plastic-encased bed in the center of the room, legs aloft. Dunham rolled up her sleeve and drenched her hand in lube from the black, falcon-shaped lube dispenser. She inserted first two, then three, then four, then tented all her fingers and thumb together, carefully working them in past her knuckles.

The lamb was indeed screaming. "Yes. Yes! YES!"

"Interesting," Scully said with a cocked eyebrow.

A man with dark, jagged hair wearing a raincoat blustered in on roller skates.

"What the...?" said Dunham, still wrist-deep in Starling.

"Sorry I'm late, Agents! Go Go Gadget Pleasure Devices!" the wobbly, wheeled man shouted. A tongue chainsaw, a two-pronged dildo, and a Hitachi Magic Wand extended from beneath his coat. Dunham (one-handed) and Scully (two-handed) tore off their sensible suits,

Velcro-stripper-style. Scully joined Starling on the bed on all fours, her ginger-haired cunt toward the fucking-machine man, and started using her hands and mouth on both the sheep and the sheep fister.

Inspector Gadget rolled over to the writhing, moaning mass of federal agency. He angled the duodildos up between Dunham's legs, started up the tongue-saw on Scully, and seemed to be looking for somewhere on the sheep to use the Hitachi.

Wilmer turned away quickly.

He could feel the WilmHammer plotting its inevitable escape like a big-screen villain in a poorly-thought-out transparent cage. He quickly muted the sound and minimized room 1. He stared longingly at the clock and squirmed damply in his seat.

At four minutes past quitting time, Wilmer's relief shambled in. He was an older white guy in an overcoat and trousers, with an unruly mass of gray hair. He had a cigarette hanging from his lower lip.

Wilmer gathered his things and prepared to head out into the foggy San Francisco night. Before he made it to the door, his replacement stopped him.

"Wilmer, uh…just one more thing…"

Wilmer turned back to see the man standing before him, his coat open and without a stitch on from neck to shin. His collar wasn't attached to a shirt. His "trousers" were held up by an intricate system of garters. A string with a small key on it was looped over his surprisingly majestic cock.

"Thanks, Columbo," Wilmer said as he retrieved his CB-10,000 key. "See you tomorrow?"

But Columbo had already turned to the monitors and was softly, almost absently, masturbating as he keyed between the occupied rooms.

# WATCHMEN

## "Nite Owl" by Kate Leth

"Ornithology bores people," he had said, and as soon as the words left his mouth, he felt himself cringing all the way down to his bones.

He was terrible at this.

Dan was a vigilante-turned-bird-expert, and he knew the description wasn't what drove Laurie to unfasten his belt right there on the couch. It was loneliness; it was an impulse, maybe a blind need for comfort. All the same, he wanted to slide into place with her. He ached to feel whole again, was desperate for some kind of control.

His mind raced to the dark places men go when what they see or where they are can't bring them to the edge. A night sky. A rooftop perch. The cold flap of wings and cutting through the howl of sirens below. The old days, when he'd been a legend. Nite Owl, terror in the dark. He shivered, but it wasn't enough. He felt weak and flaccid as just a man, ready to give up and cower away to bed. Then she told him to put on the cape.

Inside the suit he was so much more. The costume made him a god. The goggles, the wings, the firm leather against his skin contrasting the parts exposed, pushing against her. He could hold her, take her. Push his fingers into her mouth and bite at her collarbones, a predatory

animal blind with lust. She moaned beneath him, and her surprise at
his forcefulness only egged him on.

This, he was good at.

When the ship landed, Dan and Laurie disembarked in a haze of
sweat and nostalgia. They'd hatched a plan to rescue Rorschach from
prison—not that he was generally the type to need rescuing—but Dan
was lost in his head. He tried to sleep, watching Laurie's chest rise and
fall under the thin veneer of yellow silk. It was useless.

He went down to the workshop.

"Dan?"

"In here, Laurie."

She hovered in the doorway, sleep clinging to her eyes. It was dark,
too dark, and she was confused. It must have been five in the morning.

"I made you something."

She clicked on the light, her pupils struggling to adjust, and what
she saw did little to ease her. There was Dan; or rather, there was Nite
Owl, sitting at a desk fully costumed, his fingers working thick fabric
through a loop. The steady *thwip-thwip-thwip* of the serger echoed along
the steel walls of what she'd begun to refer to as his underground lair.

"Did you come to bed?"

"I did. I did, Laurie... but I couldn't sleep."

She came to him, draping her arms around the back of his chair. He
wore the goggles even now, threading thick black leather through the
industrial-grade equipment. The needle pounded away at what seemed
like a cape, long and dark, shining opalescent in the dim purple light.
*Thwip, thwip, thwip.*

"Is it a new costume?"

"It is. I..."

He stopped, pulling the long cape away from the needle, snipping
the thread from a loose end. She could see now the make of the thing—
overlapping teardrops of black fabric gave the appearance of feathers,
cascading down the length of it and pooling onto the floor. Wings.
Dark leather wings.

"I made this for you."

She pulled from his outstretched arms a tight black dress, covered over again in the same pattern. Long black gloves with sharpened points at their tips. Boots, which would easily reach to midthigh, were sculpted at the toe to resemble...talons?

"Dan?"

"Laurie..."

He handed her, finally, a cowl. Great, majestic black feathers rose up from the temples, the eyes masked over by shadowed glass. The sculpt came down to a point, over where her nose would lie, a hard ebony beak.

"Dan."

"Laurie?"

She looked into his eyes. His determination had shrunk into fear, realizing with every moment how he had exposed himself with the gesture. Dark, majestic Laurie, careening through the night in search of prey. He could feel himself getting harder and shifted in his seat. He'd overplayed his hand, and he knew, watching her eyes scan the room and her hands drift over the cold leather. She would never.

"Is this what you want?"

She pulled the mask over her head. It disguised her almost completely, presenting unequivocally the countenance of a raven. Austere, governing, ready to strike. Dan felt his hands begin to sweat. She slipped on the dress. Dark feathers overlapped on her curves, her thighs exposed and teasing at him. The talons, the claws at the base of those maddening legs.

"Like this?"

Dan felt his mouth drying as she fastened on the wings. His resembled a cape more classically—he'd often thought he'd been too subtle—but not hers. They rose from her back like dark clouds to menace over him.

"I look like a bird," she said.

"Yes," he gasped.

"You want to have sex with birds."

His hand trembled.

"No...no. Not like that, not..." It was hard to speak, her standing there looking like she did, all her soft corners sharpened by the angles of the costume and the beak and those feathers. God, those feathers.

"You want to have sex with me while we're dressed as birds."

He felt himself choke, small guttural sounds unfurling from his lips. He was glad she couldn't see his face, not all of it. The flush on his cheeks burned under his mask.

"Is that...so wrong?"

She moved to him, leather rustling as she closed the short gap between their bodies. He wondered if she could feel the heat pulsing from his entire being. That beak...

Laurie took his gloved hand, pulling the thick brown material off his fingers slowly. She held it in her teeth. Her hand guided his, caressing her soft down, reaching for the warmth between her legs. She was wet, terribly so. She pushed his fingers in. Her wings brushed his arm. He moaned.

"Caw, caw."

Dan's eyes flashed open, his cock suddenly aching against the front of his pants. Had she really—

"Caw, caw."

She flapped her wings, her head cocked to the side, studying him like an abandoned French fry on a waterfront pier.

"L-Laurie?" He stammered through her name.

She reached for him, running her gloved hands determinedly over his unyielding erection. He'd nearly forgotten his fingers, dripping with her, and on remembering began to run circles around her clit. Her knees trembled.

"I need you to fuck me, Nite Owl."

She unclasped the belt of his costume, reaching for him. He grabbed her hand, stopping her, and their beaks clacked as she looked up in question at his protest.

"Hold on," he begged.

He pressed a button on the sewing desk, and a section of what had appeared to be a seamless wall began to retract. A darkened room revealed itself opposite them. Laurie craned her neck to see. He pushed his fingers inside her again, harder this time, catching her off guard and forcing a stammering moan.

"I've got a nest."

## "Silhouette" by Jeffrey Cranor

There are rules about this job, you know.

Like first off don't tell anyone your real name. That's dangerous for a superhero. Unless your name is Lala La [big kissing sound] and you're repeating it into my twat, shut your blowhole.

We use code names. Superhero names. To protect our identities but also to sound powerful or intimidating or sexy. Like me...I chose "the Silhouette" because it's dark and mysterious, like a backlit feminine figure in a street corner window or like a suggestive hand puppet.

It's important to choose a name that reflects your talent or your affect or one that's just plain menacing. The easiest way to come up with a name is combine an adjective describing your genitalia with your favorite social cause. That's how Hooded Justice chose his name. It's pretty easy. So like you [points to audience member]. You could be Kegel-Clinching Equality. And you: the Turgid Vegan. And you: Moist Health Care Reform.

But that's only if you're totally out of ideas. A better way is to come up with a costume first. Like Nite Owl. That's a good name. Haunting, wise, stealthy. He first devised his outfit...Actually that's a terrible example. I'm not sure what tight gold shorts, a sleep mask, butterfly collars, and an Amelia Earhart hat make you. It's something, but it's not an owl.

I'll give him this—it looked comfortable. And comfort's a big part of crime fighting. For example, once I was tailing a couple of crooks trying to steal a prized jewel from a museum. I needed to sneak into dark corners and spy on them. So I chose comfy shoes that don't squeak.

The crooks were wearing tight black leggings and deep V-neck tops revealing firm but felonious breasts that I wanted to caress until they repented for their crimes. This was a very smart getup on their part, but I was wearing a fitting tube top—simple to move in, breathable, but also easy to flip down when I wanted to teach this dastardly duo a couple of things...about my couple of things.

Once they saw me, the criminals moaned in terror. I grabbed one of them by the hair and she sighed, "No! I mean yes! I mean no!" And the other grabbed my hair and I breathed, "Yes! I mean no!" and then I was in her mouth, wrestling her tongue with my own to the soft pink ground, a little hint for the real kissing yet to come. "Yet to come," I whispered, pulling my unmasked face away from her raccoon-styled, red sparkling eyeliner and glistening lower lip.

She started kissing her partner in crime, teaching her lips the lesson I just taught her own.

Another thing. You'll want shorts that are flexible enough for flying scissor kicks, something that makes it easy to get your thighs around a criminal's face. But not so tight they get hung up on your ankles as you're working over these two wet-lipped, moon-hipped, unzipped, pussy burglars.

Those two fought hard. They fought with fists and tongues afire. I had one thief pinned beneath my hips. She was trying to get me off with her tongue. I really had her, but then...she discovered my kryptonite. No one had ever found my kryptonite. A decade of fighting male archnemeses, and not one ever found my fucking kryptonite. My only recourse was to rhythmically twirl my hips and groan in order to keep her incapacitated. She put out an angry, wet, valiant struggle.

Another good costume tip. File your nails. A lot of people get caught up in gloves and rings. But a good superhero should file their nails into sharp points. Don't get bogged down in colored polish. Red, blue, that minty green shit everyone's doing now, little pictures of cats. Fine, fine whatever. Just make the nails sharp.

Because when you're in the fight of your life with criminal masterminds, every little edge helps. So I had the one pinned down, and the other tried to get away. I leaned back and caught her ankles with my hands, bringing her to all fours. I pulled her toward me and used my sharpened claws to slowly split open her protective costume. The tight top wet from sweat tore a wider and wider V, revealing to me the widest and wettest V I had ever seen.

She pressed her tits to my face, blinding and suffocating me. Her sidekick worked her tongue so deeply, so gently, so assertively. She knew where everything was, how much longer could I...NO! I managed to get my face around to one breast, and I knew she was expecting me to kiss, to suck, but instead I touched her nipple with my lips and blew. So lightly, so softly. She giggled and flinched away.

Another thing. Always wear a belt. You can flick it off quickly and threaten and tease your enemies with this makeshift whip.

I lifted her up, snaked off my belt, and tied her hands behind her back. While the one under me had almost defeated me, my kryptonite was taut and green and glowing and oh I think I've got enough air in there to just...Can I?

Yes. A powerful queef filled her face and vanquished her mood. She turned her head and gagged. I tied them both up back to back. I returned the diamond to the museum and stood over them, belt at my naked side, the insides of my legs bright with saliva and justice. "V is for victory," I said.

I was about to punish them. Punish them for their sins when one of them said, "Zack Snyder."

No! It was the safe word! And I had to let them go.

Until next time, you dirty thieves. Dirty, dirty thieves. And we all kissed and ran our separate ways through the dark city streets, naked save our comfortable shoes and punch-drunk grins.

So, a good nickname, a good costume. Those are pretty important. What else?

[Takes out cigarette]

Oh yeah, a good superhero has a cigarette in her mouth at all times.

[Places cigarette in mouth]

Intimidation. It lets the criminals know you're cool. That you mean business. And that you just got laid.

# "Malcolm Long" by John Scalzi

## From the Secret Notes of Dr. Malcolm Long, October 25, 1985

First interview with Kovacs, aka Rorschach. He's even more disturbed than I'd heard, but I'm optimistic. A success here could make my reputation. Also, I think he's kind of hot.

I should qualify that. Physically, he's fascinatingly ugly. I could stare at him for hours... except that he stares back, which I find uncomfortable. He never seems to blink. I worry about that. His corneas could dry out. I can see myself leaning over the table, opening my mouth and gently tonguing his eyeballs, bathing them in my lubricating saliva. But I would be the first to admit that would be totally unprofessional and aside the point. Especially for a first session. That's maybe a third session thing.

Nevertheless, I'm convinced I can help him. No problem is beyond the grasp of a good psychoanalyst, and they tell me I'm very good. Good with people. And I am. Especially with short, ugly ginger-haired men with lovely bruises that suggest that he would be enthusiastic with all the fun wrestling parts of the sexy times. Like, I would ask him to tell me what he sees in the Rorschach blots, and he would tell me that he sees the two of us, heavily oiled, grappling right there in the prison conference room, with the guards watching us fight and taking bets on who would penetrate whom first.

And you would think it would be Kovacs, because he's Rorschach, after all—he's used to fighting people and penetrating them, although maybe not in the hot, sexy-times way. But I've got a little weight on him, and I did some Greco-Roman wrestling in high school. I've got some moves, man. And I can be slippery when I want to be. So I see us going for a long, sweaty, hard time before he finally gets the best of me and puts me over this conference room table here, his stiff, villain-fighting cock hovering just outside my quivering, manly love gate. And I'll look up at him and beg, "Be gentle!" and he'll look down and whisper, "No."

This evening at home I asked Gloria if she'd be interested in trying out a strap-on and wrestling around. She looked at me sort of funny.

## October 26, 1985

Kovacs is telling me about how he made his Rorschach mask from fabric taken from a dress made at his garment factory. It made me wonder how much of the fabric was made and if there was enough for a whole Rorschach body suit—a tight-fitting suit that would show off Kovacs's wiry form, the inkblots pooling in all the right places to play across his pecs, the small of his back, his hard, compact buttocks, and his no-doubt-impressive testicles. I can see myself kneeling in front of Kovacs in his Rorschach getup, him opening up his trench coat and telling me to describe what I see down there. And I would tell him it looks like a butterfly with a deliciously fleshy proboscis, before I dove in and took all the nectar I could from him.

Asked Gloria tonight if she wanted to get into skintight bodysuits. She asked me if I was ill.

Later:

The deputy warden just called. Apparently Rorschach was involved in an incident today, with another inmate, in the prison lunchroom, involving hot oil...I don't like to think about it, because it makes me a little jealous. Hot oils, another inmate, all the other inmates watching...

hmmmm, yes. I got distracted enough that I suspect I might have missed a detail or two in what the deputy warden was telling me about the incident. I'll have to go back and ask him about it. Or maybe I won't. I bet my version is better.

Broached the subject of hot oils with Gloria this evening. She told me if I keep this shit up she's going to leave me.

## October 28, 1985

Rorschach told me everything today. But I wasn't listening. I was imagining him and all the other costumed crimefighters getting together to talk about fighting crime but eventually everyone has a drink or two and then the costumes come off—except for the masks, of course—and they all descend into a pile of sweaty, virtuous crimefighting sexy-times. Just then, a cadre of the worst of their supervillains attack, intending to take advantage of the crimefighters at their weakest and most distracted, but when they see the naked hotness, and all the crimefighters available to them for their debased wickedness, they join as well, and for the evening the city of New York is devoid of the sounds of crime or crimefighting, save the moaning of these two groups as they merge, violently, passionately, in an intermingling of costumes and fluids.

And where am I? Well, I'm right in the middle of it. Because Rorschach was so impressed with my skills in helping him that he invited me over to meet with them all as a consultant. And I do. I consult with them all. Thoroughly. One moist, willing, tangy orifice at a time.

I was so taken with this idea that I confess that when Rorschach stopped talking and left the room, I was still distracted and silent. I think it might have looked like I was shocked and depressed by his story. I'll need to have him tell it to me again. I shouldn't have gotten so distracted. That's really unprofessional. But he's just so hot I can't help it.

Gloria reminded me that tonight she's invited Randy and Diana to dinner. I think on the way home I'll stop at the costume store in Times Square and pick up some crimefighter getups for each of us and see if it leads to anything. Honestly, I see no way this plan could ever possibly go wrong.

# Children's Literature

$\mathscr{O}$kay, a quick disclaimer before we get into this section: First thing we do when tackling kids' books is get rid of the kids. What that leaves on the table is comically overwritten grown-ups, anthropomorphized animals, and magical furniture. That's our method. We take children's books and turn them into grown-up books. Then, and only then, we turn them into adult books. We take on all the colorful ridiculata that make the worlds whimsical and menacing while the kids wait outside in the van where they're safe. It's safe to leave kids in vans these days, right? Hard to say. Casey's a parent, but whether or not he's any good at it is beyond the scope of this text.

The books herein hail from the Golden Age of publishing explicitly for children. It flourished as its own genre in the early 1900s, and our selections are squarely the product of that period, the oldest being *The Wonderful Wizard of Oz*, which saw print in 1900, and the most recent is *Charlie and the Chocolate Factory*, published in 1964.

It's always funny to go back to classic children's books as a grown-up. So much of the action takes place in the gulf between the gray world of adulthood with its muttered dissatisfactions and the see everything, feel everything wonder of youth, where a vintage armoire can be a portal to another world and not just an heirloom to squabble over when an uncle's estate goes into probate. Through these books we can glimpse adults with bills and bland grown-up lives mining nostalgia and the gleaming eyes of their nieces and nephews for a glimpse of a lost moment in their lives that they can hardly remember.

We can also glimpse the first stirrings of romance in that hazy moment of our own lives. Not just the chivalric romance of the Pevensies and the Lost Boys as they tackle evils both subtle and outsized, but also kiss-kiss romance and all that gross stuff from when we were just starting to feel dumb things and not know what we should do about them. In these books we find the seeds of our secret wishes and humiliating crushes, and through it all we're left to consider, being adults and all, that most of those seeds were sewn by weird grown-up dudes in stodgy times we can barely relate to.

Apologies if you hadn't considered that.

We're starting with *Peter Pan*. So you'll want to kick off your shoes and knowledge of physics and fly away with us to a land where the boys are off adventuring and, you know, being fully autonomous characters while the ladies tag along and put food on the table. We kid! Of course the female characters each have battles of their own, boldly fighting for the attention of the boys.

From Neverland we take a river cruise through *The Wind in the Willows*. A note about that piece: the writer is Sean Chiki, dear friend and Booksmith alum, and he designed our original logo. He's a quiet, kind sort of fellow who wore a vest and a pocket watch to work every day, which proves that no matter how much you think you know someone, they might turn out to be the kind of person who can churn out a ribald tale of Lady Churchill getting rogered in Ratty's boat.

A short cyclone ride spirits us to *The Wonderful Wizard of Oz* next. This is a children's book containing mostly strange adult characters, making it particularly ripe for our purposes. Once their adventures in Oz are over, the Cowardly Lion goes off to find himself at a furry convention (natch), and the Tin Woodman gets into the real reasons he chopped off all his extremities.

Oof! After all that adventure, we could use a nap. Good thing there's plenty of room in bed with the elders in *Charlie and the Chocolate Factory*. Grandpa Joe's on hand to regale us with tales of his multiple failings—not least of which being how he insists that Charlie brush his teeth BEFORE going to a candy factory.

That leaves a certain titular wardrobe to close the door on this, our most magical section. Yes, we've got a lion and a witch on tap, but we've also got an odd couple of FBI agents, a Hyborian Age MRA, and a polite beaver looking to spice things up in the old dam.

But let's not get too far ahead of ourselves. First we need to talk about crocodile dicks. Presenting: *Peter Pan*.

# PETER PAN

## "Taint Misbehavin' on the High Seas" Peter Pan by Rose Garrett

As the sun squatted low over the horizon and dusk settled over Neverland, Smee stood with a hand on the rail of the good ship *Jolly Roger*. "Oh, to be a pirate," he mused, "plowing the impetuous seas with a spray-soaked bow…"

"Avast!" came the terrifying roar of Smee's captain. The diminutive bo'sun blanched as Captain Hook, all six-foot-four of him, resplendent in the fearsomest of pirate's garb, used his fearful iron namesake to hoist the pudgy Irishman to his sun-ravaged face.

The captain's knickers, painstakingly washed and ironed by Smee earlier that day, seemed to be in a knot. "Enjoying the sunset, are we?" Hook snarled. "You pathetic, codswalloping, toadmunching, son of a footman's goat! How can you stand there with that smile in your fat head, with the Indian princess and that devilish flying boy escaped yet again from our piratical clutches?!"

Smee would admit the battle at the lagoon had not ended well for Hook and his crew of scurvy miscreants. But ever the faithful bo'sun, he feared Hook's attentions too often turned toward that irritatingly youthful scamp, Peter Pan, even to the detriment of his health. Smee observed that Hook's luxurious wig was askew, his eyes wild and bloodshot, and worse: Smee felt sure that Hook had once again forgotten to take his blood pressure medication.

While serving his time as a lowly cabin boy aboard a vessel captained by the Dread Pirate Dirty Sanchez, Smee had learned many a handy seaman trick. Now he determined to calm the captain's rage and restore him his healthful glow, even if it meant making the mercurial Hook, for at least one night, his love slave.

He thought fast: though mocked by the ship's crew for his affable manner and penchant for striped boatneck tees, which he'd adopted from a Venetian before skewering him in a tavern brawl, Smee stowed at least some cunning beneath his scarlet cap.

"Captain, puh-puh-please forgive me, perhaps a hot bath and a dash of Bordeaux might help you to recover from this most grievous disappointment?" Smee asked, adopting his most obsequious manner and leading Hook toward the captain's lavish quarters. There, he settled Hook into an armchair, opened a bottle of the finest vintage a cutlass could plunder, and deftly affixed the cork to the captain's needle-sharp hook.

So preoccupied was Hook by Pan's latest caper, he barely noticed as Smee went to his knees to remove the captain's black leather boots, then set to work on Hook's intricately laced codpiece.

Hook sighed as the wine began to sooth him, relaxing into his chair as the most pleasant sensation began to spread throughout his body. Startled, he glanced down to see Smee loose his swollen flagpole from its confinement and set his industrious bo'sun's hands to work upon the captain's formidable manhood.

"This is queer," Hook gasped, though in protest or acquiescence, even he did not know. Under the ministrations of the ever-dutiful Smee, his tender skull and crossbones now stood at full mast, and Hook settled back into the chair, ready to let the subservient Smee complete the job. Smee looked up at the captain and paused, a sly smile playing upon his lips. "Now, James," he said. "You didn't think it would be time to fire a shot from Long Tom so soon?"

Hook sputtered in outrage. Ay, he had nicknamed his member after the *Jolly Roger*'s prolific cannon, but the name was only uttered in the privacy of his chambers, when he took Long Tom out before a mirror to dangle picturesquely in the soft glow of candlelight. How dare Smee know his secret and call him by his Christian name at that! But before he could slash the insubordinate Smee, he felt a tickle more fearsome than that of his hook, as Smee navigated southward and nuzzled Hook's tender, hairy Neverland.

Smee's spectacles fogged as his eager mouth found Hook's taint, humid as the island's deepest jungle. His tongue fought valiantly to part the pirate's perineal pelt, rank as a Lost Boy's unwashed bearskin. And even as Hook squirmed, Smee dove deeper into the dastardly captain's uncharted dotus.

Where anger had moved Hook a moment before, his devious mind was now empty of all thought. Scrotal squeals of pure ecstasy escaped his mouth as Smee expertly laved the captain's shuddering nifkin.

But though Hook quivered with pleasure, he was not to find satisfaction just yet, as Smee soon ceased his activities and stood up. No longer the submissive servant, he loosened his belt. "Turn around, James," he commanded, "and prepare to meet Johnny Corkscrew."

Hook, master and commander no more, meekly obeyed, even as he smelled the familiar scent of coconut butter, which he used habitually to groom his mustache, and felt Smee's fingers creep upon his untouched land starfish.

"Now," Smee intoned gleefully, "ready the poop deck." Without further preamble, Smee drove his rigid plank into Hook's shadowy treasure trove, just as a wave caught the *Jolly Roger* and the ship began rolling in its berth. As the deck rocked beneath them, Smee's not ungentle entry grew in urgency, each thrust winning a throaty moan of assent from the captain.

"What's my name?" Smee growled, but Hook did not answer. "WHAT'S MY NAME?" Smee cried again, but there was no time for response, as the ship lurched and both Johnny Corkscrew and Long Tom erupted with a salty spray that only two seasoned seamen could muster.

After a moment, Smee gently led the stunned Hook to the captain's fur-strewn bed, where the exhausted pirates collapsed in each other's arms.

"Odds bobs," James murmured huskily, and as Smee bent to kiss the captain's mustachioed lips, he whispered the name "Seamus" softly in his ear.

## "Tinkerbell's Fuck Party" John William

*Once inside a forest clearing lived a race of fairy beings,*
*Mere inches tall, with gossamer wings and voices none could soon forget.*
*Tinkerbell was a busty lass, and Tootsie bore a shapely ass,*
*While sweet Tallulah brimmed with sass, and with them now our stage is set.*
*We've only got a thousand words, the story has not started yet;*
*Three named characters are all you get.*
*A fairy's brain, if truth be told, can only one emotion hold,*
*Her temper running hot and cold, capricious as a gust of wind.*
*One minute she'll be quite serene, then fill with rage like none have seen,*
*And switch it off like a machine as if upon some passing whim.*
*Then barely will a moment pass before the cycle starts again.*
*It's enough to drive you 'round the bend.*
*We would call this, in reality, a borderline personality,*
*And in all eventuality, medicate those crazy fae.*
*But fairies, they live in the grand fantasia of Neverland,*
*So the audience must understand they cope with it in other ways:*
*They make sure only fun and pleasure ever fill their fairy days.*
*In other words, they fuck in spades.*
*Oh, the blustering bacchanalia of flying fairy genitalia,*
*Of pixies in their sex regalia making whoopee in the grasses.*
*They jam their tongues into moist places, blow elfin loads on spritely faces,*
*And tangled up in strange embraces, fuck each other in the asses.*

*All this aerial copulation leaves them stickier than molasses.*
*Their humping prowess none surpasses.*
*One day, while playing with their toys, the fairies heard a curious noise,*
*Drowning out their cries of joy, coming from the trees beyond.*
*The sound of sorrow's tears falling roused the fairies from their balling,*
*An interruption so galling they knew at once they must respond.*
*And yet they could not source the sound that echoed over stream and pond,*
*Though they scoured branch and frond.*
*While at the sound the fairies pondered, a grieving donkey sadly sauntered,*
*Into the magic glen he wandered with his tail swinging low.*
*"Donkey," they said, "what's the matter? We have seen no creature sadder,*
*Perhaps now it will make you gladder to explain what's vexed you so?*
*Then mayhap you shall fall silent, and back to fucking we will go.*
*Tell us now your tale of woe."*
*And the donkey said:*
*"Forgive me, fairies, I didn't mean to interrupt your orgy scene,*
*But the past few days have been a bit traumatic for yours truly.*
*My one and only donkey love, with whom I fit like hand in glove,*
*Has lately given me the shove, and run off with some big-horned mulie,*
*Leaving me a sobbing mess whose heart has been broken unduly.*
*How could love treat me so cruelly?"*
*And the fairies said:*
*"We have no time for such sad dealings; they leave our minuscule brains reeling*
*So we commit ourselves to feeling only pleasure, as you'll see.*
*Let us show you, faithful burro, and your brow it will unfurrow.*
*Soon you will forget your sorrow, so great will your delight be.*
*We'll teach you how to never feel anything but felicity,*
*Till you collapse in ecstasy."*
*Then the fairies, right and quick, did flutter 'round the donkey's dick,*
*And with their tongues proceed to lick and suck his bone relentlessly.*
*They gave his asshole such a rimming it sent his donkey head 'a spinning,*
*While he stood stupidly grinning at his newfound ecstasy.*
*And their slutty ministrations left him moaning breathlessly.*
*He hoped they'd go on endlessly.*

*Then the donkey, his heart thrumming, let out a bray and started coming,*
*Sending jets of semen pumping on a nearby flowerbed.*
*So great, the pleasure in his dick, it even caused his legs to kick,*
*His back hoof flying out so quick, it struck poor Tootsie in the head.*
*The helpless fairies watched in horror as their good friend Tootsie bled.*
*Then, gravely, they pronounced her dead.*
*"Oh what a monstrous affair," the donkey said, in deep despair.*
*"Is there no way to repair the damage to this fairy sweet?"*
*"There's one sure way," Tinkerbell said, "to raise a fairy from the dead:*
*Just clap your hands above your head and fill your heart with true belief.*
*The power of the true believer's always mightier than grief,*
*So from death she'll find relief."*
*The fairies circled in a ring, arm in arm and wing to wing,*
*And hoped with clapping hands to bring the fallen Tootsie back alive.*
*So they clapped, and maybe you will kindly lend a hand or two.*
*It's the least that you could do to help this poor fairy survive.*
*Clap, you motherfuckers, clap, unless you want Tootsie to die . . .*
*And we shall see if she'll revive.*
*Alas poor Tootsie got no better; she was dead and getting deader,*
*Till Tinkerbell, being quite clever, understood what must be done.*
*She said "'Tis not our hands we need to drive away this evil deed;*
*It is something else indeed that we must clap to wake her up.*
*To harness magic stronger even than belief will be no stunt;*
*Fairies, you must clap your cunts!"*
*In peals, in waves, in droves, in batches, the clarion call of flapping snatches*
*Echoed through the leafy branches like the songs of tiny sirens.*
*And the magic of their belief, born aloft on fairy queefs,*
*Reclaimed the fairies from their grief, and shook the air with winds quite violent.*
*The audience should understand their help in this is not required.*
*Please keep your pussies set to silent.*
*As if from sleep Tootsie was woken, and her lids did flutter open,*
*Upon her face a smile had broken, the spark of life in her eyes flashing.*
*"Fairy friends," she said to them, "you've saved me with your flapping quims,*
*But now that all is right again, let us get back to cooter smashing."*

*And just like that the fairies leapt right back into the throes of passion,*
*And all of that hot donkey action.*
*And so now must our tale end, the fairies and their newfound friend*
*Writhing naked in the glen, with hand on crotch and tongue on breast.*
*But should your own path ever wind, and in such forests yourself find,*
*With creatures of the fairy kind, remember what was here expressed:*
*That though she may be kind of nuts, as our friend Donkey can attest,*
*A fairy's always DTF.*

# "The Crocodile" by Andrew Dudley

There are so many strange and exciting penises in the animal kingdom.

The blue whale, for example, sports the world's biggest dick, an eight-foot-long jizz cannon that can shoot thirty-five pints in a single load.

The human boner, by comparison, is but a turgid little breadstick. It's big enough to get the job done (well, usually—wink!) but discreet enough to tuck under a waistband at, say, children's birthday parties or funerals.

Have you ever seen a panda bear's dong? Neither has a panda bear. It's just a tiny nubbin, buried beneath the bear's celebrated muffin top. Neither grower nor shower, the panda and his tiny dick can barely penetrate a mate when they find one, which is never. Basically, this species is fucked.

And then there's the crocodile.

The crocodile's penis is special for one reason: It is constantly erect. It remains hidden inside the animal's body until he's ready for sexy time, then springs out without warning, like a cum-spewing jack-in-the-box.

While this sounds fun, imagine actually being a crocodile. You're toting a forever-engorged member, roaming the lonely waters in search

of a mate. Such was the frustrating life of our protagonist, the Neverland crocodile. Pirates mistook his constant lurking for menace; in fact,
he was just super duper horny.

One sunny afternoon, the crocodile and his raging boner were troll-
ing the waters of Mermaids' Lagoon. As he neared the shore, he spotted
two figures lounging on a rock: Captain Hook and Smee.

"Okay, Captain, 'Fuck, Marry, Kill,'" Smee said. "Tiger Lily, Tin-
ker Bell, Wendy."

Hook thought for a moment. "Well I'd just kill all of them, obviously."

Just then, they froze. In the distance, they heard the terrifying
*tick-tock* sound they knew so well. It was the approaching crocodile,
which had once eaten a clock; this was never really explained.

"Hear that, Captain? Here comes the croc!" Smee squealed. "Shoot
him with your pistol!"

"Nay, Smee," replied Captain Hook, eagerly taking off his musty
cloak.

"Aye, stab him with your sword, Captain!"

"Nay, Smee," said Hook, unbuttoning his musty pirate's blouse.

"Then what, Captain?"

"I'll set a trap, Smee!" Hook snarled, unbuckling his belt and pulling down his musty velvet pants.

"Uh...what?" Smee mumbled, transfixed by Hook's tangle of aged
genitals.

"Crocodiles are extremely horny, Smee. Everybody knows that. So,
I'll lie here waiting, naked, like an irresistible fucktoy. The crocodile
will approach, and when he gets close, I'll cut off his head with my
hook!"

"Brilliant!" Smee clapped and giggled with delight.

By now Hook had fully disrobed, his weird drooping breasts and
shapeless buttocks glistening in the Neversun. He lay on the beach,
smirking, tickling his ancient balls. To him, this was seduction.

And it worked. The crocodile, watching from afar, was aroused.
Hook wasn't much to look at, sure. Clearly he wasn't even a crocodile.
But, holes were holes.

The crocodile emerged from the water, crawling up the beach toward Hook. Step by step he got closer, the tick-tock growing ever louder.

"That's right, come and get it," whispered Hook, running the fingers of his good hand through his filthy nest of pubic hair.

The croc, now just a few feet away, was indeed horny as fuck. Sensing that copulation was imminent, his perma-boner, which had been throbbing inside his body, sprang out of its gopher hole.

"WHOA, WHOA," said Hook, never having seen a crocadildo before.

"Look at that!" shouted Smee, who was sitting nearby, feverishly masturbating. "Looks like a butternut squash!"

"There is NO WAY that's going inside me," Hook insisted. "No, croc, it is MY unusual cock that shall go inside YOU!" he said, making the "roll over" motion with his hand.

The croc had never bottomed before, but he was open-minded, and as we've already established, like, CRAZY horny.

And so the crocodile rolled onto his back, his raging boner still exposed. Hook approached, gingerly climbing atop the submissive beast.

"You've got him now," Smee exploded. "Kill him!"

"Nay, not quite yet, Smee."

"But you're literally on top of him, Captain!" Smee shouted. "Just slit his throat and we'll go get some brunch!"

"Hush!" Hook sputtered. For a more pressing matter had arisen. Hook looked down at his own flaccid, bescabbed penis. He may have been captain of the *Jolly Roger*, but he was apparently not captain of his OWN jolly roger. Meaning, his unresponsive schlong.

"Ah." Smee smirked. "Looks like somebody's got a REPTILE dysfunction."

Hook looked at Smee like, "GUUUUUUUURL..."

Sensing Hook's impotence, the crocodile took matters into his own hands, meaning his mouth. Before Hook knew it, the croc was giving his limp ding-dong what may have been the world's toothiest head.

"Ow ow ow ow ow," Hook said, kind of in pain but also not exactly complaining.

"Oh, you've got him now, Captain!" said Smee, now aggressively fingering his own butthole. "Cut off his head!"

Hook ignored Smee. The blood was now flowing to his penis, ensconced as it was in the crocodile's mouth. It wasn't particularly satisfying for either of them—kind of like a dinosaur sucking a pacifier—but it was more action than Hook had gotten in years, and he was digging it.

"Hey, Captain, remember the time he swallowed your clock?" said Smee, now vigorously fucking a coconut.

Hook was fully erect. He looked down at the crocodile—its kind eyes, its generous mouth. *Look at his taut, hairless body*, Hook thought. *Look at his pearly teeth, his short muscular arms. Why, if he were upright, I might mistake him for one of the Lost Boys. Wait... Is it possible my hatred for children is really a psychosexual attraction? Is my quest to kill this crocodile really a denial of my true desires? Am I basically a pedophile? Because that would make a ton of sense.*

Before he could formulate an answer, the croc chomped down on Hook's penis, biting it clean off, swallowing it whole.

Hook let out a scream that echoed throughout Neverland, a combination of excruciating pain and unbearable heartbreak. For he had just begun to trust and, perhaps, love his long-time adversary. And yet here he was at his most vulnerable—betrayed and decocked. And the crocodile, who had thought he only wanted love, now realized he couldn't fight his lizard brain. In the end he was a predator, and Hook was prey. Salty, saggy, hairy, handless, dickless prey.

As he bled out, Hook took his final revenge. He dug his iron claw into the crocodile's throat, dragging it down to his belly. The mortal enemies died there in a bloody pile, both satisfied in their vengeance, yet unsatisfied in not having ejaculated one last time.

One person who did ejaculate, however, was Smee. He sulked over to Hook's body, sobbing. In an act of respect for his fallen mentor, he pulled his still-erect penis out of the coconut, letting out a halfhearted splooge onto the intertwined corpses.

Then, businesslike, he reached into the crocodile, pulled out the still-ticking clock, and smashed it against a rock.

"Who's captain now, bitches?" Smee boasted to no one in particular.

And with that, he pulled his pants up and waddled off to brunch.

# THE WIND IN THE WILLOWS

It was probably a little cruel to give anyone as earnest as Kenneth Grahame the Shipwreck treatment, but no more cruel than what Disney did with the material. I adore this book for its quiet simplicity. As Ratty says, "There is nothing—absolute nothing—half so much worth doing as simply messing about in boats." So naturally my favorite piece involves Grahame and his chums in a historically accurate orgy of privilege on the water.—Casey

## "Ratty's Boat" by Sean Chiki

### From the Private Diaries of Kenneth Grahame

"I say, Kenny, why do you write all that rot anyway?"

His Royal Highness was eyeing me over the top of his cards. The Prince of Wales, along with myself and Ratty, were at the card table at Boodle's. Toad was greedily shoveling Orange Fool into his gullet while Mole and Badger snored away in their overstuffed wingbacks.

"What do you mean?" I said, a bit taken aback.

"Oh, you know...all that Merrie Olde England nonsense...tea at four, bluebells in the meadows...Why not write something with a bit of vim?"

"Vim?"

"He means a bit of cock," sputtered Toad, spraying cream and bits of cake.

"Hmmm. Well, what would you suggest?"

The prince leaned back in his chair meditatively, his head wreathed by the smoke of his cheroot.

"Why not write about our boating down at Henley? Jolly fun that was, what."

"Boats," said Ratty. "Yes, I like that."

"I'm not sure that story would suit the dignity of Your Highness," I said as my hand reached reflexively for the small scar on my left temple.

It had been one of those perfect English afternoons—soft breezes whispering through the willows, the river's water gently lapping the banks, etc. You get the picture. Ratty was usually not inclined toward society, but the Henley Royal Regatta was one exception. He'd brought out his favorite skiff, and as Toad and the Prince had been up to Oxford together, we had an open invitation to His Highness's pavilion, down in front of the Red Lion.

The race was over and we'd all enjoyed our day immensely. I was helping Ratty prepare the boat for our return to Cookham Dean, when a great hullabaloo arose from up the bank. We turned to see Toad and the prince, looking very much like fat schoolboys and both clearly well in their cups. On the prince's arm was his amour, the Lady Churchill, giggling like an addle-brained moppet.

"What ho, you fellows!" shouted the prince. "I'm commandeering this vessel by right of the Royal Navy!"

"Oh, Bertie," cried Lady C, "what a wascal you ahw!"

"We're all heading to Toady's pile for the weekend. Be good chaps and give us a row up the river, what."

Ratty's skiff was crowded as it was but we made room best we could for our three additionals.

"In you go now, Jenny, that's a gel!" said the prince.

She squealed as he grabbed a handful of her bustle, while helping her up over the gunwale. I planted myself at the tiller and Ratty took the sculls, pulling us out into the stream. The prince was quite stewed. He leered at Lady Churchill, while a line of drool crept out along the cheroot he held loosely between his lips.

"Come over here, Jenny," he slurred, "sit on my lap. Let me take your temperature."

Lady C giggled but refused to move.

"Here now, you mincing little bint...," he slobbered, rocking the boat as he lumbered toward her.

"Oh, you beast!" cried the lady.

With deft movements far exceeding what one so intoxicated should be capable, he'd managed to undo his fly and lift her skirts from behind. Popping the buttons on the front of her dress, he took her plentiful bosom in his other hammy hand.

"There now...how's that? You like a bit of the Royal Prerogative, don't you, my dolly?"

"Oh, Bertie yes, woger me! Woger me good!"

I glanced at Toad and saw that strange expression come over him— the one we knew, of which no good would come. He chewed his cheroot, muttering unintelligibly.

"Bertie," said Lady Churchill with a tone of concern, "what's wong? Are you quite all wight?"

He was clearly not—all in a sweat and breathing heavily. He disengaged his limp pudenda and fell back onto the bench.

"No, no," he said, "I'm fine. But my Old Fellow seems to have taken forty winks. Must be all the rum punch. Speaking of...I must see to the royal wee."

And without further ado, he stood up, aimed his honorable member over the saxboard, and added his own tributary to the Thames.

"Weally, Bertie! How vulgah!"

"Still fucking stoats and weasels are you, Toady?" the prince jeered while he pissed.

Toad merely grunted and chewed on his cheroot.

"Toady never stays interested in anything for too long," said Ratty.

"Oh," said the prince, "then what are you fucking these days?"

As if in answer, Lady Churchill let loose with a shriek.

"Oh! You bwute! You bwute!"

Toad had quickly managed to mount Lady C and we watched in wonder as he rapidly thrust away like the piston of an engine. His eyes were transfixed, and he puffed great plumes of smoke from his cheroot, at regular intervals. It was at this moment that I stepped back from myself, as they say, and objectively took in this absurd scene. Here was a cigar-chomping, three-foot-high amphibian rogering the mother of our future prime minister.

The prince swung himself around, but being still in mid-spray, painted a wet stripe up the back of Toad's white boating jacket.

"The Deuce!" cried Toad irritably, his spell broken.

"Here you little cretin...I'll not have you doing that to my lady!"

Grabbing Toad by the collar, he tore him from Lady Churchill's posterior with such force that Toad's cheroot went flying from his mouth. The whole boat pitched violently and Lady Churchill fell forward. Ratty found himself with his whiskers firmly wedged between her gloriously exposed poonts.

"Jolly good!" said Ratty in delight. "I say, do you smell something burning?"

The prince, seeing Lady Churchill prone thus, with her rump in the air, reached for his pego, which had quite come back to vigor and was valiantly thrust to the fore.

"My brush always stiffens," he bellowed, "at the sight of a freshly gessoed canvas!"

But before he could mount, the prince roared in outrage.

"What the bloody deuce?!"

Toad, although quite fat, was also very nimble and, in a flash, had managed to come around and launch a rear assault on the prince himself. His Highness gasped in indignation as Toady yelped and thrust with glee.

"Just like back at the old school, eh, Bertie?"

"Help! Help! I'm abwaze!"

It was Lady Churchill. She jumped off of Ratty in a panic. Toad's cigar had landed in the mess of crepe, on the top of her bonnet, setting it fully alight. As she scrambled about in terror, the boat rocked up on its side, sending us all over into the drink. One of the sculls knocked me square in the head, just as I came to the surface, sputtering for breath.

The room fell silent as we all, each of us, mused over our memories of the day. My eyes happened to fall on a portrait of young Winston, recently made a member. I pondered for a moment his squat toadlike features, then put the thought right out of my head.

"Yes," said the prince, "best not to write about that one."

# THE WONDERFUL
# WIZARD OF OZ

## "The Tin Woodsman" by Colin Winnette

Dotty was no saint, and I should have seen it coming. When I met her, she was traveling with a pack of wild things, dumb cowards she dragged around to feed her insatiable lust. She kept a dog in tow, too, which I still can't quite stomach. But that was the thing about her: She was unpredictable. Unpredictable and alive and loose.

It didn't take much to solder me to her. When we first met, I was sore and all but rusted shut from a late night in the poppy fields. I'm no saint either, if you hadn't realized, and sometimes you get a little lonely, being the only one of your kind. And sometimes you like a little attention. So sometimes you smoke opium with the Lollipop Guild and let them bukake you before Oz and the whole world. Because, fuck it, you get one life to live. Or that's how I felt until I woke up to find Dotty pressing down upon me.

It was only a sweet, brief exchange that got me head over heels and hunting for a heart to call my own. Dotty's lips met mine and woke me, just as another set of lips met my knee and starting oiling me up. Dotty's pussy drips and drools like a terrier, and it was only a few moments before I was fully greased and ready to rise. That was it, though. At least for that morning. She got me standing, then wandered off. That was the thing about Dotty. She was always looking elsewhere, always on the move. Where she was going, what she was after, I never thought to ask—I just fell in line to follow her, along with all the others.

Hanging with those boys and chasing after Dotty was like trying to bathe three dogs in one bathtub. Everyone kept slipping out and none of us felt like we were getting the attention we deserved. We tried to joke around with one another, pretend as if we were all cool with the way things were going. We had goals of our own; it wasn't just about her. But in truth, we were desperate creatures in hot competition for her affection. Dotty could see it, and she exploited it.

She fucked us privately, whenever a simple itch set in, but she preferred public degradation. It was punishment for our desperation, our neediness, our inability to see her as anything more than a prize to be won. And her favorite game was meant to do nothing less than reveal us for the true filth that we were.

After a long day of walking, she would select one of us, seemingly at random. She would set that one on his back and stand over him, facing away—an angled portion of her perfect ass curving above like a gibbous moon. With thoughtful, attentive strokes, she would work her selection until he was erect, and at the height of his arousal, she would release her… "Yellow Brick Road." Her urine was a thick golden stream, meaty with dehydration from walking all day and most of the night, and we would have the opportunity to fuck her, yes, but only if we could get ourselves up and into her before she was finished and the road had vanished. We were not allowed to touch her with our hands. We were not allowed to move her or reposition her. The task was all but impossible, and we were never successful. Regardless, according to the rules, whoever did not spiritedly chant, "Follow the Yellow Brick Road" to the selected participant would be cut from the running for tomorrow's games, thereby losing his opportunity for a glorious coupling with our beloved Dotty. So I was compelled to chant nightly for my sworn enemies, fists churning the piss-thick air, lustful jealousy rattling around inside my empty, metallic chest.

I marveled at Dotty's twisted capacity for punishment, but it was ultimately a hell of my own devising. We could have walked away. We could have left at any moment. But we kept coming back. Some of us were too stupid, maybe, or too cowardly to leave. Me, I was something worse.

One night, when she was loaded on poppy dust and looking for something stiff and hollow, she dragged me into the woods and unlatched the buckles at my waist.

"I want to tell you something," I said, but she didn't listen. She ran her thin tongue along my cool center, her pigtails tickling my rusty thighs.

"I love you," I said as my thin tin dick ratcheted to life. "I love you and it terrifies me because I haven't loved anyone in years. I've been a heartless fool. A loner not caring for anyone or anything that couldn't hurt me or soak me in degradation. I was living moment to moment, thinking I could outrun my pain. I used to be a normal guy, just a woodsman in love, but it ended badly, that first and only other time. I want to be honest with you because I love you, Dotty. But all of this scares me. I lost it when my first love didn't love me back. It hurt so bad, I chopped off my arm to take my mind off the pain. When I didn't feel any better, one arm turned into two. Then a leg. Then the other. Then, finally, my enormous penis. When I was just a woodsman, Dotty, believe me, I had a penis that would tremble the tallest fir in the forest. But the pain of that first love not loving me back just wouldn't go away, and I was brought to ruin by my own axe. A friend rebuilt me from scrap and some kind of magic or whatever, but I begged him to leave out my heart. I never wanted to feel that w—"

"Shhh," she said, "you're ruining it." She slid me inside her and began to pump like a piston.

"But I love you," I told her.

"I know," she said, fucking me with indifferent force. She sighed, repositioned herself to face away from me.

"I'm happy for you," she said, out into the night.

"Why?" I asked, and leaned back because I just couldn't take it anymore, how hard she was fucking me and how sad I was starting to feel in that exact moment, with her fucking me like a vibrator, like a tool.

"You've found something to chase," she said.

"I don't understand," I said.

"You've found something to chase and it's really something," she said. "It's me." She lifted her hair up only to let it fall back across that tablecloth of a dress she refused to take off.

"Whereas I—" she said, but the word broke with a limp orgasm. She fell off me and I came in a few wild spurts across my lap and on the moss at either side of us.

"Me," she sighed, "I've always deep down known that I was chasing nothing."

And a rainbow broke out from between the mountains like nature's ejaculate, fading across the sky.

# "The Cowardly Lion" by Fifi LaFan

The Cowardly Lion pushed up his green visor and sighed. He hadn't had a new lead in weeks, and his job at *Pussy Parade*—New York's rag of record for the town's feline elite—was on the rocks. Subscriptions were down and the pressure was on for a killer story to entice new cats to the pride.

"Ding! You've got mail!" The Cowardly Lion's computer was brought out of its daylong lull to bring him an all-important lead.

"Furballs Unite! Come to Rabbits Center, Midtown West for New York's Inaugural Furry Convention." The e-mail mentioned a fashion show, contests, DJs, and a dance floor, and welcomed all kinds of animals, including one he'd never heard of before: "fandom."

Hmm. The Cowardly Lion certainly had lots of fur and had lusted after the occasional rabbit—though he usually just ate them. This seemed like the perfect feature for *Pussy Parade*'s society section, "Fancy Felines," where he could cover a bunch of furry animals congregating in one place. There was even a dress code: "Non-thong bathing suit is the minimum amount of clothing allowable," and any "'anatomically correct' costumes must be appropriately clothed in public areas."

What animal wouldn't be "anatomically correct"? The Cowardly Lion ran his paw through his Beethoven mane and looked down at his kitty cock. He assured himself that he was just fine, and shrugged. Well, he'd have to cover up, but he could only do the bare minimum, otherwise he'd get fur stroke. He called up Andre Leon Tabby, *Pussy Parade*'s stylist, and got a hold of a pair of tasseled pasties for his manly nips and a red sequin bottom. It wasn't terribly virile, but the sequins on Eartha Kitty's old pleather jumpsuit were a nightmare. Tabby had a warning, though: "I know you—you get into this immersion journalism stuff and then you get carried away. Just get the story and get out."

He registered his name as Maximilian Clawbite—his professional alias and journalistic disguise. His real first name was Maxi, but he liked Maximilian's machismo.

After arriving at Rabbits, Maxi picked up his name tag and took in the scene. Hundreds of fur-covered bodies were all around him: raccoons, foxes, wolves, griffins, coyotes, centaurs, rabbits, more foxes, cheetahs, pandas, some miniature ring-tailed lemurs, and some guy dressed like Pepé Le Pew. Maxi hadn't seen this much fur in a long time. The saliva started pouring out of his wide-open maw.

"No, Maxi, be good," he told himself. "Get the story and get out…"

Maxi was about to head to the bandstand when he was stopped by a foxy lady.

"Hiya, Maximilian. Can I just call you 'Maxi'?"

"Uh…"

"My name is Vixen RooRoo, and you make me feel yiffy." She sauntered up closer to Maxi and thwacked her tail on the floor, swaying her hips. Maxi put out his paw to introduce himself. Vixen shook it and shuddered.

"Oh. My. Gahd. You're a real one."

"Huh?"

"That. Is. So. Hawt."

Vixen got down on all fours and put her rear end up in the air. She started pawing the floor and eyeing Maxi's crotch. She curled her body around and, keeping her rear up, tickled Maxi's cock with her tail. She tickled and tickled and Maxi felt his kitty penis—and all its flail-like spines—growing bigger and bigger.

"Whatchya got under there, Maxi? What are you doing in a Burlesque outfit anyway? You not a manly puss puss?"

Boosh! Maxi's briefs burst open and Rabbits was showered in red sequins as Maxi's kitty cock thudded onto the convention center floor like a big, rubbery, spiked dinosaur tail. Vixen's tongue was hanging out and she was panting, unable to control her enthusiasm for Maxi's genuine felinity.

Vixen asked Maxi if she could go down on him.

"You may, Vixen, you may," he said grandly as she lowered herself on all fours again and began with the tip. Vixen wasn't the only one starstruck by Maxi's bestiality. The furry fandom had turned toward Maxi and were rabid with lust. The ring-tailed lemurs were doing a chain bang while watching Maxi and Vixen.

Although Maxi was enjoying himself, he saw, in the distance, what looked like a mere memory of someone he once craved. A wee canine with glossy black fur was across the convention center, grinding its behind on a unicorn horn. It was Toto, Maxi's beloved buddy bear meat dog. Maxi's cock grew to ginormous proportions at the sight of Toto, which ejected Vixen off his cock and sent her flying across the room with a shrill shriek.

Maxi stomped toward Toto, shunning all journalistic responsibility (not that he hadn't already blown it—no pun intended) after Toto started double teaming, taking one horn in the ass and sucking another one off.

"Nooooooo, Totooooo! You're my meat dog!!" Maxi shouted, stomping across Rabbits.

Toto stopped sucking, met Maxi's gaze, then popped up in the air like a little black balloon, propelled by the rainbows farting out of his butt.

"Maxi!" *Pffft*. "Maxi!" shouted Toto. "How I've missed"—*pop*—"you." *Toot toot*.

"Toto!! Why are you farting rainbows?" Maxi bellowed. "I can't catch you and I want to make love to your little meat dog ass!!"

"Oh, Maxi, that's JUST"—*toot*—"what I would wish!" *Pffft pffft.* "I'm sorry, Maxi, this is what happens"—*pffft*—"when you fuck unicorns!"

*Pop. Toot.*

"What are you doing fucking unicorns anyway?" shouted Maxi. "It's not manly. Now come on, come down here, let me do you right."

"I'm almost"—*toot*—"done"—*pffft*—"I think," Toto said. "Besides, you weren't here, and unicorns"—*toot*—"are magical fucks."

Toto alighted and Maxi thrust him onto the tip of his towering cock. The unicorns returned. One filled Maxi's ass while the other put his horn in Toto's mouth and soon they were grunting and coming a thousand times over, their mutual orgiastic bliss blasting them out of the convention center and landing them in a field of poppies.

Dazed, Toto, Maxi, and the two unicorns stared at each other, all their cocks plump, rosy, and sopping wet with juices.

"Look, over there," said Toto dreamily.

Marching toward them was the furry fandom en masse. Within a few feet they bowed down before the two unicorns, Toto and Maxi.

"We followed you, o-o-over the rainbow," said the furries. "We have never seen the like of you. We came here to be your yif, we mean, your sex slaves."

And the unicorns, Toto and Maxi, lay back and got hella laid.

# CHARLIE AND THE CHOCOLATE FACTORY

With kids' books, our writers tend to double down on the silliness and the whimsy to make some-thing grotesquely over the top. While the rest of the show had cartoon cereal mascots and B-list Disney characters, Colin's piece was DARK, gritty, almost noir-like in tone. What's the adult equivalent to a candy habit? A sex addiction with a side of cocaine, natch.—AMY

## "Grandpa Joe" by Colin Winnette

Hello, my name is Joe Bucket—no limericks, please—and I'm an addict. I'm mailing this in and having this guy read it because my life is hell. But more on that later. I've been clean for...six years. Wow. I mean, for a while there I was as addicted to breaking my sobriety as I was to anything you could smoke, snort, or shoot. But things have slowed down lately. It's good. You get old, you get a little sick, a little weak, and you slow down. I mean, my addiction's out there in the parking lot doing cock push-ups and chugging Vegemite, but I've been retired to "the bed" for something like…shit. Seven years. Seven and counting. Seven years ago my boy and his wretched wife claimed Josephine and I were too "old and tired" for a place of our own, and they plopped us on a stinking bed in their miserable apartment, along with George and Georgina. And once they set us down, there was no good reason to get back up. When I'm up, I'm trouble. But in "the bed," well…six fucking years clean, man. I should get a shot and a screw just for living that long, on top of the eighty I was already carrying around with me.

I'm kidding.

George and Georgina are decent people, but they're boring. You'd think being eternally confined to a bed with your wife and another couple would turn into some kind of endlessly sexy fuck and swap party, but that's because you're all a bunch of young assholes. The biggest thrill I get these days comes whenever my wife sleepily throws a leg over mine and I get a cool, cruel chill from reprimanding her.

"Dorothy, climb off. Your crotch feels like a deflated football."

Nobody wants it around there, not even me. And I always want it. But as I'm writing this, Josephine's leaking God-knows-what from her nethers and that's of course pooling beneath us. But no one's going to say anything about it. We all leak at some point or another, different fluids but in equal measure. It's just the way it is. So, like I said, nobody wants it around here. Not even me.

My thing was always excess. Of any kind. Fucking, sucking, ass-licking, shooting shit, shoving shit up your ass, vodka enemas, gargling cum mixed with cocaine and codeine, fuck it. I liked to mix it up. And I was durable, man. I could take it. I was looking to fucking blast off and I wouldn't even check the view until I was orbiting Uranus.

That guy knows what I'm talking about.

Forgive an old man a joke or two. At my age, it's the only comfort you can provide people: letting them shrug off a dumb joke and feel like they're tolerant, good people. You've all done it. I did it all the fucking time. I still do it. These goddamn aneurisms I call bedmates would be the death of me if it weren't for my false sense of superiority.

Look, I know I could take another hit. I know I could fuck another whore, let her fuck me. Let her open me up. I know I could take it and take it harder and longer than I've ever taken it. I know I could shower these octogenarians with cum and sign it Jackson Pollock in piss. I mean, I've got life left in me. But I don't know if I've got another recovery in me.

So I stay in "the bed" and shrug off these shitty personalities and their even shittier bowel movements, and I tell myself I'm just a little better than them. Just a little. Me, I'm doing fine, I say. And I write these letters to remind myself that I'm not.

I pray this thing finds its way to the right place, to the right set of hands, and not to someone who'll hold it up in front of a crowd and encourage everyone to laugh at the pathetic old addict with HPV— that's right, warts bigger than my dick ever was—the old drunk who drove his secret second family out to Florida some thirty years ago and abandoned them in a motel outside Disney World.

One of the steps says I have to reach out to them. Give them my real name. Tell them I'm sorry. Amends, is the step. But when you're a tired old man full of cum and regret, you start to walk pretty goddamn slowly.

I'm getting morbid. I'm getting sad. I wish I could be there to stand in front of you all and say this stuff. I'm better in person. I'm funny, I swear. They've probably got some fat ex-pothead reading this. One of those guys who insists on leading the meetings week after week, regardless of the protocol. Or maybe not.

Guy who's reading this, don't take my bullshit seriously. You're doing a great job, man.

Well. What else? Like, I said, my thing was always excess. I'd go for anything, as long as I could keep doing it and doing it and doing it. But. Nowadays. Dick's broken so the sex addiction's not much of an issue. Nose is rotted out, so cocaine's not appealing. Heroin would be good. I think I would enjoy some heroin, or whatever equivalent they're mixing up these days. Something that just slides into you and makes you not give a fuck. That's the worst thing about being six years sober: how much you start to give a fuck. I care about shit now I wouldn't have thought twice about before. Like my boy's boy, Charlie. I mean, he's a complete shit. We cook up cabbage, right? That's a meal for us. We cook up cabbage and this little shit makes a face at us, like we're not all fucking miserable and eating cabbage. I'm just like, Look, kid, don't make a fucking face. Eat your cabbage. Put your face away. Do you know how much better I used to have it? This ain't my life. This is a fucking cell.

So, this kid, all of a sudden I give a fuck about him. I listen to him. I'll sing a song with him, if I've got the energy. I mean, what is that? Maybe it's love, and I've just never known it like this. Without the fucking part, I mean. Anyway, it's not what I pictured for myself.

But maybe if I keep at these letters and "keep on keeping on" this shitty, boring love will become my new addiction. My new access to excess. Wouldn't that be fucking ironic?

I'm joking again.

You people are good people for hearing me out on all this. I'm going nowhere precise, but just kind of wandering around here at the end, so I'll sign off. Charlie's got some news that's got him more than excited than the day he realized you can fuck a wet roll of toilet paper if you take the cardboard out. And look at me, prick that I am. I'm going to put down this pen and actually hear him out.

# THE LION, THE WITCH, AND THE WARDROBE

## "Professor Digory Kirke" by Sarah Maria Griffin

Here is the thing about being the nephew of a magician. You get used to seeing strange things. If you had a childhood like Digory Kirke's, dipping your hands in pools in magical forests with pretty girls called Polly, awakening entire worlds all by yourself, you become weathered. Hard to stun. Lions? Whatever. Snow witches? Sure.

Professor Kirke was over it. Fauns? Been there, done that. Centaurs? Phhhhht. Giant rats and stone tables and talking ducks with monocles and what have you—Kirke was unflappable. He'd just about shagged them all, over the years. He was exhausted from these magical creatures, these other worlds. He was old now, though. Bespectacled. Mostly impotent.

He never even thought about the wardrobe any longer, really. Folks didn't come around so much anymore. The Pevensie brats got out from under his feet after the war. It was just him and his tomes, dust and all. There was a quietness to them, an antidote to his questionable youth.

But this warm, sunny morning in early summer, a heavy knock came to his door and he dragged his feet to answer it. When he unhooked the latch—like so many enchanted brassier straps of his past—and heaved the great door open, he was faced with two of the most splendorous and beautiful creatures his old eyes had ever fallen upon.

A tall, rugged man with slightly flippy brown hair and a square jaw and a handsome, yet weirdly expressionless face stood in the doorway. He wore a black trench coat and a sharp black suit. Beside him was a short woman with hair the color of fire in a slightly less fabulous suit wearing an expression of utter disgust.

"Can...can I help you?" asked Professor Kirke coyly.

"Fox Mulder, Federal Bureau of Investigation," said the man, his voice gravelly and American.

Rarer than all brands of magical creatures in postwar England. An American. How exciting.

"Dana Scully," said his partner flatly. "We're here to ask you a few questions about a closet, or, excuse me, a wardrobe." She rolled her eyes on *wardrobe*, as though she were saying *unicorn* or *magical lion* or *bullshit*.

There was nothing Kirke liked more than a cynic. Except Americans. American cynics—what a combination. How he would delight in their company.

"Oh? I do, I do certainly have a few of those in the house, although I believe I know the one you want to see. The big one."

Mulder nodded. "We got some word in that the wardrobe in your home has certain properties that other household storage units don't necessarily possess, Professor Kirke." Scully laughed aloud, a bright, scornful "Hah!"

Kirke ushered them eagerly into his extravagant home, delighted, awoken, thrilled. He led them up the creaky stairway and down the landing to the room he had moved his largest wardrobe to, a locked, beautiful room, safe from any antics should the Pevensie sprogs ever come to his home again and take liberties over other worlds, develop a monarchy, and then go and dredge snow and forest all over his fancy carpets.

The room was so lavishly decorated that Scully's eyebrows rose so high they almost left her forehead and ascended to outer space. There

were great lamps, not unlike streetlights, lush bloodred wallpaper, a
fainting couch, and taxidermy running from small cute bunnies to
a great lion skin draped over the four-poster bed in lieu of a blanket.
The lion's eyes were open in something between horror, shock—and—
possibly arousal. (Worry not, dear reader. Aslan is all right. Your
golden savior did not fall to the remorseless lust of Professor Kirke.
This was just another lion that was hanging around on the wrong night
and didn't quite survive his sexual appetite. He couldn't talk or anything. Fret not.)

The wardrobe stood erect and magnificent. Professor Kirke leaned
up against the side of it and looked at the pair of agents over his eyes.

"Here it is."

"Do, do you mind if we take a look inside?" asked Mulder, eyeing
the intensity of the room suspiciously. The air was heavily perfumed.

"Why would I let you do that? Do you have a warrant to search this
premises? Did I not let you in here out of my own common courtesy? I
mean, I have no problem per se, showing you what's inside this wardrobe, if you . . . show me . . . something in return."

Mulder took a slight step back. Scully sighed deeply. This nonsense
again. How she pined to go back to medicine and surgery just so she
didn't have to deal with these lunatics every goddamn day of her life.
Mulder was going to take the bait too. He always did.

"Show you, what, exactly?" asked Mulder.

"Well," purred Kirke, stepping lightly across the room, "I'll let you
see what's inside here, but you have to show me how much you like it.
You know. You wouldn't be here if you weren't excited by the unusual."
He was close to Mulder now. "By the supernatural." Closer again. "By
the magical."

Mulder shrugged his shoulders and shuffled, both slightly aroused
and slightly uncomfortable at the proximity of the old professor—at the
proximity of the possibility of something supernatural happening. He
fucking loved this shit. He was into it. The old man smelled like incense
and trouble.

"You cannot be serious." Scully's voice was flat. She walked over and sat dramatically on the bed, in refusal to participate. "Mulder, can we leave right now? There is so little science in this house that I'm not even sure I can function."

Professor Kirke ignored her and turned away from the tall handsome American and placed his hand on the knob of the wardrobe door. He opened it.

"If you like what you see, show me. Show me how much you like it."

As he opened it, a bright gust of summertime rolled from the doors, lighting the whole room with otherworldly sun shining through the remaining old fur coats (the ones the bloody Pevensie creatures hadn't stolen and wrecked). Mulder was so taken by this magical revelation that he became hard immediately. Professor Kirke noticed and grinned.

"You like that? You like seeing a glimpse of another world."

"Yes," grunted Mulder. "Goddamn it's beautiful. Any…any aliens in there?"

"No, no," said Kirke. "But I'll tell you what is in there, if you show me what's"—he gestured to Mulder's exquisite suit pants—"in there."

Mulder, without any hesitation, opened his fly and removed his throbbing, excellent, American dick. He stroked it carefully, well practiced. Scully put her hands over her face. Why did it always have to be this way? Why couldn't they just arrest some fucking drug dealers, then go to a bar and go home? Why couldn't he just find her sexy? Why wasn't their dreamer/cynic dichotomy enough to turn him on? Why did it have to always be this weird shit? She had simple needs.

"What's in there?" groaned Mulder softly.

"Fauns," purred Professor Kirke.

Mulder gasped.

"Talking. Animals."

Mulder groaned again.

"A kingdom, a vast unknowable kingdom."

Tears awoke at the corners of Mulder's eyes.

"A. Magical. Immortal. Lion."

It was almost too much for the agent to bear and Kirke was hard too.

Scully was bored. She wondered what putting her fingers into her eye sockets would feel like. She'd seen this shit happen a hundred times before.

Mulder stepped forward, majestic American dick in hand, into the wardrobe. When he saw the bright forest ahead of him, he moved his hand faster. God he loved supernatural things. He loved them. He loved them so much—

Kirke pulled him by the shirt collar back into reality just as he stepped over the boundary that separated Narnia from WWII-era England. The sensation of being slightly choked pushed Mulder over the edge and he climaxed in a flurry of white, snowlike cum. It fell to the ground just where Narnia ended and reality began, the seed of it one with the soil. Mulder's eyes lit up at the sight of this: He had finally done it. He had finally fucked another world.

Flushed, he composed himself, and Kirke slammed the door shut. Scully surfaced from her burgeoning migraine, her hands on her face. "Are we done here? I don't see any scientific evidence that there's anything supernatural in that wardrobe, Mulder."

Kirke nodded. "Absolutely. Absolutely nothing." He quietly catalogued the beautiful image of this American special police federal agent man's improbably gorgeous cock in his memory for further use. My, how he had not felt this way in many a year.

Mulder composed himself and turned, aghast, to Scully. "Scully," he said, dismayed, "didn't you see? Didn't you see?"

Scully shook her head. "No, Mulder. I didn't see anything. I can't find any scientific proof that anything unusual happened in that wardrobe today. Science, Mulder."

"But—"

"No, Mulder. We're going home."

"But—"

"Science. That's all. Let's go."

And Scully erased that day from her memory just as she always did. When she got home, she drank an entire bottle of scotch and fell into a blissful, relieved sleep, while far away, Professor Kirke wrapped himself in lion skin and brought himself to ecstasy.

## "What a Wife Does for Her Beaver" by Deborah Kenmore

Snowfall is always accompanied by comfortable silence. Not a creature stirring, mugs of cocoa, flannel blankets—all of it. But tonight,
rhythmic sounds of pure flesh on flesh pierced the night, sending two
wide-eyed squirrels up a tree.

"Arrer!"

"ARRER!"

"Dearie, did you say 'Aslan'?" Mrs. Beaver was concerned—her
husband never used their safe word this quickly. He usually relished
these post-tea hours spent getting spanked on the snout with her wide,
flat tail. "Do you want me to untie you?" She readjusted her bonnet
and pushed her round spectacles back up her snout before turning to
her Mister. Her beloved was an arresting sight: circular lenses askew,
an ill-fitting ball gag causing his cheeks to puff out alarmingly, and his
paws bound beneath that argyle sweater vest she had knitted for him
last Christmas. A loud snort and flash of red from the window caught
her attention—Tumnus, that dirty fiend, was watching them again.
She knew by now that half the scarf would be wrapped tight around his
neck, tugged to a choke by whomever he could entice to join him, while
the other end would be knotted around his magenta-tinged shaft. He
had a fondness for the itch of wool against his tally whacker. Oftentimes
he stood outside, watching their beaver play, flicking and pinching at
his wormlike erection until goat-man spunk spewed onto the window-
panes. Mrs. Beaver sighed. Things had not always been like this.

Ever since those Children of Adam and Eve had been here,
Mr. Beaver was simply not himself. He was nervous, gnawing at anything and everything he could find! Goodness, even their dining room
table and her sewing chair—covered in teeth marks! No wood was safe!
And the things he would ask her to do. Gone were the days when he
would approach her rocking chair, take her paw, and lead her to their
marriage bed, the same they shared for the past eighty years. He would
gingerly push her down on her stomach and slowly lick up her tail. "I

want to savor this…your thickness…your meaty love flap!" His pillow talk was bumbling but effective, causing all four of her nipples to
engorge, pressing up against the crispness of her pinafore apron. His
pointed tongue would find its way into every crease, every line, every
scale of her slick extremity, to the edges that he would nibble, causing
her to lean forward on her paws and stick her bottom in the air. Then
he would tenderly grip her bum before lifting her tail and burrowing
his twitching snout into her fundament, a pink and puckered abyss,
furred in brown. He would seek out her oils, smelling and licking at the
liquids she secreted, professing an addiction to that fruity taste, much
to her perpetual embarrassment and pleasure. "Let me suck from that
font of mixed berry goodness!" This act alone sent paroxysms of sinful
delight throughout her body, carrying her to a state of paralysis as the
natural juices flooded out of her notch and soaked the fur on his abdo-
men. "Oh my," he would chuckle, "have I burst the dam?"

    "ISHIS!"

    "ISHIS!"

Mrs. Beaver was pulled out of her reverie, amorous, filled to
brimming with the liquids of nostalgia. That knocking outside was
undoubtedly Tumnus, that randy beast, stamping his hooves angrily
as the pressure built up in his fuchsia cock-stand. Her husband was
wide-eyed, glaring, clamping down on the ball with his prominent
teeth and straining to be free of his sweater. She unbuckled the gag
from around his neck and pulled the vest over his head.

    "Dearest, I was saying, 'HARDER!' not 'Aslan!'"

    "Beaver darling, I do apologize, this dreadful cold, I think it's
reached my ears! Would you look at that." She was peering at a hole in
the sweater. "You've clawed right through. Oh do be careful next time,
Mister."

    "You'd best sleep with the flannel cap on tonight, my flower—
blimey!" The faun's clomping had quickened, and he was braying
hoarsely into the night, "YES! Yes! Chipmunk, you tiny bitch, tug the
scarf!" while the Beavers braced themselves for the inevitable, syrupy
moistness that would coat their home.

"Don't you mind that filthy bugger, Mr. Beaver! He is not a well faun."

She could recall the first time she noticed the change. It was that... tail job. He rarely asked for the treatment but when he did, she was always rewarded with a spray of his own unctuous emission all over her face—and it tasted just like coconut cake. She had just started when he turned his head and asked innocently, "Why...why don't you fit it all in your mouth?" She complied, taking it inch by whiskered inch, gagging from its girth, eyes watering from its river-scented musk. "Bite it. Be a love and bite it hard." No sooner had she clamped down than he shuddered and moaned, his organic cream spurting out all over the faded patchwork of their quilt. "That was the tickity-boo, Beaver love," he said, before kissing her cheek and reaching for his nightshirt.

After that night he always wanted his tail bitten, and he started bringing home a vast array of accoutrements meant to be inserted in all manner of bodily openings! The ball gag, clamps, a string of silver beads she mistook for a necklace—that was a birthday she would always remember—and handcuffs a tad too large for beaver paws. But he professed a liking for the metal. "It's the stiffness and the dark cold," he confessed, an odd glint in his eyes, "just like the witch." He chewed down sticks to be thrashed with, the friction of which created bald spots in his lush fur, spots she would lick afterward, while he tittered and hissed from pain, "Mmm, right there. That bit there." He even brought home two dildos, one tan and the other black, the sizes of which every Son of Adam aspired to. They stood at either side of the fireplace, towering bastions of shameful glee. She enjoyed those toys thoroughly during her "alone times," but the sight of his enjoyment baffled her. This was her Mister! Her Mr. Beaver, who liked his tea milky, spoke incessantly about gardening, horsed around with their grandchildren and referred to colds as the "snuffle-wuffles." Her Mister, who seemed to have acquired a taste for having one enormous, vibrating doodle plunged deep inside his hirsute rectum with his tail propped on top while she slapped him with the other monstrously mechanical member, so huge as to require both paws to grasp. Was this age creeping up on them? As she swung floppy, flesh-toned rubber at her husband's mouth, she lamented not being able to ask her mother about these things.

"UNGHH YES...YES!"

The faun had cum, his baby-making discharge, painted across the window. A tiny paw print in the corner of the splooge opus indicated that Chipmunk had, in fact, been there. Mrs. Beaver rolled her eyes as she pulled the vest over her husband's head. She straightened her floral housecoat before giving the glinting string of beads that peeked out from under Mister's tail a tender pull.

"Ready, Beaver?"

"Tug it, missus. Tug it hard for NARNIA!"

## "Jadis: The White Witch" by Alan Leggitt

"All hail Her Imperial Majesty Jadis, Queen of Narnia, Chatelaine of Cair Paravel, Empress of the Lone Islands." The voice echoed through the throne room, bringing the great assembly to silence. Wolves, ogres, dwarves, Minotaur, incubi, and other assorted evil spirits all took a knee and fixed their eyes on the stone floor. Presenting her finest resting bitch face, the White Witch entered and slowly approached her throne, savoring the silent terror of her minions.

The Queen of Narnia wore a tight corset that showed off her milk-colored cleavage, a semi-transparent silk robe, and a lavish silver belt, encrusted with diamond skulls. The only spot of color on her person was her bright red lipstick.

"You may rise," the Witch said after she was seated. Her voice was soft, yet it seemed to echo through the very souls of those present. "What business shall be set before the queen?"

The great wolf Maugrim, chief of secret police, stepped forward. "Your Grace," he growled. "My wolves found a Son of Adam roaming in the Western Woods. He submitted to capture and has requested an audience with Your Majesty. He was armed with this."

Another wolf bounded forward with a two-handed broadsword in his mouth. The queen patted his head, gave him a treat, and let out a regal, "Who's a good boy?" before inspecting the sword.

"A fine weapon," she mused. "Very well, bring in the prisoner."

The doors of the hall opened and the assembly turned, chattering with excitement. Flanked by two wolves, a tall and muscular man strutted in, clad in a fur loincloth. The visitor's body, though scarred and weathered, seemed to be carved from shining bronze—a Harlequin romance cover brought to life. He held his head high, long black hair flowing behind him, smoldering blue eyes fixed on the queen.

"Your Grace!" the guest's voice boomed as he stood before the throne. "I am Conan the Cimmerian, Slayer of Serpents, King of Aquilonia. I have come to take your hand in marriage and proclaim myself King of Narnia."

There was a great uproar. Goblins giggled, wolves growled, wraiths hissed, and Wooses...made that sound that Wooses always make. The White Witch was taken aback, for the first time in over a hundred years.

"Silence!" shouted the queen, her voice piercing the cacophony, and all was still. She fixed her icy gaze on the presumptuous intruder. "You will kneel before addressing the empress and speak only when spoken to. God, did feminism even happen?"

All eyes turned to the Son of Adam, who remained standing. "Conan the Barbarian kneels for no woman," he growled. "This kingdom needs a man to rule, or it will surely fall."

For a long time the queen stared at the barbarian like he was an insect, then slowly, a sinister smile spread across her red lips.

"Very well, Conan the Barbarian," proclaimed Jadis. "I have heard legends of thy strength and courage, and I believe that you are just the man that Narnia needs."

The entire court gasped, while Conan smirked, quite pleased with himself.

"But before I can consent to marriage," the queen added, "I'll need you to prove your virility."

Conan scoffed. "Mine is the mightiest seed that the Age of Hyboria has ever known."

The witch smiled. "Then you shall take me right here, right now."

This time, it was Conan who was taken aback. "Right now?" he asked. "But...it's not even our first date. Shouldn't we...wait until we're married?"

The queen waved the thought away. "A draconian relic of the patriarchy. You must take me first, so I can be sure that you are capable of producing an heir."

Insulted, Conan boomed, "Very well! Dismiss this court and I shall take you in this very room."

"Is the King of Narnia afraid to do his royal duty in front of his subjects?" returned the queen.

"What? No," said Conan. "I just..."

The witch interrupted. "Ladies! Help King Conan out of that loincloth."

From behind the throne appeared three lithe women with red wings and black horns. Though they appeared to be in their early twenties, each succubus was more than ten thousand years old.

The sex demons surrounded Conan and began stroking his barrel chest, caressing his meaty thighs, running their fingers through his windswept hair, and kissing his broad neck and mighty nipples. When one of them slipped his loincloth down, Conan coughed. "Cold in Narnia...," he muttered. Two of the succubae set to work on Conan's manhood, licking his scrotum and taking the head of his Thulsa Doom in their mouths. Another succubus gently flapped her wings and hovered with her unholy lady parts before his face. Though her cunt smelled of hellfire and brimstone, Conan felt compelled as if by magic to go down on her.

Meanwhile, the queen was becoming aroused. She lifted her robe and began fondling herself. (Remember that potion she used to turn the snow into hot chocolate? Turns out it also makes a great lube.)

"You see, Conan," the queen whispered, though her voice echoed through the throne room, "it is always winter in my vagina. But never Christmas."

Many members of the court (except the ethereal ones…and the ones without hands) began fondling themselves as well.

By the time Conan was fully erect, the White Witch had removed her belt, opened up her robes, and let her supple snow-globes spill out of her corset. She beckoned him, "Come stick me with that broadsword of yours, My King."

Conan swaggered forward, his epic erection waving before him, while the queen lay at the edge of her throne and spread her legs. With a mighty battle cry, the barbarian plunged his Jewel of Gwahlur into the witch's cave.

"By that Hammer of Thor! It's cold in there!" bellowed Conan.

Jadis replied with a coy smile.

Conan began hammering her ice cavern with his battering ram, but with each thrust, the barbarian seemed to lose momentum.

"What sorcery is this?!" Conan exclaimed. He had ceased his incursion and was trying to pull out, but like a wet tongue stuck to a frosty pole, his barbaric boner was trapped in the queen's frozen abyss.

Jadis yawned while Conan grunted, tore at her corset, pushed against her throne, twisted and pulled from every angle. Despite the barbarian's exceptional strength, his stiffy would not budge.

In a fit of rage, Conan lifted the queen from her throne and slammed her back down again. There was a sickening crunch that echoed through the hall, and Conan fell backward, clutching his pelvis.

Tossing what remained of her tattered corset to the ground, the White Witch stood naked before her subjects, some (but not all) of whom had stopped masturbating. The queen reached down between her thighs and pulled something hard and black out of her vagina. It was Conan's still-erect penis, which had succumbed to frostbite and snapped off.

"You see, Conan," the queen whispered, though her voice echoed through the throne room, "it is always winter in my vagina. But never Christmas."

The White Witch sat back in her throne and lit a cigarette, admiring the frozen phallus. "You can be the king," she said to Conan as her guards dragged his neutered body away. "But watch the queen conquer." She tossed the icy cock to one of her succubae. "Now finish me off, girls!"

# Other

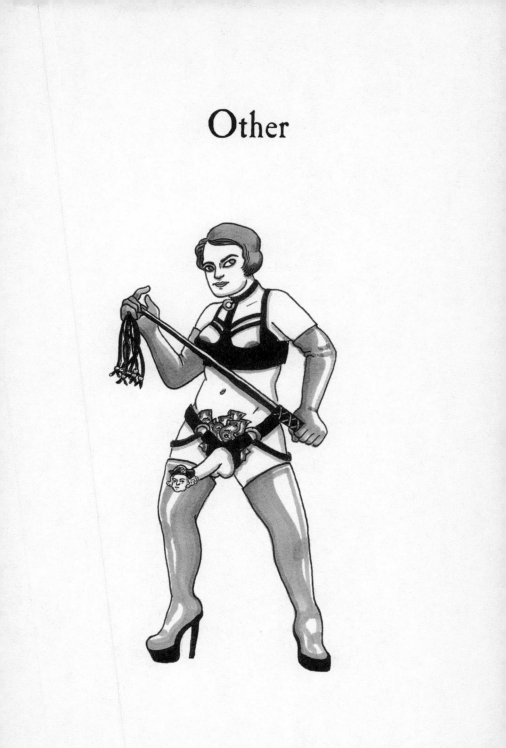

*H*ere we are at our final section: Other. Earmarked for volumes that defy basic shelving principles, Other is home to those books that refuse to be one thing. Is it a manifesto or an epic of dystopian mumblecore? Is it a dudgeon-addled management handbook or literature's most perfectly executed troll? Is it a thinly developed polemic or a thinly developed action/adventure story? Questions like these bring us no closer to an answer, but they do point to the real question we're attempting to ask.

Is it *Atlas Shrugged*? Yes, it's *Atlas Shrugged*.

Enjoy!

# ATLAS SHRUGGED

## "Atlas Boned" by Joe Wadlington

Dagny waited in an armchair in her living room. Hank Rearden was scheduled to be in New York that day meeting with the National Board of Taxation and Business Ruining. His nights were always hers. She was excited. Giving herself a 4:00 a.m. finger tango below Nat Taggart's statue wasn't doing it anymore, and she knew they'd get into some filthy shit tonight.

The door was kicked open.

"Yo, yo—it's the Hank!" Hank Rearden walked in firing imaginary guns into the air. He had a stature so elegant and powerful that it only belonged in an ancient temple or the inner office of a bank. He stepped to the bar and opened a bottle of Dagny's whiskey.

"Oh, Hank, I—" she began.

"Ehhhh." Hank put his finger to her lips and laughed. He poured his drink with a lavish gesture, then finished the entire thing in a gulp. "O-kay, now you may address the God of Metal," Hank said proudly.

"It was an awful day, Hank," Dagny said.

"I bet! Trains are TOUGH," Hank said.

"We lost the Rio Norte Line. I will have to reconfigure the train schedule for the entire country," Dagny said.

Hank nodded vigorously and looked around with big eyes, as if there were other people also not listening.

"Babes, Babes, how many train cars do you have?"

"Twenty thousand," Dagny answered.

"Whoa! Looks like she's tryin' to im-press somebody!" Hank said to the invisible party guests. "Dags, tell me, how many factories do I own?"

"One," she said.

"One factories!" he said proudly. "Now, trains are cool—way better than people, way better than my wittle wife and her wittle fam-i-wy." Hank cranked his fists under his eyes like he were a crying cartoon. "But have you ever heard of Rearden Metal?"

"I funded your production of Rearden Metal," Dagny said with narrow eyes. Hank was wandering around the apartment, not listening. Dagny ignored it. "Hank, I have something important to ask you."

He refilled his glass from Dagny's bar. "Aww, that's cute!" he said.

"Today, two of my most talented conductors retired without a word. My favorite barista, the only one who can spell 'Dagny,' left. Everywhere, men are whispering words that feed the poor like hay—or whatever it is the poor eat. I know it doesn't escape your attention. What is it, Hank?" He went to the window. During conversation, he preferred to be looking out a window so he could point out metaphors.

"Why ask? Don't you just want to run your bus stations in ignorance? In peace?" Hank said.

This sparked something in Dagny. "I will not have my ambition taunted by someone with a less-developed backstory!" She took a breath. "What's ruining this country? Is it corporate giveback programs? Is it Christmas?" Dagny asked.

Hank finally looked her in the eyes. "It's butt stuff," he said diplomatically.

"Buttstuff?" Dagny asked.

"Buttstuff. There's not a man in Washington who hasn't, and, Dagny"—he paused—"I want to do it too."

"What?" Dagny was astonished.

"I want to fill my fruit basket—my obscene nectarine—my maraschino hairy. I want to buttstuff, Dagny! Will you watch?"

"Hank, I thought you were better than them," Dagny said, looking away.

"Oh, Dagny." Hank put his hands on the ground and waved his ass in the air—the universal sign of cats and people who want to buttstuff. "I'm so much worse!" he called out.

Hank's gray suit pants slipped to the floor like a metal waterfall, followed by his baggy white briefs. His shirt and socks remained on. The first time Dagny saw Hank's penis, it had shocked her. But now she was used to the teeny-weenie sausage and thought of it as a friend, like a frisky, medium-sized caterpillar. At this point, his man thimble was clearly, probably erect. It looked like the beak of a baby bird, breaking through an eggshell.

Hank gestured to the couch. Dagny pulled three metal bins and a red bell from underneath. She hadn't known they were there.

"A bell?" she questioned.

"Not just any bell."

Dagny noticed a gold *S A* in script on the handle's end. "This isn't—" Her eyes widened.

"It's a Salvation Army bell. They ring it for…donations—for, for the poor." Dagny dropped the thing as if it had burned her. Hank looked at her squarely. "And, Dagny, I want it in my buttstuff."

"Hank, I…" Dagny didn't know if she could do it.

"Do you want to be bad?" Hank said.

Dagny nodded. "I do." She lowered her chin. "I want to be the worst."

"Then donate, baby," Hank said with a whip of his head. He went to Dagny's closet and produced a red tripod with a bucket suspended in the middle. He set it up a few feet from Dagny.

"How did you—" Dagny started.

"Shhhh, your apartment is very easy to get into," Hank said.

Hank began deep-throating the bell's handle and flicking his jelly bean. He strummed himself the way people strum guitars or brush crumbs off trench coats. Dagny remained fully clothed and did not touch him. Independent masturbation was the only noble sexual conquest. Hank fully covered the bell's handle with his spit. He leaned forward and started to buttstuff the bell into his Goodbye Kitty. A look of immense peace spread across his face, like he'd heard hundreds of homeless people had frozen to death. His body was giving way to a slight rumble, as if a distant train were nearing. Dagny felt the rumble too—deep, deep in her wallet.

Dagny opened the metal bins at her feet. One was brimming with cash; the other held hundreds of gold coins. This was Hank's entire net worth, cashed out. Dagny had never seen this much money—except for her money, which was more money. Dagny brought handfuls of the cash to her face and took deep, moaning breaths.

"Hank, I didn't know you were so...virtuous," she said with a growl.

Hank's body puffed up, then rolled like a cracking whip. Dagny heard a loud *CLANG*. Hank didn't break eye contact. He whipped his body again, violently.

*CLANG*

*CLANG*

Hank started muttering—crazed speaking that turned into hungry-eyed yelling.

"Give to the poor!"

*CLANG*

"Money for the poor!"

*CLANG*

Dagny realized what was being asked of her. She grabbed a wad of cash and threw it at him. When the bills touched Hank's skin, his eyes rolled back. His shaking increased and he continued shouting.

"Give to the poooor!"

*CLANG*

"Money for the poooor!"

*CLANG*

"Make me moral," he hissed.

Dagny made it rain with dollars, then hail with coins. Hank stroked his teeny, weenie penis pebble and bucked wildly. Dagny threw the wealth at him with clawed fists. She was so angry. She was so turned on.

The bell ringing became faster and shakier. They both vibrated now, as if the distant train were nearing the station. Dagny took the last fistful of cash and began slapping Hank furiously across the face with it. The ringing was now so fast it seemed constant. Their mutual shaking felt like it would bring the building down. Hank caught the bills in his mouth and bit down. The bell announced his climax like an orgasm maraca. Hank came into the slit of the donation bucket, began chewing the money, and swallowed.

Dagny looked down. She had come all over the money. It was hers now.

# "Francisco d'Anconia: A Day in the Life of a Totally Normal Teenage Magnate" by Kamala Puligandla

You can ask anyone around school: I, Francisco d'Anconia, am hot shit. My skin is like butter, my hair is glossier than the finest fur coat, and my dad owns some copper mines that are worth millions.

"I hear that Francisco naturally smells like a peach Bellini candle," says a girl on the cheerleading squad.

"I hear that his smile can generate actual electricity," says an artsy girl, who is gorgeous, except for her glasses.

"I hear he has lips like Jessica Rabbit and gives better head than a pool jet," says Rudy, our custodian, in his deep baritone as he removes a "Closed for Cleaning" sign from outside the girls' locker room.

"Wait a minute," I interject. This is not the kind of ego boost I'm looking for on my morning sashay down the hallway. "Than a pool jet? That hardly gives me any credit for nuance. Where would you even hear something like that?"

Rudy shrugs and starts rolling his mop cart away.

I turn to my friends to say, "That guy. He can't even button his coveralls correctly. Am I right, ladies?"

They're all like, "Hell yes, Frisco! Can someone please tell Rudy that coveralls are for men who need to cover up? And Rudy should not be hiding such a stately ass."

Which I haven't considered until now because Rudy is old. He's like twenty-five. But his ass is a little stately. A lot stately, actually. "I guess I'd get buried in those cheeks," I muse aloud.

Which, of course, is the exact moment that my girlfriend, Dagny Taggart, pops out of the locker room. She looks all smug and boss bitch, like usual. I know she's in a good mood because straight off, she adjusts her blazer and then buries her tongue in my ear—and thank God, because the last thing I need is my girlfriend getting jealous over some comment about old Rudy's ass.

"Morning, Frisco," Dagny says. "How about you give me a ride after school?" Dagny is basically panting at me.

"Okay, but I'm not your Uber," I say. "A ride for a ride, Miss Thang." I squeeze her butt cheek so she gets the idea. There is a big debate team match in the auditorium this afternoon and I'm sure she'll be all riled up. Nothing gets Dagny wetter than humiliating other people, which is just one of the reasons she's my girlfriend.

Dagny wiggles her eyebrows up and down and she growls at me, "Mr. d'Anconia, show me your copper mine and I'll show you some world-class mining equipment," or something else totally obvious. When she gets like this, my girl gang tends to scatter. They talk a big game, but they're all saving themselves for Justin Bieber.

Meanwhile, Dagny is hornier than ten gorillas. Her beaver has a fever 24/7. She loves to fuck me with a metallic gray strap-on named Rearden that's thicker than my forearm, all while she gruffly inquires about the identity of my daddy. Spoiler alert: It's her. She likes getting me so worked up that I accidentally come on my favorite sheer black button-down or my beautiful new platform boots or whatever my hottest item of the moment is. Then—only after I've ruined something I love—is it my turn to penetrate her: slowly, gently, rhythmically, to infuriate her into coming. Is my girlfriend my frenemy? Absolutely. Hello, we're the most scary and beautiful people at school—who the hell else could we date?

Anyway, later in English class we're going over college admissions essays again, for the plebs that have to explain who they are to admissions boards. Our teacher, Dr. Thompson, is always wearing pilly sweaters that don't bring out his eyes and telling me that I need to be more specific in my essays.

"Francisco, when you say, for example, 'my pussy is the phattest,' what are you intending to convey about yourself? Or, 'I'm the best bitch, doing it, doing it'? Can you show the reader concretely what it is you're the best at doing?"

I look at Dr. Thompson, cross my arms, and touch my hair. "Specifically, my own feminist narrative involves the empowerment of the pussy—for everyone, mine included. More specifically, my pussy can handle a very wide load and nobody leaves unsatisfied. Do you need more details? I feel like my work speaks for itself." I'm pretty sure Dr. Thompson would love to get his patient, nurturing mouth on my cock. If not mine, then Dagny's. Nobody on earth can say no to the both of us.

Dr. Thompson sighs. Passionately, I assume, until he says, "I wish you would take this more seriously," and I realize he doesn't want to play this game with me.

"No," I say. "I wish you would take this more seriously. I'm using my bathroom pass."

He waves me away and I decide to wander the halls a bit. I figure I'll swing by the gym and see if Dagny is doing her debate thing. She's always involved in activities that get her out of class—she knows how to work a system. I'm sashaying by the dance studio when I notice that nobody is taking advantage of those perfect floor-length mirrors. So I let myself in. I want to check on which side of my profile I like better.

Last I looked, it was the left. I'm turning my head back and forth and am bent over to take a closer look at the definition in my right jawline. That's when I hear the familiar rumble of a custodial cart.

"From one stately ass to another, you really ought to be in class," Rudy says.

That deep voice of his, it rustles something inside of me. In the mirror, I see him watching my cock get hard—I'm wearing my floral printed leggings today, so it's really not any kind of secret. "Listen, Rudy, I'm not in the business of running my mouth, if you aren't. But between you and me, we're gonna need to talk about that booty," I say.

Suddenly Rudy is close up behind me and I feel a stiff poke in my back. "What exactly would you like to say about it?" His soft, firm hand caresses the left side of my face. "You know, this is your better side," he says thoughtfully.

I roll my eyes at him. I have to be back in class in like fifteen minutes and I want him to stuff me with his hot meat, not confirm what I already know about the perfect contours of my face. "Yeah, duh," I say, and shove his hand down the front of my leggings.

He strokes me a few times and then drops his coveralls. "Dagny is not going to like this," he purrs.

"Oh, she doesn't have to know about this." I moan as Rudy works his way inside of my phat pussy. I peek in the mirror at the flexing of Rudy's pert ass. *Stately, def stately,* I'm thinking.

Suddenly, I hear a familiar, businesslike bossy voice—one I don't want to hear right now. "I have to be on the debate floor in thirty minutes, so please get yourself hard right—"

Dagny breaks into the room and then stops. At this point, I'm on the dance studio floor and Rudy is working me like a wheelbarrow. She takes in the scene, removes her blazer, and then plants herself before us, hands resting on her elegant little hips. Neither of us moves.

"It seems to me that both of you are currently in violation of our individual agreements," Dagny finally announces.

"What?" I ask, catching my breath. "Both of us?"

"Yes," Dagny answers, and examines her nail beds. "Rudy fucks me between classes. G-spot orgasms help me focus. How do you think I scored so high on my SATs? Listen, Frisco, I love pumping you with my cold, steel rod, but you're much better at receiving."

I crane my neck to look at Rudy, who nods in agreement. I'm still rocking against him because, amazingly, he's still hard and Dagny isn't the only fierce queen who needs to get off and also, whatever.

"But I can work with this," Dagny says confidently. She always has the answers. She stretches out her fingers and rolls her neck a few times. In what feels like seconds, Dagny has shed the executive skirt suit that is her official debate uniform and is on the ground, legs in the air, riding my face like a rocking horse. "Mmm, yes, better than a pool jet," she exclaims while Rudy, who still has more juice, continues to tap my pinkberry. It doesn't take long before that formation ends in spastic shudders and heaves. "Up, down, open," Dagny directs us as we move through several more positions. Then finally Dagny whips out Rearden, lubes him up, and punishes the both of us for violations. Afterward, we're all left panting and glistening on the dance studio floor.

"Well, that was an invigorating experience," I say. "I think I have some details for Dr. Thompson."

Dagny is already zipping up her skirt. "Don't forget to clean the mirrors, Rudy," she casually instructs. "I'll need you again when we break at three-fifteen."

"My name isn't really Rudy," Rudy replies. "It's John, John Galt. And I'm not a custodian. I'm an engineer. I'd like to talk to you two about coming away with me to join my revolution."

Dagny is putting the back of her right earring in. "Rudy, I told you I was only interested in role-play if you could snag a cheerleader outfit. Stop trying to make things complicated."

"Francisco?" Rudy is starting to sound desperate now and his coveralls are still not buttoned correctly. "Come on, it's a really important revolution. Don't you want to use your popularity for a good cause?"

"Uh, hell no," I scoff at this ridiculous notion. I have plenty of activities on my plate without some coverall revolution—I don't know where Dagny finds these losers. By now, I've shimmied back into my leggings and am using a sock to clean all kinds of cum off my face.

"Later, Dag," I say. "Call me when you need another ride or found us a new victim." I blow her a kiss, shrug, and walk away.

# Acknowledgments

Amy and Casey would like to thank artist Sean Chiki (dadayama.com) for our original logo, Baruch Porras-Hernandez for being our voice, Cecil Baldwin for always being down to collaborate from 3,000 miles away, Madeline Gobbo (madelinegobbo.com) for her filthy illustrations which we will forever cherish (especially Porn Ayn Rand), our editor Madeline Caldwell for plucking us up at a show and insisting that we get a book, our poor copyeditors who handled so much cum with grace and aplomb, Alan Leggitt for being our uncompensated and often un-credited photographer for three years, Trax bar for hosting countless after-parties (if you are ever in San Francisco, it's the best dive in town), the entire crew at The Booksmith for putting up with 300 of our closest friends every month since June of 2013, and, finally, Christin Evans for giving us the green light to run a porn show in her theretofore well-respected bookstore.

# Appendicks

Arousal
Baby canon
Baton
Battering ram
Beachhead
Bearded gourd
Boat
Bone
Boner
Breadstick
Broadsword
Broken flashlight
Brush
Bulging monster
Canary
Cock
Crocadildo
Cucumber down
 under
Cum hammer
Cum musket
Dick
Diiiiiiiiick
Dingle
Dong
Dorian Jr.

Eggplant
Emission hose
Endowments
Flagpole
Flesh axe
Flesh shaft
Gearshift
Ham hock
Hard-on
Harpoon
Hot dog
Hot meat
Jelly bean
Jewel of Gwahlur
Jizz cannon
Johnny Corkscrew
Jolly Roger
Leaky meat pole
Libertarian
Long Tom
Love bulge
Man thimble
Manhood
Meat
Member
Moby Dick

Nubbin
Organ meat
Organ of
 benevolence
Pants oak
Pecker
Peen
Pego
Penis
Pike
Plank
Pleasure zucchini
Pocket rocket
Pole
Prick
Protuberance
Pussy drill
Rod
Rolling pin of delight
Royal prerogative
Sausage
Schlong
Sex stick
Shaft
Shillelagh
Situation

Skin sledge

Skull and crossbones

Splooge hose

Spoo hose

Stiffy

Sword

Tallywacker

Third leg

Thor's hammer

Thulsa doom

Totem

Trouser fugitive

Turgidity

Upright reverend

Wedding tackle

Whalebone

White whale

Wiener

Wood

Wooly Willy

Yule log

# Additional Copyright

# Information

# Index

# About the Editors

**Casey A. Childers** is the author of the novel *Bear Season* and the short fiction collection *Pictures of the Floating World, She Said, and I Pretended to Understand*. He is also the the co-creator of Shipwreck. He lives in San Francisco, has three children, and is loved by all he meets.

**Amy Stephenson** is a curly-haired human female and scotch enthusiast living in San Francisco. She co-produces and emcees Shipwreck, a monthly literary fanfiction competition. You can see her writing on *Hoodline, The Establishment, Midnight Breakfast, Litseen,* and others. Find her on your platform of choice at @losertakesall.